The R

Libby Ashworth was born and raised in Lancashire and comes from many generations of mill workers. It was while researching her family history that she realised there were so many stories about ordinary working people that she wanted to tell.

Also by Libby Ashworth

The Lancashire Girls

The Convict's Wife
A Mother's Fight
The Runaway Daughter

The Runaway Daughter

LIBBY ASHWORTH

CANELO

First published in the United Kingdom in 2023 by

Canelo
Unit 9, 5th Floor
Cargo Works, 1–2 Hatfields
London SE1 9PG
United Kingdom

A CIP catalogue record for this book is available from the British Library.

Print ISBN 978 1 80032 659 0
Ebook ISBN 978 1 80032 658 3

Look for more great books at www.canelo.co

Printed and bound in Great Britain by Clays Ltd, Elcograf S.p.A.

1

Chapter One

February 1818

Betty Knowles looked at her elder daughter and willed Lydia to at least acknowledge the offer that the relief committee was making to her. But the girl continued to stare down at her boots and twist her mouth in an expression of distaste, whilst her arms were folded firmly across her skinny chest in a gesture of self-preservation.

'Lydia? What do you say?' Betty prompted her, hoping for some expression of gratitude for the opportunity.

'I don't want to go,' mumbled Lydia.

Betty looked at the three men sitting behind the desk, watching her daughter with frowns on their faces. Their irritation was clear. She knew that if Lydia refused the apprenticeship they would no longer pay anything towards her keep. They'd been fortunate that the payments had continued this long, thought Betty. At fourteen, Lydia should have been in work long since, except that there was none in Bolton during these days of hardship and poor trade. She'd taught her daughter to spin but there was no market for hand-spun yarn now that the factories were being built all around. The town was taking on a different aspect from the past with chimneys that poured

1

smoke into the skies all day long, except on Sundays. And the sound of hand-loom weavers at their work had been replaced by the clatter of clogs on the cobbled streets as people rushed to work early in the morning, leaving their homes and their looms empty.

'What did she say?' asked Mr Hamer, the grocer. It was well-known that he was a little hard of hearing and hated anyone who didn't speak up.

'I think she said she doesn't want to go!' Mr Hewitt, the ironmonger, shouted in his ear.

'Doesn't want to go? What nonsense! Of course she wants to go. Should be grateful!' he replied as he glared first at Lydia and then at Betty as if it were her fault that her daughter was less than eager to travel to the cotton spinning mill at Caton and live there in the apprentice house, far from her family.

'I'm sure she'll be glad to go when she's had time to think on it,' ventured Betty, wishing that one of these men had forewarned her. If she'd been able to broach the idea with Lydia first it wouldn't have come as such a shock to her. She would have had time to get used to the idea rather than having it sprung on her, like a trap, in this boardroom with its panelled walls and heavy furniture.

'This is what happens when a family is without a father,' commented Mr Lomax, who worked as an over-seer in one of the mills. 'If the father had been here, we wouldn't have had any of this nonsense.' He fixed Betty with his cold blue eyes. 'Single mothers always have problem children,' he said. 'God intended children to have two parents. The girl needs a father to set her straight. And if she goes to Caton she'll be subject to proper discipline as well as learning a trade.'

Betty was tempted to speak out, but she knew it would do no good. Perhaps she had been a bad mother, she thought, suddenly doubting herself. Heaven knows, she'd tried to bring up her three children as best she could since Jimmy had been sent away, but it had never been easy. It had been a long hard struggle to survive all these years on the pittance called parish relief that these men, in their long-tailed coats and carefully tied cravats, had handed out to her.

'Lydia,' said Betty, turning her attention back to her daughter, who was crushing a stray hairpin that had fallen onto the floor under the sole of her boot. 'Thank the gentlemen,' she told her in a tone that she hoped wouldn't meet with a refusal. There'd be trouble later, she knew, but if she could get Lydia out of the room without her spoiling all hope of improving her lot in life then perhaps she would be able to talk some sense into her.

'Thank you,' mumbled Lydia, still without looking up. Betty hoped the men of the committee would interpret it as humility.

'What did she say?' shouted Mr Hamer again, cupping a hand around the back of his ear.

'She said thank you!' Betty told him in a raised voice.

'Should think so as well,' he muttered.

'We'll make the arrangements then,' Mr Hewitt told her. 'You'll have to come back on Monday for the indenture to be signed, and we'll give her a ticket for the coach and happen a bit of clothing if we can procure some,' he added, frowning at the threadbare clothing that Lydia was dressed in. 'She can't go like that,' he went on, turning to his fellow committee members. 'It'll reflect badly on us.'

3

'She could walk,' suggested Mr Lomax, glancing at Lydia, who despite being underfed gave off the impression of being strong.

'She's too young to walk all that way alone,' protested Betty. 'And I'm not sure it's safe for a lass on her own.'

Mr Hewitt nodded in agreement. 'We'll pay for a seat on the mail coach,' he told the committee firmly. 'Outside seat, of course. I'm sure someone will meet her if we let the mill know to expect her,' he added.

Betty nodded and thanked him. She knew it was generous. 'Come on,' she said to Lydia, knowing it was too much to expect her daughter to thank the men again.

Lydia needed no encouragement. She burst from the room like a gust of wind rattling the window panes.

'I don't want to go,' she repeated as soon as they were out of earshot of the committee.

'Tha'll do as tha's told!' Betty reprimanded her, feeling guilty for feigning anger. The truth was that she didn't want Lydia to go either, but she couldn't see any alternative.

Their lives had been left in ruins since the judge at Lancaster sent Jimmy away for seven years to New South Wales. Betty remembered how shocked she'd been when she received the news. She'd collapsed to the floor when the letter had been read out to her by the schoolmaster and he'd had to run and fetch Ann Booth, her neighbour, to help her up.

'Why?' she'd kept on asking him. 'Why are they sending him away? He's done nowt wrong.'

'Your husband was at the meeting up near the Rope Walk,' the schoolmaster had said. 'They're making an example of everyone who was caught there to put a stop to them causing any more trouble.'

'But he were never set on trouble,' Betty had said. 'He just wanted to know about trade and how to get fair money for his work. That's all.'

She remembered how she'd sobbed into her apron and Ann had made a pot of tea and told her to shush because she was frightening the children. The image in Betty's mind, of the faces of Lydia and Simon and Rose staring up at her wide-eyed with fear, would never fade. She'd known that she was scaring them, but she'd been so afraid herself that she couldn't control the tears and the trembling until, in the end, Ann had shepherded them out and taken them to her own cottage whilst Betty tried to calm herself.

She'd never seen Jimmy again. She hadn't had the money to travel to say goodbye to him in the prison. All she'd been able to do was send a letter to the government, pleading for him, for leniency, and failing that the chance to sail with him on the convict ship. But the answer had been no – as it had been to all the wives whose husbands had been sentenced to the same fate at Lancaster. They were to be left with no husbands to support them and their children, forced to throw themselves on the mercy of the parish guardians as they struggled to keep themselves and their families out of the workhouse.

Jimmy had been a hand-loom weaver like most of the men who lived at Tonge. Betty had been brought up as a spinner, but now that the spinning was being done in mills there was no prospect of her getting work and even less prospect of her daughters working beside her at their own spindles. There'd been so much change in recent years. The inventions of men with good intentions, like Sam Crompton, that were supposed to make their lives better had done the opposite. The jennies and looms that spun and wove as much as a hundred workers had stolen the bread from their mouths. All the machines had brought were hunger and hard times for many.

'Why do I have to go away?' asked Lydia mutinously as they walked up the track towards home. 'Why can't I work here?'

'Because no one needs workers here and Mr Greg at Caton has a huge mill where there's employment for as many lasses as the parishes can send,' Betty told her. 'It'll be all right,' she added as Lydia continued to walk with her head bent and her lips downturned. 'Tha'll learn a trade and when th' apprenticeship's finished tha'll be able to take on paid work.'

'But it's over six years 'til that'll happen,' she complained. 'That's nearly as long as they sent my dad away for.'

It was almost six years since Jimmy had been sentenced back in May 1812. Betty had counted every day since then, even though she doubted that their punishment would ever end. For what use would it be for him to be freed when she was in this place and he was on the other side of the world?

She sighed as she turned her attention back to her daughter. 'It'll soon pass,' she told her. Betty hoped that Lydia wasn't going to fight her over this. Even though she would be heartbroken to see her go, one less mouth to feed would be a relief.

Lydia didn't reply. She walked on ahead of her mother and Betty made no hurry to catch up with her. She didn't want any more argument. She was too weary to deal with it.

When Betty reached their little cottage and lifted the latch on the door, there was no sign of Lydia. Simon was sitting by the cold hearth whittling a stick and she knew that Rose would be with Ann next door. She kept her shawl wrapped around herself for warmth as she began to make some dinner from the few things she had in her pantry – some oatcakes spread with a thin layer of lard. She knelt down at the hearth to coax a fire with some twigs and branches that she'd gathered. The storm of the previous week had at least brought her some bounty, she thought as she blew on the small fire and hoped it would be enough to boil a kettle of water for some weak tea.

'Pass some more of those thinner branches,' she said to Simon, who was watching her closely. He was a bright little lad, who reminded her so much of Jimmy that it broke her heart afresh every day when she looked at him, tousle-haired and bleary-eyed from sleep.

'I could have had it going afore,' he told her. Betty didn't reply. She knew that she was over-protective of him and that he resented not being able to do the things that other lads did. Heaven knew, lads of his age were working down the mines and on the farms and doing far more dangerous things than tending an open fire, but still she wanted to keep him safe. She didn't know if she would be able to bear it if something happened to him – or to any of her three children. They were doubly precious to her since Jimmy had gone.

The door opened and the gust of wind almost blew out the few flames. Betty moved to shield them with her body as she heard Rose come in, followed by Ann.

'Everything all right?' asked her neighbour. She understood. They all understood the fear that came with being summoned to appear before the relief committee – the fear that the help they were given could be denied them on a whim.

'They're sending our Lydia to Caton,' Betty said, rocking back on her heels as the fire began to burn. 'Keep adding those branches,' she told Simon as she got up and reached for the kettle to fill it with water. 'Tea?' she asked Ann.

Her neighbour shook her head. 'No. Thanks. I'd best get back. I'm sorry about Lydia,' she added. 'It's a long way off.'

'Aye,' replied Betty. 'I'll not see much of her.'

'Where is she?' asked Ann.

'Gone off in a huff somewhere. She doesn't want to go.'

'She'll come round,' said Ann.

'Aye.' Betty nodded. Neither woman spoke of how shocking the news was, but Betty could feel the sympathy oozing from Ann. She had daughters too, but they were grown and married and lived near enough to visit. Her neighbour was one of the more fortunate ones. Her husband, Peter, still had work as a silk weaver. They were better off than a lot of folk, but everyone knew that life was precarious and that another slump in trade could make all the difference between just getting by and having to beg for charity.

Betty and her two younger children ate their oatcakes sitting on boxes in front of the feeble fire. Once, she'd had chairs and a rag rug, but they'd been sold long since – along with the table, the dresser, and the beds.

She wondered where Lydia had got to. She could hear the pattering of rain on the window and hoped that the lass wouldn't allow herself to get wet through because it would take days for her clothes to dry out in this cold winter weather. She put a few oatcakes to one side for her to eat when she came in, even though Rose's eyes followed them longingly as she watched the plate being put up on the mantlepiece to warm. Although Betty managed to provide food most days, none of her children knew what it was like to eat until they were full.

As they sat and watched the fire, too weary to do anything much, Betty began to fear that Lydia had run away for good. It wasn't like her to be out this long and the rain was coming down steadily now with the threat of sleet. It could well turn to snow before long, thought Betty as she fretted about where Lydia had gone.

–

Lydia kept on walking with no clear intention. She had no purpose, no destination. She only knew that she didn't want to go home and face the prospect of being sent to Caton. She couldn't get the image of those men out of her mind, sitting there, behind that big oak desk and telling her how she was to spend the next six years of her life. If her father had been here he would never have allowed it to happen. She was certain of that. But because her mother was alone, they were bullied and told what they could and couldn't do. They were serving a sentence just the same as her father was – and it was all so unfair.

She thought about her father as she walked, head down, not looking where she was going but just needing the freedom of being out, alone, on the moorland. Most of her memories of him were hazy, but there were a few that remained clear, etched on her mind for ever. There was a day when he'd taken her fishing in the little brook near to their home. He'd taught her how to cup her hands in the fast-flowing stream and close them quickly around the little tiddlers that thrashed about and tickled her palms as they tried to escape her grasp. He'd shown her how to throw them into the bucket he'd brought. Later they'd taken them home and he'd added them to the little tank he'd set up in the parlour, made to look like a real river with stones and gravel and little plants growing in it for the fish to hide. Counting back, she thought that she must have been about eight years old – the summer before he was sent away. Simon had been too young to join in properly and had just spoiled things by splashing in the water and frightening the fish, and Rose had been a baby, at home with their mother.

As Lydia walked, she tried to remember what had happened to the fish and the tank. They didn't have it now. It had been there and now it wasn't, but she couldn't think of the day when it had been taken away. It was the same with her father. He'd been there and then suddenly he wasn't. She could remember her mother crying and crying. She could remember the neighbours coming around, the whispering, the furtive glances and the warning looks. She'd known that something was very wrong, but she hadn't known what. She'd known that the grown-ups were keeping something secret from her and that whenever she asked when her father was coming home her mother would begin to cry again. For a while, Lydia had believed that her father had died. She'd heard of another lass whose father had been killed in an accident at one of the new mills and she'd thought something similar had happened to her daddy. It was only when she'd asked her mother if they could go to the churchyard to see where he was buried that her mother had realised her attempt to shield Lydia from the truth had only made things worse. She'd explained to her then that her father had been sent to the other side of the world for attending a meeting.

Lydia wished that her father would come home. Two of the men who'd been convicted with him had come home, so why hadn't he? He hadn't even written, except for one letter before his ship sailed. A horrible thought sometimes gnawed away at her – an evil little voice that said her father really had died. Why else would he not have come back to them? Yet, she'd thought he was dead once before and it turned out not to be true, so she wasn't going to give in to the temptation to believe it now. He would come back. He must come back and when he did he would rescue her from that awful place at Caton that she was to be sent to.

It was hunger and thirst rather than the aching in her legs and the rain seeping through the thick woollen cloth of her shawl that made Lydia stop and look around. She wasn't lost. She'd walked on these moors often enough to know whereabouts she was even though the landscape looked similar in every direction, especially in the pouring rain. She needed to turn back. She knew that she couldn't go on walking no matter how much she wanted to. Her mother would be angry with her for going off and getting wet. She might not even have saved her anything to eat, thought Lydia as her stomach rumbled again. But she was used to being hungry. It rarely bothered her any more.

Rain dripped from the shawl that was wrapped around her head and shoulders. Her boots were covered in mud and the bottom of her petticoat was black. Reluctantly, Lydia headed downhill towards the track that would eventually take her towards Tombling Fold where they lived. Her stockings squelched where the rain had soaked through her boots and the wind that had turned northerly stung her face with a smattering of sleet. It would snow before morning, she thought and she hoped for snow that would come again and again and pile up against the walls of the cottage and block all the routes and roads in and out of Bolton so that there would be no question of her setting off for Caton just yet. Perhaps, if she had more time, she could talk her mother round, find some work nearby, do something to prevent herself being sent away.

–

Betty felt relief flood through her when she heard footsteps approaching the door. It opened and Lydia stepped in. The lass was covered in snow. It clung to her shawl in a layer at least an inch thick. She was shivering and her hands and lips looked blue with cold.

'Where hast tha been?' demanded Betty, her anxiety turning to anger now that she knew her daughter was safe. 'What were tha thinkin' of, goin' off in this weather?'

Lydia eased off the shawl and shook the loose snow from it. The white crystals fell to the floor and melted into a puddle. Betty could see that her daughter's jacket was soaked through beneath it and the rest of her clothing was filthy and wet. She wouldn't be surprised if the lass caught cold and was unable to go to Caton after all – she wondered if that was Lydia's intention. The lass exasperated her with her stubbornness.

'Tha'd best come to the fire and get dry,' she told her brusquely. 'What on earth were tha thinkin'? Goin' off and gettin' wet through like this? Hast tha no sense at all?' she demanded as Lydia sat down and stretched her icy fingers towards the flames. 'Look at the state of thee!' Betty added, not knowing what else to say. She wanted to hug her daughter and she wanted to slap her as well for all the worry she'd caused. But mostly she wanted to talk to her about the decision to send her to Caton – except she didn't know where to begin.

Instead, she reached for the plate of oatcakes and gave them to Lydia without a word. Her daughter mumbled her thanks but wouldn't meet her eye. What was she going to do? wondered Betty. How could she refuse to let Lydia go and risk her other children starving to death? But how could she bear having her family rent apart once more by those in authority over her?

Chapter Two

The next morning, the snow was thick on the ground. Betty wondered how long it would last and if she could use it as an excuse not to send her elder daughter away. Somehow, she doubted it. But she had a few days, she reminded herself. Lydia couldn't go until the papers were signed on Monday, and maybe something would turn up before then. Maybe a miracle would occur. She felt she was owed one after everything that had happened these past six years.

Lydia came down the narrow twisting stairs wrapped in the banket she'd slept under. Betty watched as her daughter felt at the clothing that had been hung around the hearth before they went to bed. The fire had gone out and the clothes were still cold and damp to touch. Betty knew, because she'd already felt them herself.

'Tha can't put those on. They're still wet,' she told her daughter.

'What am I supposed to do then?' asked Lydia.

'Tha'll have to stay wrapped up like that until they're dry,' Betty told her, not adding that it might take days and only then if there was enough fuel to light a fire.

Lydia sat down on one of the boxes. They would have to be burned to get the clothing dry, thought Betty. Their last bit of comfort would be gone and she would have to drag the sacks of straw that they used as mattresses down the stairs for them to sit on. They would need to come down anyway, she thought. It was freezing cold up there under the eaves, so they might as well all sleep together near the hearth. It would help them to keep warm.

Simon and Rose came down the stairs. They were still young enough to be excited by the sight of the snow outside but Betty was firm when they asked to go out.

'No,' she told them. 'I can't cope with any more wet clothes and I don't want all three of ye sitting wrapped in blankets like urchins.'

'I can look for more logs,' pleaded Simon.

'No. Everything's buried,' Betty told him. 'We'll find no more logs until the thaw. The boxes'll have to go on the fire instead. Get up, our Lydia,' she told her daughter. 'Tha might as well start by breaking that one up then we can put the kettle on to boil.'

Betty had to break ice on the top of the bucket in the back kitchen before she could fill the kettle. She spooned some of the oats from a sack into bowls and waited for the water to boil so she could make some porridge and tea. There wasn't much left of either and she didn't know when she would get to the market again, but it was so cold that they needed something to fill their bellies and she decided that she would worry about tomorrow the next day.

They were still huddled round the warm ashes of the wooden box when there was a tap on the door and Ann came in, wrapped from head to toe against the weather with only her eyes peeping out. She was carrying a bucket with a few cobs of coal.

'Our Peter says tha's to have these,' she told Betty. 'He's worried about the childer,' she added when she saw that Betty was reluctant to accept the gift. 'Tha can pay us back later,' she went on, although Betty knew that they would refuse to take her money when the time came.

'I'm grateful,' she told her neighbour, knowing that the words were inadequate. 'Tell Peter that I'm grateful, and I'll pay ye for them when I can.'

Ann nodded and carried the bucket across to the hearth. 'Let's get some on,' she suggested. 'It should take hold if it goes on now.' She picked up a couple of the smaller cobs with her gloved hands and settled them onto the hot ashes. They smoked at first, but then the blue flames began to lap at the edges and soon they were burning steadily. Ann hadn't lingered. She'd refused the offer of a cup of tea and gone back home, probably to sit on a proper chair, thought Betty, hating having to be the poor relation and the object of pity.

Steam began to rise from the wet clothes and Lydia rearranged them as they gradually dried. There was nothing else to do and Betty felt restless that she had no work and wasn't even able to get outside to tend the little patch where they grew vegetables to supplement their meals. At one time she would have sat spinning yarn for Jimmy to weave on his loom, but those days seemed a lifetime ago. So much had changed, and none of it for the better.

Lydia was unusually quiet and Betty knew that she was brooding on her impending journey to Caton. She wanted to talk about it with her daughter, tell her that there was no other option and make things right between them. The tense silence was exhausting her and Simon and Rose seemed to sense that there was something wrong too. They both sat and warmed themselves at the fire, but said nothing.

Lydia felt at her petticoat. She'd washed the dirt off the hem and it was almost dry enough to put back on, but she was cosy inside the blanket, with flames searing her face, and was reluctant to shift. She wished she could sit there for ever and not have to face the future. Several times she'd taken a breath to tell her mother that she wasn't going to go to Caton, but the words never reached her lips. It wasn't the work she was afraid of. If there had been work locally she would have done it gladly. It was being separated from her family that she couldn't face, but she didn't know how to express the feeling of emptiness inside her that made her want to weep every time she thought about it.

She took another breath and turned to her mother.

'Don't tell me again as tha won't go,' said her mother before she could speak. 'It's not that I want thee to go. I don't. But tha heard what t' committee said. I've no choice.'

Her mother did have a choice, thought Lydia. She hoped that if she'd been in her mother's position, she would have had the courage to tell those men what to do with their apprenticeship and somehow find a way to feed them all. But she knew that she was being selfish. She knew that her mother couldn't afford to keep her at home any longer. And there was her little sister and brother to consider too; if she stayed, they would go hungry. But that didn't make it fair. It wasn't fair that she should be sent away like this without having any choice in the matter herself. It was all very well for her mother to keep telling her that she was an adult now, but she didn't treat her like one. No one listened to her or asked what she wanted.

'It'll be all right when tha gets there,' her mother told her, trying to sound reassuring. 'Tha'll get three meals a day, and there'll be other lasses that tha can make friends with. Tha'll enjoy it.'

'No I won't!' snapped back Lydia. 'I'll hate it. Tha knows I will.'

Her mother sighed. 'I don't know what else to do, Lydia,' she told her. 'Look at us,' she implored. 'We've barely enough to keep body and soul together as it is. If I don't get rent money and a bit o' summat for food we can't even stay here. We'll end up beggin' on the street, or in t' workhouse – and then they'll send thee to Caton anyway.'

Lydia pulled the blanket around her head to disguise her tears. It was becoming clear that she had no way out, and that for the next six years of her life she would be an apprentice whether she liked it or not, unless her father came home.

Chapter Three

The cold snap kept them in the cottage for most of the weekend. The thaw, when it came, happened overnight and they woke on the Monday morning to the sound of the melting snow dripping from the eaves of the thatched roof.

Betty went to the window and looked out. The banks of snow were still white, but where it had been trodden to ice on the paths it was melting and turning to slush. She had been half hoping that the freeze would last longer and put off the inevitable return visit to the relief committee. Every day that had passed with her family all together had been precious to her and the grey skies that had come with the rise in the temperature added to her gloom.

'It looks like we'll be able to go,' she said, trying to sound bright and enthusiastic. Lydia glanced up from her bowl of porridge with a sour face.

'Can I come too?' asked Simon hopefully.

Betty hesitated. 'Tha'll have to wait outside and mind thy little sister,' she warned him.

'I will,' he promised and although Betty could have done without the little ones slowing them down on the long walk, she was reluctant to leave them alone in the cold cottage.

After breakfast, they wrapped themselves in every item of clothing that they still owned and stepped out into the drizzle that was making light work of turning the accumulated snow into fierce streams of water that poured down the hillside.

Lydia walked sullenly by Betty's side as they trudged towards the town centre, and the boardroom where they'd been instructed to present themselves at ten o'clock. Mr Hamer, Mr Hewitt and Mr Lomax were seated on the other side of the desk when Betty went in with her daughter. Water dripped from their sodden clothing onto the floor as they waited for the men to speak and Betty saw the irritation in Mr Lomax's eyes, as if he thought they had wet themselves through simply to annoy him. She wished with all her heart that she didn't have to go through with this agreement, but she knew she had no choice.

They stood in silence until a door burst open from an inner room and Colonel Fletcher, the local magistrate, came through. He was a middle-aged man with a paunch that settled onto his lap when he sat down and peered at Betty and Lydia. Betty averted her eyes. She hated the man. He was the one who was responsible for Jimmy being sent away and she would never forgive him.

'Is this the girl?' asked Colonel Fletcher. 'And is this the mother who can't provide for her?'

Betty bit her lip. It would do no good for her to answer back, but how she longed to give this well-fed man a piece of her mind.

'We're recommending that she's apprenticed to Mr Greg at the Caton mill,' Mr Hewitt told him, placing a parchment document in front of him. 'It simply needs your name here on the indenture, and then the seal.'

Without hesitation, the colonel took the pen and made a flowing signature. Mr Hewitt blotted it then added a seal to the warm wax that had been poured onto the paper. The colonel stood up and left the room and the document was passed to the two other poor law guardians for them to add their names. It seemed little to do with her or her daughter, thought Betty, wondering why their presence had even been needed.

'There,' said Mr Hewitt as he looked up again. 'All done. If you go through to the other room you'll be given a bundle of clothing and a ticket for tomorrow's coach,' he told Lydia. 'Don't lose it. Don't be late. The mail coach leaves at a quarter to seven in the evening.'

'Tomorrow? So soon?' asked Betty in alarm. She hadn't expected them to send Lydia the next day.

'No need to delay,' interrupted Mr Lomax. 'One less mouth to feed will benefit our parish funds.'

–

Lydia didn't sleep at all that night. She lay awake on the thin, straw mattress, wrapped in her blanket and listened to her brother and sister and mother sleeping. She was finding it impossible to believe that this was the last night she would spend in her own home and that tomorrow she would be sleeping in a strange place with people she didn't know. Once again, she wished that it would snow hard so that the walk down to Bolton would be impossible, but the steady drip of meltwater from the roof told her that no such reprieve would come.

When the all-consuming black of night faded into an early morning grey, Lydia got stiffly to her feet, her teeth chattering with cold, and put the last of the coal onto the fire so she could prepare some breakfast. She tiptoed into the back kitchen and hit the ice on the top of the bucket hard with the handle of a spoon, struggling to break the thick layer to get to the water below so she could fill the kettle.

It was coming to the boil before her mother woke.

'I wish tha hadn't used t' last o' that coal,' she complained as she tied her shawl around herself. 'Any wood we collect today'll be too wet to burn.'

Lydia didn't reply. She'd tried so hard to be helpful on her last morning, but it was being thrown back in her face. Her mother would miss her when she was gone, she thought. Simon would never have got out from under his blanket to help – and because he was a boy their mother wouldn't have even expected him to.

They made a thin porridge with the hot water. Lydia sat cross-legged in front of the fire and tried not to think about her impending journey. She was still hoping for some miracle – like her father appearing in the doorway – to save her.

'We'll have to set off in good time if tha wants us to walk down with thee,' said her mother. 'I don't want to walk back when it's gone dark. It seems an odd time to send thee off, so late in the day.'

'There's no need to come,' Lydia told her, knowing that her words would hurt her mother.

'Nay. I'll see thee safe to the stop,' she replied.

Lydia scraped her bowl and spooned the last of the porridge into her mouth. Her mother was probably worried she would run away if she didn't make sure she went to Bolton, thought Lydia. And part of her did want to run away, although she had no idea where she would go.

Sometimes, in the past, she'd thought about going to New South Wales to look for her father. Boys ran away to sea. She'd heard stories about them and she'd wondered if she could disguise herself and get taken on board a ship as a cabin boy. But those ideas had been nothing more than daydreams. They lived a long way from the sea and she had no idea how to get there.

Lydia took her time over washing the pots and tidying away the bowls. She fussed about straightening the straw mattresses and folding the blankets, then began to sweep the floor with a broom – anything to put off the inevitable hour of departure.

When she was done, her mother made her wash herself all over in a bowl of water by the fire. She sent Simon and Rose to play outside to give Lydia some privacy.

'Be a good lass and do as tha's told,' her mother instructed her as she helped her daughter put on the new shift and petticoat that the relief committee had given her. 'Don't go answering back,' she went on as Lydia pulled on the thick stockings and fastened them with garters. 'Tha's lucky to be given these clothes,' she added as Lydia fastened the stays and the jacket. 'But tha'd better put that shawl around thee as well. It'll be cold on yon coach.'

When she was dressed and ready, her mother called to Simon and Rose and they set off for the Old Man and Scythe. All the way there, Lydia hoped that the coach wouldn't come. Perhaps it had become stuck in a rut along the way or had a wheel come off. Such accidents were common.

Her mother walked beside her in silence. Lydia didn't speak either. There wasn't much left to say, but when they reached Bolton and her mother hugged her tightly, Lydia clung to her like a child, remembering all the times when she'd trusted her mother to make things right. If this was what it was like to be a grown-up then she was sorry for it, she thought as she hugged her brother and her little sister and hoped that they would never need to face such adversity as this.

'We can't wait with thee,' said her mother, choking back her tears. 'We'll have to get home afore it goes dark.'

'I know. Go. I'll be all right,' lied Lydia.

Her mother nodded and, after she'd looked back to wave as she turned the corner from Churchgate, Lydia slumped down and wept until a passing man threw her a ha'pence as if she were a beggar.

–

Every step that she took her away from her daughter felt harder than the last to Betty. All she wanted to do was turn around and go back for Lydia and take her home. She knew that the sight of her daughter's brown eyes, brimming with tears as she'd left her outside the inn was an image that was burned onto her memory for ever. She felt as if she'd let Lydia down. She ought to have tried harder to find work for her in Bolton so that they didn't have to be wrenched apart like this. It was too cruel of the parish guardians to send her away.

She only had Simon and Rose now, she thought as she tried to reassure her younger children that their sister was perfectly safe and would enjoy her new life at Caton. Simon seemed doubtful. He'd said nothing, but Betty knew he was wondering if he would be next. Boys his age ought to be working and it probably wouldn't be long before he was taken from her as well. Betty wasn't sure how she would survive if he was sent to Caton too, or worse, apprenticed out to one of the butties who found children to work underground in Colonel Fletcher's coal pits.

If only they'd been allowed to go with Jimmy to New South Wales. She knew that it wouldn't have been easy, but at least they would all have been together. It was the prospect of her family being split apart for ever that troubled Betty the most.

Darkness fell before they reached home and Betty had no lantern. She'd thought it would be easy to find her way because the track was so familiar, but the dark was confusing and more than once she found that they'd gone astray before she saw the welcome sight of a candle burning in her neighbours' window. Bless Ann and Peter for putting it there, she thought as she urged the children on.

'Nearly home!' she said. 'Then we'll have a bite to eat before bedtime.'

'Did she get off all right?' called Ann from her doorway as she heard them approaching. She must have been concerned and watching out for them, thought Betty.

'Aye. I hope so,' she replied. 'We left her at the stop. She should be on her way by now.' The thought of Lydia being rushed away from her through the night was too horrible to contemplate. She hoped she would get to Caton safely and had begged her daughter to try to send word if she could. Her biggest fear was that it would end like it had with Jimmy, and that she would never see Lydia again.

It seemed a long time to Lydia before she heard the notes of the bugle that heralded the mail coach's arrival. The horses came panting and steaming with sweat, pulling the red and black coach behind them. The ostlers hurried out of the stables, some to unharness the horses and others to bring the fresh animals that were tossing their heads and dancing on the cobbles as the ostlers tried to back them between the shafts and buckle up their harness.

'Are you for the coach?' a man in a red braided coat and top hat barked at Lydia.

'Aye. I've a ticket here,' she said, fumbling to find it.

'Outside seat. Up there, next to the driver,' he told her and she almost gasped as she caught sight of the pistol tucked into his belt as he turned away to grasp the sacks of letters that the postman had brought.

Lydia gathered her skirts and clambered up to the wooden bench at the very front of the coach. The driver was watching the horses and once he was assured that everything was secure he climbed up beside Lydia, giving her a curious glance. She averted her eyes and tried to make herself as comfortable as she could whilst staring at the flurry of activity below her.

There were some other passengers getting into the coach – a middle-aged man, a woman wrapped in a rug, who returned her gaze with a sympathetic look before disappearing through the door, and a young man with a pointed nose, whom Lydia took for a clergyman.

Too soon, the inside passengers were settled on their plush seats, out of the wind and the cold, and the letters secured in the sturdy metal post box. After the guard had consulted his pocket watch, he climbed up at the back and sounded his bugle to warn any bystanders to move out of the way. Then, the driver cracked his whip and the horses leapt forward, their hooves scrabbling to get purchase on the slippery cobbles. Lydia's stomach lurched along with the coach. There was no turning back now. If she tried to jump down she would be trampled under the hooves or the wheels. The wind began to whistle past her as they picked up speed and soon they were on their way, rushing through the darkness with only the coach's lanterns to guide their way along the road that would take them north.

They travelled at a fantastic speed and Lydia marvelled at how the horses could see which way to go. In different circumstances she might have found it exciting, but the parting from her mother and siblings made it too hard to find any pleasure in this adventure and she was glad that it was dark and the driver couldn't see that she was gulping back tears and struggling not to sob out loud.

Lydia had no idea how far it was to Caton. They galloped through the night until the long journey lulled her into a state of sleepiness. Then, after time had passed, she had no idea how much, she saw lights up ahead. The cottages clustered more closely together and there were people about. The guard sounded some notes on his bugle again and soon they were rushing through streets with buildings on either side – cottages and shops and beerhouses. The driver pulled hard on the reins and the wheels began to slow. They came around a corner with the horses slipping and the coach lurching to one side. Lydia clung on as people leapt out of the way and they rolled to a halt outside an inn where more ostlers ran out to change the horses.

The inside passengers got down. The young clergyman hurried on his way, but the woman paused and peered up at her anxiously before being hurried inside the inn by her husband.

'Where are we? Do I get off here?' Lydia asked the driver, worried that she would be forgotten and taken on goodness only knew where.

'This is Lancaster. Stay put,' the man told her irritably. 'You're to get off at Caton.'

When letters had been exchanged and the fresh horses harnessed, the guard shouted out the next stop was Kirkby Lonsdale and a man with a tall hat hurried towards the coach, removing it to give him enough headroom to duck under the doorway and take his seat. Once the door was slammed shut, the driver cracked his whip over the heads of the fresh horses, the bugle sounded and Lydia grasped the seat as they set off again into the cold, dark night.

After a while the driver began to slow the horses even though there was no sign of an inn or a town.

'This is Caton,' he told her. 'We're to put you down here. Whoa!' he shouted as he reined in the eager animals to a halt. Lydia glanced about in alarm. Everything around her was black. They seemed to have stopped in the middle of nowhere.

'Get a move on!' shouted the guard, making her jump as he swung his lantern into her face, blinding her with its light. 'We have a timetable to keep.'

Lydia fumbled her way to the edge of the seat and felt for the steps with her feet. The horses were restless and the coach kept shifting as she climbed down. At last, she felt the ground beneath her feet, even if her boots did sink into the mud.

'Stand away from the wheels!' cried the guard as the coachman cracked his whip once more and the horses surged forwards. The wheels spun, throwing out a smattering of mud that Lydia felt hit her in filthy spats. She almost cried for the spoiling of her new clothes as the coach was swallowed up by the darkness, leaving her with just the fading sound of its wheels.

Lydia stood alone, not sure what to do. She could hear the wind howling and there was a sheep baaing mournfully somewhere in the distance, but the sound of the coach's wheels had long faded and the pinprick lights of its lanterns had been swallowed by the night. There wasn't even a moon or stars. The sky, if she'd been able to see it, would still be cloaked with thick cloud and as if to prove it was so, Lydia felt the first drops of a rainstorm splashing down around her.

She hugged her arms around herself as she puzzled over what to do next. She had no idea which direction to take to find the mill. There seemed to be a few cottages scattered around; she could see the flickering of candles at one or two windows. She was wondering if she dared to go and knock on one of the doors and beg for shelter when she realised that one of the lights she could see was moving towards her. She waited, watching its approach until a man materialised out of the night.

'Lydia Knowles?' he asked her.

'Aye, that's me.'

'This way,' he said, turning back the way he'd come.

Lydia followed his steps down the track, trying not to step in puddles as the lantern swung to and fro, casting shadows all around them. She wondered if he was Mr Greg, but she didn't dare ask. Whoever he was, he didn't seem pleased to have come out in the dark and the rain to fetch her.

They walked only a short distance before they reached the mill. Lydia could see glimpses of the towering building with its tall chimney and firmly locked wooden gates as they approached, but the man didn't take her inside. He continued to a large house where he rapped on the doorknocker and stood aside. Lydia stood on the edge of the circle of light cast by his lowered lantern and waited, wondering if this was where she was to live. A moment later, the bolts were drawn back and a woman in a cap and apron peered out at them.

'Lydia Knowles,' said the man before leaving them alone.

'Come in,' said the woman. 'You look wet through.'

Lydia stepped inside, waited until the woman had relocked the door and then followed her to a parlour where a fire was lit.

'Come to the fire,' said the woman, leading Lydia past the rows of benches and tables. 'Take off that shawl and I'll hang it to dry. Sit down.'

Lydia did as she was told, realising how tired and hungry she felt. The new jacket and her petticoat were wet and covered in mud from the coach's wheels. She could feel her hair dripping from the strands that had escaped her cap and she saw from the woman's glance that she looked a mess – not the clean and neatly dressed lass who had left home earlier that day.

'I don't know what they were thinking of, sending thee at this time,' complained the woman as she put the shawl to dry. 'Here.' She handed Lydia a rough linen towel. 'Dry thyself as best tha can and I'll fetch thee summat else to put on. Tha'll be no use if tha catches thy death of cold on thy first night,' she remarked as she went out of the room.

Lydia rubbed at her face and hair as she heard the woman's footsteps going up the stairs. A few minutes later she returned with a clean shift and a blanket.

'Get out of those wet clothes and put this on,' she instructed. Gladly, Lydia took off the wet jacket and found that she was damp right down to her skin. But the fire was blazing and she rubbed herself dry, enjoying its warmth.

By the time she'd put on the shift and wrapped the blanket around her shoulders, the woman had returned with a bowl of thick porridge and some slices of brown bread. Lydia accepted the food eagerly and ate it all, trying not to look too greedy. Perhaps things wouldn't be as bad as she'd feared, she thought. Although she missed her home and her mother and her eyes kept welling up with tears, it was good to have warm toes and a full belly for a change.

'Tha looks all in,' remarked the woman who had told her she was Mrs Simms and that she was in charge of all the female apprentices. 'I'll show thee where tha's to sleep.'

Lydia followed Mrs Simms up the stairs to a long room under the eaves. As she held up her candle to light the way, Lydia saw that there were rows of box beds down each side of the room with just enough space to walk between them.

'Tha's in with Violet,' said Mrs Simms as she stopped at one where Lydia could see a huddled form already under the blankets. At home, she'd shared her bed with her sister, Rose, when they still had beds, but she was reluctant to get in with a stranger. 'Hurry up!' chided Mrs Simms. So Lydia climbed into the bed and pulled the blanket over her. The other lass moaned in her sleep, but didn't wake and without even wishing her a good night, Mrs Simms went back to the door with her candle and closed it behind her. Lydia was left in darkness once more, listening to the shifting and breathing of the dozens of other apprentices.

Chapter Four

Betty woke with a hollow feeling in the pit of her stomach. It was a moment before she realised what was wrong. Then she remembered that Lydia wasn't with them and her heart yearned for her. She wished that there was some way she could find out if her daughter was all right and if she was being treated kindly, but other than sending a letter and hoping for a reply there was no way she could get in touch – and even a letter was impossible. She had no money to pay for one to be sent and Lydia had no money to pay to receive it. Even if she did earn some wages, Betty wasn't sure that her daughter would want to spend her money on a letter from home. Lydia had been so upset when they'd left her at the coach stop, and Betty couldn't blame her. She knew that her daughter thought she'd failed her by not keeping the family together and she was right. Betty did feel as if she'd failed.

She pulled herself up from the floor and stared at the few tired sticks on the hearth. They wouldn't make much of a blaze and she needed to gather more before she could boil water. She pushed her feet into her clogs and went to the door. It had rained earlier, but was fine now. There was the acrid smell of coal smoke coming from the chimneys of other houses around the fold and a few folk had opened their curtains to welcome the new day. Betty glanced back at Simon and Rose, who were still sleeping, and pulled the door quietly closed. The sharp air bit into her lungs as she walked towards the woodland that lay behind the houses. She hoped that the wind in the night had brought down a few more branches.

She trudged through the trees, picking up a branch here and there and a few twigs. Her haul wasn't as much as she'd hoped for, but it would be enough to get the fire going for now. The next day, she would have to go before the relief committee again to see how much money they were willing to pay her this week and whether she would be able to afford a bucket of coal when she'd bought food, or if they would be forced to sit in the cold if they were to eat.

Back in the cottage, Simon and Rose were awake and they'd rolled up the straw mattresses and put them aside. Simon was trying to break the ice on the bucket of water. Betty's heart went out to him. He was doing his best to take on the tasks that would have been Lydia's.

'Here, I'll do it,' she said, moving him aside and hitting the ice hard with the wooden spoon. It was thick this morning.

'I could have done it,' he complained as he watched her fill the kettle.

'I know,' she said. She ought to have let him. It would be his eleventh birthday in a few weeks. Her own brother had been in work for five years at the same age and yet she still thought of Simon as a baby. It was as if she didn't want to acknowledge that he was growing up. She was terrified of losing him as well.

They got a small fire going and after they'd eaten the last of the food in the pantry, Betty was surprised by the sudden knock on her door. The rent wasn't due today and most folk just called and came in. Fear almost overwhelmed her that something terrible had happened to Lydia – there had been a coach accident; she'd run away; she hadn't arrived at Caton and they were here to look for her!

Betty caught herself automatically straightening her cap and her threadbare apron as she went to answer the knocking. Perhaps it was because she couldn't possibly receive bad news if she was neat and tidy, she thought, as if it were a charm.

She eased back the door a fraction and peeped out. The vicar of the parish church, the Reverend Brocklehurst, was standing there. He took off his hat when he saw her.

'Mrs Knowles. Good morning! May I come in?'

'Aye. Of course.' Betty opened the door fully and stood back as he passed her. She closed it against the rush of cold air and turned to see that he had gone across to the hearth to warm his hands.

'Have you no coal?' he asked when he saw the remains of the few sticks in her grate.

'No. It's all gone. But tomorrow's the day I get my relief.' She watched his face, trying to find some clue as to why he'd come. It must be bad news. 'Is it Lydia?' she whispered, hoping that she wasn't going to disgrace herself by having a fainting fit. She could see the darkness encroaching the edges of her vision already as all manner of frightening ideas streamed through her imagination. She wished there was a chair for her to sit on.

'No. No.' He shook his head. 'I've had a letter,' he told her, drawing an envelope out from an inner pocket of his coat. 'It's from the Home Office,' he explained. 'Your husband has sent a request for you to join him in New South Wales.'

'My husband?' Betty stared at the clergyman, not quite comprehending what he was telling her. 'But I've never heard from him in years.'

'Even so, it seems that he wants you to join him.'

Betty began to shake her head. 'But I asked to go, when he was first convicted,' she told the vicar. 'All of us Bolton wives who lost a husband that day asked for passage, but we were turned down.' She couldn't believe that Jimmy was sending for her now, after all this time, that he was alive and that he wanted her to go to him. It made no sense. She'd long since resigned herself to never seeing him again. There had been so many disappointments and she wasn't going to be tempted by hope again only to have it dashed away from her.

'Yes, I remember writing some of those letters,' said the vicar. 'It was disappointing, I know. But things have changed,' he told her. 'Governor Macquarie – the man in charge of the colony down there – is keen for more families to be reunited. He believes that wives will be a good influence on the men and will keep them out of any further trouble. But I'm getting ahead of myself,' he told her with a slight frown. 'The letter doesn't actually grant you a passage,' he explained. 'It only asks if you would be willing to go if you were offered a place.'

Betty knew that it was too good to be true.

'What's the use of it then?' she asked, thinking that the vicar had wasted his time bringing her a letter that was just another false promise. 'It's cruel of 'em to keep taunting folk like this,' she said, 'when they've no intention of keepin' their word.'

'I understand how you feel,' sympathised the vicar. 'But the Home Office have asked me to approach you about this matter and I have no reason to believe that they are not sincere.'

'But it isn't a definite offer of passage?' said Betty.

'No,' he agreed. 'That's what the letter says.' He paused. 'I don't know all the ins and outs of it,' he admitted. 'It's the first I've heard of this scheme, but I think it probably depends on how many free places there are on the convict ships.'

'Aye, that'll be it,' replied Betty.

'So what shall I reply?' asked the vicar. 'Would you be willing to go, if there is a place for you?'

'What about my childer?'

'Your husband has asked for the children to accompany you,' the vicar reassured her. 'He's named them on his application – Lydia, Simon and Rose. How old is Simon?' he asked, glancing at her son, who was watching warily from the pantry door.

'He's ten.'

'That's all right then.' The vicar nodded. 'It says that boys aged ten and under are eligible for passage. Shall I tell the Home Office that you would like to be considered?' he pressed her.

Betty wasn't sure how to reply. Of course she wanted to see Jimmy again, but this news had come as a shock after she'd convinced herself that he must be dead and had resigned herself to the life of hardship that she was leading here in Bolton. The prospect of leaving everything that was familiar to sail to the other side of the word filled her with trepidation.

'How soon do I need to decide?' she asked. 'I need time to think about it.'

'Why would you need to think about it?' asked the vicar, clearly puzzled by her reluctance. 'You couldn't be any worse off than this,' he added, waving a hand around the empty parlour. 'A fresh start in a new country might be the best thing for you. And surely you want to be with your husband? It's only right that a man and wife should be together.'

'It's been such a long time since I saw him. And it's such a long way to go. I was hoping as he might come back to me, like Thomas Holden came back, aye and Jack Fisher as well.'

The vicar nodded. 'It is quite an undertaking,' he agreed, 'but I'm sure that you are capable. You're young and strong. The sea journey shouldn't trouble you.'

The idea of it frightened Betty but she didn't like to admit it. It seemed wrong to say that she was afraid of being reunited with her husband, especially to a clergyman.

'So shall I write back to say that you would be willing to go?' the vicar urged her.

'When will I get a reply?' she asked him. 'How soon will I know if there are places? How would we get to the boat?' She had so many questions that she didn't know where to begin, but it was clear from the vicar's perplexed face that he didn't know the answers either.

'I really couldn't say, Mrs Knowles. The letter doesn't go into much detail. I think it's just a preliminary enquiry as to whether you would like to be considered. Shall I say that you would like to go?'

Betty realised that he wasn't going to leave until he had her agreement. 'Aye, all right,' she said after a moment, thinking that it would probably come to nothing anyway.

'Good!' said the vicar as he folded the letter and put it back into his pocket. 'I'll write back to them straight away.'

As he turned to go, a thought struck Betty. 'Could I ask a favour?' she ventured, unsure how to ask.

'Yes, of course. What is it?'

'I need to write a letter as well,' she told him. 'My elder daughter's gone as an apprentice to the spinning mill at Caton and I want to send word to make sure she arrived safely. I'm worried.'

'Yes, of course,' replied the vicar. 'I don't suppose you have pen and paper here?' Betty shook her head. She had nothing. 'Then come down to the vestry this afternoon and I'll gladly do it for you.'

'Thank you.' Betty watched as the Reverend Brockle-hurst put on his hat and hurried away from the cottage. He was a kind man and never reprimanded her for her poor attendance at church. She ought to make the effort to attend service more often, though it was a long way to go down to the parish church and most Sundays she was too tired, preferring the worship at the non-conformist chapel that she knew the vicar disapproved of.

After they'd eaten a few scraps of stale bread, Betty told Simon and Rose to wash their hands and faces, then they set off to walk down into Bolton. As they passed the Old Man and Scythe on their way to the church, Betty stared at the spot where she'd last seen Lydia. Where was she now and what she was doing? Betty hoped that they were being kind to her at Caton and that Lydia wasn't pining too much for home. Perhaps, if she was feeling upset, a letter would help to lift her spirits and cheer her up, especially now that Betty could write to say that there had been word from her father, that he was alive, and that he wanted them to go to join him in New South Wales.

The vicar's vestry was warm. He found a chair for Betty to sit down and she wished that she could stay there all day.

The fire was making her fingers tingle and Rose's cheeks were growing pinker as she sat on her mother's knee and ate the slice of bread and butter that the vicar had passed to her from his own plate when he saw that she couldn't stop looking at it hungrily.

'What do you want to say in your letter?' he asked Betty when he was ready, with his pen in hand, hovering above his inkwell.

'I want to ask if she got there all right. Just ask that first. Though I don't know if she'll be able to write back with an answer.'

'I'm sure she arrived safely,' the vicar reassured her. 'And she'll be glad to hear that you are thinking of her.'

'I hope so,' said Betty, remembering Lydia's glum face and hoping that her daughter would forgive her for sending her away.

'What are you going to tell her about her father?' asked the vicar.

'Tell her that he's alive and he's written to us.'

'Are you going to tell her that he's asked you to go to New South Wales?'

'Why wouldn't I?'

The vicar rested his pen on the edge of the inkwell and turned to face Betty straight on. 'I began to think about what you told me after I saw you this morning,' he said. 'This matter of the indenture may make things difficult and it isn't certain yet that you will be offered a passage.'

'The indenture?' repeated Betty, unsure what he was trying to say.

'Yes. The paper that is the agreement of her apprenticeship. Did you not sign it?'

'No. The parish guardians and yon magistrate put their names to it. I just watched.'

'Yes, of course. It would have required her father's signature,' mused the vicar. 'In his absence, the parish would be responsible.' He drummed his fingers on his desk as he became lost in thought for a moment or two. 'Best say nothing to Lydia about going to New South Wales for the moment,' he advised. 'I'll try to make some enquiries, but it's a new situation so there will be no precedent,' he remarked as he picked up the pen again to continue writing the letter. 'You mustn't think that I know everything about this because I don't,' admitted the Reverend Brocklehurst. 'It might need someone with better knowledge of the law than me.'

'I don't understand,' Betty told him, puzzled by what he was saying. 'What does going to New South Wales have to do with the indenture?'

'It's a legal document,' explained the vicar. 'Lydia is indentured to Mr Greg until she is twenty-one years old. She can't simply leave the mill and go with you without breaking the agreement. I'm not sure if it would be allowed.'

Betty didn't reply. The thought of having to leave Lydia behind if she went to join her husband was a prospect she couldn't comprehend. Surely Mr Greg would not be so cruel as to prevent Lydia from going with the rest of her family?

Chapter Five

Lydia had no idea where she was when she was startled into wakefulness by the sound of a bell being rung. She thought that it was the middle of the night and wondered what was wrong because dozens of girls in the crowded attic were stumbling from their beds and vying for space to pull on their clothing.

A face loomed over her, contorted by the shadows from a nearby tallow candle. Lydia realised it was the girl she'd shared a bed with who was looking at her with such distaste.

'Who are you?' she asked. Her accent was strange and it was a moment before Lydia understood her. 'Are you stupid or something?' she went on. 'I hope you're not a bedwetter.'

Some of the other girls standing within earshot began to laugh and Lydia felt herself blush and reach out a hand to check that the mattress was dry.

'I'm Lydia Knowles. I arrived last night,' she said as the events of the previous day reasserted themselves in her memory and she realised that she'd woken in the apprentice house at Lower Mill in Caton.

'Best get up then,' said the girl.

'Aye.' Lydia rubbed at her eyes. They ached and she wanted to go back to sleep. She was sure it couldn't be morning already.

She climbed awkwardly out of the bed. The floor was cold when her bare feet touched it and she realised that she needed to wee but wasn't sure where to go. She had no idea where her clothes were, either. Mrs Simms had put them to dry last night and Lydia wondered if she was expected to go down the stairs barefoot, clad only in her shift to find them.

She was still wondering what to do when she heard her name being called.

'Lydia Knowles!'

She turned and saw Mrs Simms pushing her way towards her.

'Here are your clothes. Put them on quickly,' she instructed, thrusting the items into Lydia's hands. 'They may be a bit damp still, but there's no helping that. Mr Greg asks for two sets of clothing to be sent with each apprentice but it seems yon Bolton folk were either too hard up or too stingy.' She sniffed to show her disapproval.

'Please, Mrs Simms, I'm... I'm burstin',' Lydia said, not knowing how else to ask. She blushed as she heard more laughter from the girls around her.

'There's a chamber pot under the bed,' replied Mrs Knowles. 'Get a move on.'

'But...' Lydia couldn't believe that she was expected to relieve herself in this room as all the others watched, nudging one other and whispering behind their hands about her. She fumbled under the bed and found the white pot, already part filled with waste and stinking. She wondered if it was some sort of trick designed to test her, but Lydia knew that if she didn't empty her bladder soon she would wet herself and that would really give them something to laugh about.

She hitched up her shift and squatted as best she could, trying not to make eye contact with anyone, but she needn't have worried. Most of the girls were on their way to the door, clattering down the stairs. They'd lost interest in her now.

Alone in the room, Lydia inched the pot back under the bed with her foot. It was so full that she worried it would slop over if she tried to push it too hard. She picked up her stays and fumbled to lace them with cold hands, shivering as she put on her jacket and pulled the apron over her head. Hurrying, she didn't bother combing her hair, but pushed it under her cap before balancing on the edge of the bed to put on her stockings and boots.

As soon as she was ready she went down to see the last of the other girls disappearing through the outer door.

'Hurry up!' called Mrs Simms. 'Tha doesn't want to be late on thy first mornin'.'

Lydia followed the sound of the girls' voices out onto the lane. It was almost as dark as when she'd arrived, but a full moon had risen and cast enough light for her to find her way to the mill gates that now stood open. She followed the others into a cobbled yard then through a doorway into the mill itself. Lydia stood and stared at the sight that confronted her. The long, low room was filled with machinery and, as she watched, it suddenly sprang to life with a noise that filled her with alarm and made her raise her hands to protect her ears.

'What's tha doin' standin' there gawpin'?' shouted a voice close behind her.

Lydia turned and saw the same man who had collected her from the coach the night before.

'Come with me!' he called, beckoning her with a finger.

Lydia hurried after him, up and down iron stairs and across metal grilles that rang out beneath her feet.

'Tha'll be startin' in here,' he announced when they reached a room where the raw cotton was being spread on giant combs to be carded. 'When it's done it curls itself into one o' these tubs,' he explained. 'It'll be thy job to move the full ones, put empty ones in their place and then carry the full one down to yon spinnin' room. Dost tha think that can do that?' he asked her, peering into her face as if he thought she was stupid.

Lydia nodded. 'Aye, I can do that,' she agreed, relieved that no more difficult task was being expected of her. She'd been terrified of being asked to work the jennies when she'd no idea what to do.

The overseer lingered long enough to check that Lydia had the sense to put an empty tub in place of a full one before she took it to the spinners. He nodded his approval when he saw that she'd grasped the rudiments of her task and left her to it.

After they'd been working for a while, Lydia was surprised by the sudden silence as the machinery unexpectedly powered down. For a moment all she could hear was ringing in her ears and then it was replaced by the sound of clogs and boots as the others shoved and pushed one another to get into the queue for what Lydia saw was their breakfast.

Mrs Simms had a huge bowl on a trolley and she was dipping her ladle into it and pouring the thick porridge, not into bowls, but into the open hands of the apprentices, who were turning away, blowing on it and lapping it up like animals. Lydia wiped her hands on her apron before holding them out for the food. The porridge landed on her palms with a thick squelch. It was nothing like the thin gruel that she'd been used to eating at home. She raised her hands to her mouth and began to eat hungrily, watching the other boys and girls who perched here and there or sat on the floor to rest their legs during the break. But she'd barely had time to lick the last of the porridge from between her fingers when the overseer began to chivvy them back to their work and the machinery started up once again with its terrific noise.

Lydia's fingers were still sticky as she returned to her work, but her stomach was full. Daylight was now coming in through the bank of windows and the candles were put out once they were able to see their work without them.

The time passed fairly quickly as she rolled the tubs backwards and forwards, making sure that each was filled to the brim but didn't spill over. At noon, a bell rang out and Lydia followed the other workers out of the mill to return to the apprentice house for their dinner. Seeing her surroundings for the first time in daylight, she realised they looked nothing like she'd imagined them the previous evening. There was no moorland here. The mill was set in a deep valley that was thick with trees, although Lydia could see glimpses of hills all around and mountains in the far distance, and the high walls of the spinning mill were higher and longer than she had thought when she'd caught a glimpse of them by the light of her guide's lantern.

She was the last into the apprentice house and saw that the others were sitting in the downstairs parlour, at the tables with benches on either side. There were some boys, who sat at their own table, but the workers were mostly girls – some younger and a few older. Lydia found all the seats taken and Mrs Simms shouted at one row of girls to shove up and make room for her. Her bedfellow was sitting on the other side of the table, sniggering behind her hand to her neighbour and Lydia wondered what she'd done to make this girl so openly dislike her.

The bowls of food were passed around – bread soaked in milk with a dusting of sugar. Lydia spooned it into her mouth eagerly, ignoring the laughter from across the table. She wished that she could go home. She didn't think she would ever like being in this place and the next six years stretched ahead of her like an unending road with no clear destination.

When they'd finished eating, the girls split up into groups, chatting. Mrs Simms glared at the girls who'd been tormenting Lydia and set them to clearing the tables and washing the bowls. Others picked up their sewing or took off their caps to brush one another's hair. Lydia sat alone and watched them until another girl came to join her.

'Take no notice of Violet,' she advised Lydia, nodding her head towards the girl who was looking daggers at them from beside the sink where she was being made to wash up. 'She's a nasty piece of work. She has a few cronies that she's gathered around her, but most of us don't like her. She's a bully. No one wants to share a bed with her, not even her supposed friends. As soon as there's space with someone else they ask to be moved. That's why new lasses always end up with her. I'm Miriam, by the way,' she said.

'I'm Lydia.'

'Which workhouse hast tha come from?'

'I've not come from a workhouse,' Lydia explained. 'The parish guardians at Bolton sent me.'

'Hast tha no family?'

'I've a mother and a brother and sister.'

'Did thy father die?' asked Miriam. 'Mine did. Cholera.'

'No. He was sent to New South Wales.'

'As good as dead then.'

'No!' protested Lydia. 'He'll come back. He'll come and take me away from here,' she went on, suddenly finding some hope to cling to. If her father did return he would never allow her to stay in this place.

'I don't think people come back from there,' replied Miriam.

'They do!' Lydia said. 'I know some that have come back. I think my father will come soon.'

When their dinner hour was up, Lydia walked back to the mill with Miriam. It felt good to have made a friend and she was relieved that not all the other apprentices were as hostile towards her as Violet. They parted at the door, because Miriam worked as a spinner, and Lydia found her way back to the carding room to continue her work.

Darkness had fallen by late afternoon and the candles were lit again. At about half past five, Mrs Simms came in with more bread to eat, but the machines didn't power down and they were expected to continue with their work as they ate. Lydia wondered how long they were expected to go on for. She was so tired and found it harder and harder to concentrate; twice she was shouted at for forgetting to replace a full tub of cotton with an empty one and had to bend down to rescue the fibres from the floor.

At last, the machines powered down and the apprentices made their way back to the house. But even though Lydia was longing for sleep, she was dreading going to bed again because of Violet.

The girls went into the parlour and began to sit down again at the benches. Lydia wondered if there was to be another meal, but she was disappointed when Mrs Simms began to hand out sewing for them to do. It seemed that they were to spend their evening making shirts and shifts from the bolts of plain cloth that were being unrolled. At least it was warm, she thought as she held her cotton thread up to the light to guide it through the eye of her needle.

She'd managed to find a seat near to Miriam and some other girls who welcomed her and showed her what to do. Violet was at the far side of the room and although Lydia was aware of her and the few girls gathered near to her, she tried to ignore them and hoped that by bedtime Violet would be too tired to make trouble. But when Lydia was allowed to finish her work and go upstairs, she found that Violet was already in the bed. She'd positioned herself in the middle of it and gave Lydia a look that dared her to complain. Not sure what to do and dreading the prospect of a night on the cold, hard floor, Lydia looked about for some solution, but the other girls seemed unwilling to intervene.

Lydia was wondering whether to simply fling herself on top of Violet and fight for her space when Mrs Simms came in to make sure everyone was under the covers and the candles were blown out.

'Move thyself up, Violet Hargreaves!' she reprimanded as she passed by. 'I'm in no mood for thy nonsense tonight. Everyone else shares a bed and tha's nowt special, even if tha might think so.'

Reluctantly, Violet rolled over, turning her back, and Lydia climbed in beside her. She was so weary that she was grateful for any bed and when Violet kicked her, she nipped her fiercely on the arm and delighted in her yelp of pain.

In the darkness, Lydia lay awake for longer than she had expected. Images of her day and the constant filling and rolling of the cotton tubs played in her mind until she thought she would never sleep. But before long she fell into a restless slumber, although she felt as if she'd only slept for an hour or two at most when she heard the bell ringing and it was time to get up and go to work in the mill again.

Lydia got out of the bed before Violet was properly awake and she dressed herself quickly. She wanted to get well away from her bedfellow as soon as possible. She found her friend Miriam on the way out of the apprentice house and they walked together. It had frozen overnight and the ground was crunchy under their feet. In the mill, the candles were blazing and the machinery was powering up as the workers came yawning and shivering to their places.

Lydia ached. She wasn't used to the repetitive physical work that she'd been set to do, but she supposed it could have been worse. It was the first time in her life that she'd been certain of her next meal and she found herself looking forward to the porridge breakfast that she knew would be brought to them in a couple of hours. If only she could have gone home to her mother in the evenings she could have resigned herself to the work, she thought. It wasn't difficult and although the overseer sometimes shouted, she'd never seen him hit or beat anyone and she knew it was something to be thankful for.

Later in the morning she rolled a full tub of carded cotton down to the spinning room and took a moment to watch what the spinners were doing. The sight of the machines moving this way and that, and the workers dodging in between them looked both dangerous and mesmerising. The thick strands of combed cotton were fed into the machines that moved forwards and backwards, stretching and twisting the fibres, making them thinner and stronger until they were wound onto the bobbins. Some of the younger children were set to clearing up the fluff that accumulated under the jennies. They hurried in with dustpans and brushes to sweep, until the machines began to move back towards them and they scurried out of the way. The older girls were watching the threads in case they snapped, and if they did they hurried forward to twist the fibres between their fingers to repair them.

As she watched, Lydia caught Violet's eye. The girl mouthed something at her and she turned away. She felt close to tears as she carried an empty tub back to the carding room, unable to understand why someone would hate her so much. At home, all the neighbours had been like family. Everyone helped one another and she'd always had friends amongst the other girls who lived in the fold. She'd never come across anyone like Violet in her life – someone who disliked her for no reason and who seemed to delight in seeing her upset and afraid.

She tried to put Violet out of her mind as she worked, reminding herself that Miriam wanted to be her friend, but it seemed that Violet was determined to provoke her. As they were walking back to the apprentice house for their dinner, she felt her cap being tugged off her head and her hair pulled hard.

'Stop it!' she cried. 'Give that back,' she said as she watched Violet and a couple of her allies tossing the cap between them, jeering at her to come and try to take it back from them. Knowing that she would get into trouble for losing it, Lydia ran between them and tried to snatch it, but they were too quick for her and laughed even more at her frustration. It wasn't until Mrs Simms called from the door for them to be quick if they didn't want to miss their dinner that they threw it aside into a muddy puddle at the side of the road and trod on it with glee before they ran off, laughing.

Lydia picked up the dripping wet cap and wrung it out in her hands. She couldn't possibly put it back on and she didn't have one spare, so she pushed it into her pocket. She found a place at the table next to Miriam and tried to cheer up when she saw that they were being served bacon and potatoes to eat. It was a long time since she'd had bacon and she ought to have enjoyed it, but her appetite was spoiled by the incident outside and she found it difficult to hold back the tears long enough to swallow.

After they'd eaten, Lydia asked Mrs Simms if she could wash the cap and put it to dry.

'What happened to it?' asked the matron.

'It blew off and landed in a puddle,' Lydia told her. She found that she was unable to tell the truth because she feared it would make things worse between her and Violet.

'That was very careless!' reprimanded Mrs Simms. 'It'll not be dry for when tha goes back to work – and tha can't go without one. It's too dangerous. Tha doesn't want thy hair gettin' caught up in t' machinery,' she warned.

'I don't have another,' Lydia said.

Mrs Simms sighed. 'I'll lend thee one from t' sewing cupboard,' she said. 'But only this once. Tha'll have to learn to be more careful!'

Lydia accepted the new cap and washed the old one. She knew that Violet was laughing at her behind her back, but she refused to look round or show any sign that she cared. But silently she cursed the girl and vowed that she would find a way to pay her back.

That evening as Lydia had her head bent over her sewing, trying to make neat stitches and not fall asleep, she heard Mrs Simms say her name.

'Lydia Knowles. There's a letter come for thee.'

Fighting down the haze of tiredness that was threatening to engulf her entirely, Lydia stared at the matron and wasn't sure what to do.

'Can tha read?' asked Mrs Simms.

'A bit,' she told her as Mrs Simms put the letter in her hand. Lydia stared at it. She recognised her own name on the front of it, but couldn't understand who might be writing to her. 'Who is it from?' she asked.

'Tha'll have to open it to find out,' Mrs Simms told her before instructing the other girls to put their sewing away and go up to bed.

The benches scraped on the floor and the girls began to go up the stairs in groups of two or three.

'In bed in five minutes!' Mrs Simms warned them. 'I'll be up to make sure all the candles are out then.'

Lydia lingered, staring at her letter. She didn't want to open it in case someone was sending her bad news. What if an accident had happened? She closed her eyes and thought of her mother and Simon and Rose, and prayed that they were safe.

'What's tha cryin' about?' asked Mrs Simms, not unkindly, when she noticed that Lydia hadn't moved. 'Tha's not even opened it yet. What's to do?'

Lydia unfolded the letter with trembling fingers and wiped her eyes on the back of her hand to prevent her tears smudging the words that were written there. Then, with one finger under the letters that had been written with a flamboyant hand, she traced the words, mouthing them under her breath as she read.

> *Dear Lydia, I hope that you have safely arrived at the spinning mill in Caton and that all is to your satisfaction. I am missing you and also your brother and sister are missing you.*
>
> *We have received news of your father in New South Wales. He is alive. There is nothing more to write at the present.*
>
> *Your loving Mother*

Lydia put the letter down on the table and cried again.

'It's not bad news, is it?' asked Mrs Simms, coming to put a hand on Lydia's shoulder.

'No. It's about my father. He's alive!' she told her. And even though her mother had written nothing about him coming home, Lydia knew that he would come. He would take her away from this place and they would be a family again.

Chapter Six

Betty wondered whether to go into Bolton alone to collect her relief money. Simon was old enough to be left, but she wasn't sure that she could trust him to watch Rose – and although Ann told her again and again that she enjoyed minding the child, Betty didn't like to impose. In the end she decided to take Rose and leave Simon, giving him instructions to go gathering firewood so that they could make a broth from whatever she could afford to buy on the market. It also meant that the relief committee wouldn't see him. She was afraid that if she took him into the boardroom with her, Mr Lomax might decide that they should send her son away as well and Betty was determined to avoid that.

She set off down the track, holding Rose's hand. The weather had turned a little milder, which Betty was thankful for, although there were many weeks of winter left and the possibility of more snow and freezing conditions preyed on her mind.

The church clock was striking ten when she presented herself before the committee, hating the humiliation of each interview.

'So, how are you this morning, Mrs Knowles?' asked Mr Hewitt.

'Quite well, sir.'

'Did your daughter get away safely?'

'I think so, sir. I saw her to the stop myself, but couldn't wait to see her onto the coach on account of the darkness setting in and needing to get back.'

He nodded. 'So you just have two children at home now?' he asked.

'That's right, sir. Now that my Lydia's been sent away,' she added, feeling bitter.

'Of course. Now, we've made an adjustment to your money,' he told her, running a pencil down the list of figures in the ledger in front of him. 'There's your rent and then there'll be four shillings—'

'Where's thy son today?' barked Mr Lomax, interrupting him. 'Has he got work?' he demanded, obviously suspicious that Betty wasn't being honest.

'No!' Betty became afraid that they might try to cut her money even further if they thought that Simon was earning a wage. 'I've left him gathering firewood. We've nowt else to burn,' she added.

'How old is the boy?' asked Mr Hamer.

'Ten years old,' replied Betty.

'What? What did she say? How old?' he demanded of Mr Hewitt.

'She said he's ten!' shouted the ironmonger.

'Ten, tha says? Why's he not in work?' There was a tense silence as Betty grasped Rose by the hand. 'What about the mill?' he asked and Betty felt a shiver run through her as she feared that she would be forced to part with Simon as well as Lydia.

'They only want lasses.'

'The pit, then?'

'No!' Betty couldn't prevent the protestation escaping her lips. Not the pit, she thought. That was worse than him being sent away to Caton.

'They're always wantin' lads at t' pit,' interrupted Mr Lomax.

'I don't want him goin' down yon pit,' Betty told them. 'It's not safe.'

'Nonsense!' replied Mr Lomax. 'A lad that age ought to be in work. Tha needs to take him down and get him set on.'

Betty looked to Mr Hewitt, who was always the more reasonable man.

'It's true, Mrs Knowles,' he said. 'They always need more lads at the pit and thy son is ten years old now. More than old enough to be doing a day's work.'

'Tha can have what we've agreed this week,' cut in Mr Lomax, as he placed the pile of coins on the edge of the table for Betty to pick up. 'But next week it'll be reduced, on the understandin' that there's a wage comin' in. So make sure tha takes thy lad to the pit tomorrow,' he warned her.

Betty didn't reply straight away. She stepped forward and put the money in her purse. It wouldn't go far.

'Is there a ticket for some bread?' she asked, hoping they hadn't forgotten it.

'Only one loaf,' replied Mr Hamer, pushing the paper token towards her.

'My Simon won't need to go down the pit anyway,' she burst out, suddenly. 'We're going to join my husband in New South Wales very soon,' she told them. She enjoyed the looks of astonishment on their faces. 'My Jimmy has sent for us and the government is offering us free passage,' she went on, thinking how good it would feel never to have to stand in front of these men and beg ever again.

'I don't think that's likely,' replied Mr Lomax. 'I don't know who's put such a silly thought into thy head, but I doubt there's any truth in it.'

'It were the vicar,' she responded, enjoying having the upper hand for a moment. 'He's had a letter.'

Betty turned, with her head held high, and almost flounced from the room. But the moment she was outside, she regretted it. The offer wasn't certain, and even if it did come she wasn't sure if she would have the courage to go. If it came to nothing, her case would not be helped by antagonising these men on the relief committee. How she hated them, she thought as she led Rose towards the market stalls to replenish their food supply. She was so angry and upset at their insistence that Simon should go down the pit. She wouldn't let him go, she decided. Even if they cut her money again, or worse, refused to give her anything at all, she would find a way to manage and pray that they really would go to be with Jimmy before long.

'Come on,' she said to Rose as she hurried past the market stalls. She would go to speak to the vicar and ask if he'd had any answer from the Home Office.

'I wouldn't expect a reply so soon,' Reverend Brockle-hurst told her when she was sitting comfortably in his warm vestry. 'It's only a couple of days since I sent the letter.'

'But the committee are saying that our Simon has to go and work in the coal pit or they'll cut our money. I'm strugglin' to manage as it is,' she confessed. 'They've already reduced it because of Lydia being sent away,' she told the vicar, trying not to embarrass herself by giving in to the tears that seemed to constantly threaten her.

'Would it be so bad to set the lad to work?' he asked. 'He's not poorly, is he?'

Betty shook her head.

'I can understand your fears. It's only natural and for a lad that's not known his father it's more difficult,' went on the vicar. 'But he's not a baby, Mrs Knowles. Lots of lads work down the pit.'

Betty couldn't meet the vicar's eye. She understood what he was saying, that Simon needed to be toughened up.

'But it's not natural to be under the ground like that,' she protested.

'Yet you wouldn't say no to a bucket of coal, would you?' asked the vicar. 'Someone has to fetch it up.'

Betty supposed he was right. The fire that was warming her hands and face was burning the coal that had come from Colonel Fletcher's mine. Some mothers' sons had gone down into the bowels of the earth to dig it out and she knew she should be grateful. It was just that she didn't want it to be her son – not after all the hardship he'd suffered since they sent his father away.

'Can you not ask the committee to wait a week or two, until we hear about the passage?' she asked. 'There'd be no point setting him on if we were going away.'

The vicar seemed to consider what she was asking because he didn't speak for a moment. When he did it was not the answer Betty was expecting.

'I fear that there might be a problem about Simon going with you to New South Wales,' he told her. 'I checked his baptismal records after I spoke to you last and I think I'm right to say that he'll soon be eleven.' Betty bit her lip. She'd hoped that the vicar wouldn't realise. 'If he turns eleven before the ship sails, he may not be eligible after all.'

'But it would only be a matter of weeks!' protested Betty. 'Surely they would make an exception. I couldn't leave him behind!'

'They might ask for evidence,' explained the vicar. 'And the baptism date is written here in the church ledger.'

Betty looked away from the vicar's serious face. She knew that it would be asking too much to expect him to tell a lie.

'But why won't they let boys over ten go?' she asked. It seemed such a cruel rule. 'You told me that this reunion scheme was about keeping families together, not splitting them apart.'

'I understand what you're saying,' replied the vicar. 'But you would be sailing on a women's convict ship. You would be living in close proximity with other women and it simply wouldn't be right for older boys to be there. It wouldn't be seemly,' he explained. 'Is there anyone who would take your son in? Have you any family who would care for him?'

Betty shook her head. 'My parents are both gone,' she said. 'I have a brother, but he's got childer of his own to feed. I couldn't expect them to take on another. What shall I do?' she asked the vicar again. She'd come to ask for advice, but all that had happened was that her dilemma had deepened even further.

'Perhaps it would be for the best if Simon began work,' suggested the vicar.

Betty shook her head, although she knew that the Reverend Brocklehurst was talking sense.

'Can't I at least wait until the letter comes?' she asked, hoping for a reprieve. 'If it comes before his birthday he might be allowed to go.' Betty knew that she was clutching at straws, but she was determined to do everything in her power to prevent her son from going down that coal mine. 'Can't you try to persuade the parish guardians to give us a few more weeks before they reduce our money again?' she pleaded again.

The vicar hesitated over his decision for a moment longer than Betty was comfortable with. She thought he was going to refuse, but then he gave a slight nod of his head.

'I'll speak to Mr Lomax,' he told her. 'But I can give you no assurances. Nothing is certain about this situation.'

Betty thanked him. She knew that he was doing his best to help her even though her situation was looking increasingly impossible. She lifted Rose from her knee and stood up.

'I'm sure the pit work is not so bad as you imagine,' said the vicar as she opened the door to leave. 'The boy needs a job,' he added. 'He can't play about at home for the rest of his life, you know.'

Betty didn't reply. She couldn't. She hoped that the vicar wouldn't think her rude, but she was choking on tears of worry and frustration. Every time it seemed there might be a way forward, something happened to spoil it. How could she possibly go to join Jimmy in New South Wales if it meant leaving two of her children behind? The decision they were asking her to make was an impossible choice.

Rose followed her mother silently around the market as Betty made her purchases. It was growing late in the day and many of the stall holders were already packing up to go home. There wasn't much left except what had been rejected for being too green, too bruised or obviously rotten. The only advantage that Betty could see was that the remains were cheap and she managed to fill her basket with enough to feed them for a day or two.

As they approached their cottage she could see Simon waiting for them. Her heart churned at the sight of him. She loved him so much. How could she ever willingly part from him?

'I've managed to get quite a bit,' he told her as he proudly showed her the pile of twigs and logs that he'd gathered.

'Tha's done well!' Betty praised him and planted an unaccustomed kiss on his cheek. Simon looked embarrassed.

'What is there to eat?' he asked.

'Potatoes and cabbage. Come on. Let's get inside. We'll get a fire going and put them on to cook.'

Chapter Seven

Lydia found that each day followed the same routine until it was Sunday. They didn't work on Sundays, but they had to go to church. As they got ready, Lydia saw that some of the other girls pulled wooden boxes from under their beds and fetched out their Sunday clothes. She watched enviously as Violet put on a floral printed gown and covered her shoulders with a red handkerchief.

'What are you staring at?' she demanded when she noticed that Lydia was looking at her. 'I don't suppose you've got owt nice to wear. You'll have to put on your workin' clothes!'

The other girls began to laugh and Lydia felt herself blush. It was true that all she had was her workwear and that she would stand out as being the only one who wasn't nicely dressed.

'How come everyone has a better gown and petticoat?' she asked Miriam as they walked up the road towards the church. It was a perishingly cold morning and Lydia wished not only for a Sunday frock, but one of the warm woollen cloaks that many of the others wore. She shivered in her shawl and felt dowdy and second best.

'We mostly save up,' explained Miriam. 'If tha works overtime then tha gets paid a bit that can be set aside for clothes and shoes and such.'

Overtime, thought Lydia with horror. It was as much as she could do to get through the twelve hours of a normal day. Working even longer seemed impossible.

The church service was tedious. The pews were hard and the building was cold enough for Lydia to see her own breath as the others sang hymns she neither knew nor liked. Afterwards they went into the Sunday school where they were taught to read a passage from the bible. It held little interest for Lydia.

They returned to the apprentice house for dinner. Afterwards they were allowed some free time to go outside and even though it was bitter, Lydia went with Miriam and some of the other girls to walk down to the river.

It was the first time she'd left the confines of the mill and its grounds and Lydia turned her face to the sky as the sun broke through for a moment. She saw some rooks foraging amongst the trees, looking for sticks for their nests, and the thought of the warm and longer days to come made her feel more hopeful than she had for a while.

Before long she heard the rushing of the water and they came to the place where the River Lune flowed down the valley. The bank was grassy now that they'd left the tall trees of the woodland and she was excited to see that the first daffodils of spring were pushing up their green leaves all along the sides of the path. But her optimism was short-lived as she heard the all too familiar laughter of Violet and her friends behind them.

'Come on,' she said to Miriam, setting off at a brisk walk along the riverbank, hoping to get away from them. But she was too late.

'Ooh, look who it is!' taunted Violet. 'It's the bedwetter!'

Lydia tried to ignore her, but the sudden blow to her back almost knocked the breath from her and she gasped as she nearly fell to the ground. She turned to see Violet with another stone in her hand, ready to throw.

'Stop it!' she shouted at her as Miriam hurried on ahead out of range. Lydia wanted to run away as well, but she knew that if she didn't stand up to Violet she would never be left in peace.

'"Stop it!"' mimicked Violet, making her friends laugh. She tossed another rock and Lydia leapt back to dodge it, falling over a tussock of grass as she did and making her tormentors laugh even louder. She got up from the ground, her hands smeared with mud. The laughter from the other girls suddenly triggered her temper and without hesitating she ran at Violet and grabbed her by the hair, pulling as hard as she could to try to bring her down to her knees. Violet scratched at her as she fought to get free. The pain seared through Lydia and she saw that the backs of her hands were bleeding freely, but she refused to let loose. Her fury had overtaken all reason and she hauled Violet towards the steep edge of the sandy riverbank. Then, taking her by surprise, she let her go and pushed her as hard as she could.

Lydia had only meant to throw Violet to the ground so that her Sunday best dress would be muddy too, but she caught her off balance and Violet slipped down the banking with a scream, clutching at the grass as she went, until she landed with a splash in the water. The current was strong and it quickly sucked her away from the bank and into the fast-flowing channel. Lydia heard the other girls scream as Violet's head disappeared under the water.

'Tha's killed her! Tha's a murderess! Tha'll hang for this!' they all shouted in her face as Lydia sank to her knees and watched in horror as Violet resurfaced, choked, cried out, and was swallowed up again.

All the apprentices crowded on the riverbank. They were asking one another what they should do, if someone should go in after Violet and try to pull her out, but they all seemed afraid of the water and Violet was being washed steadily downstream towards the Penny Bridge.

Lydia pressed her hands over her ears to shut out the noise. She closed her eyes and wished that she was far, far away. It wasn't until minutes later that she realised she was alone. The toll keeper on the bridge must have heard the commotion and the apprentices were huddled on the riverbank further along where they watched him climbing down to the water's edge. He had a rope tied around his waist, which his wife was holding, and he waded into the water as Violet approached him. He managed to grab her by the arm and drag her out of the river. She was very still and Lydia thought that she must be drowned. Horror overcame her that she'd killed the girl and that she would be blamed. She could almost feel the noose tightening around her neck. Sobbing, she began to run towards the cover of the thick woodland. She had no idea where she was going, she just knew that she had to get away before anyone found her and took her in front of the magistrate.

Lydia ran until she could no longer hear the apprentices by the river. She ran away from the mill and the village, forging a path over the ragged roots of the trees and ducking under low branches. By the time she collapsed, breathless and exhausted, on the edge of a small clearing, she had no idea where she was or how much time had passed.

It was almost dark and she'd tripped and fallen twice, each time picking herself up and going on, fearful that she was being pursued and would be caught. But now, all she could hear was the dull thudding of her heartbeat in her ears as it gradually slowed and she found it easier to catch her breath.

She sat down and leaned her back against a tree trunk. She was still shaking and whenever she thought back to seeing Violet in the river, she began to cry again. She'd hated the girl, but she hadn't meant to kill her.

Lydia listened intently. She was sure that they would come after her and take her to the prison. But all she heard was the hooting of a tawny owl somewhere in the trees above her. She knew she couldn't go any further until morning. If she tried, she would have to walk with her arms stretched out in front of her like a blind man, and she was afraid of the stories she'd heard about the boggarts and goblins who infested the countryside at night and would carry people off to their lairs in the underworld to sell their souls to the devil.

The men from the mill must have decided it would be impossible to find her in the dark, she concluded. The best thing she could do was to rest here and hope that if they did come with lanterns she would see and hear them soon enough to escape.

Lydia pulled her shawl around her, although she was becoming even colder now that she'd stopped running. She realised that she could never go back to Caton. Somehow she would have to find her way home and hope that her father was there. She would explain to him that she'd never meant to hurt Violet. Lydia knew that he would believe her, and that he would protect her. Her father would never allow her to be taken away to the gallows. She was sure of that.

The night seemed to last for ever and Lydia was becoming convinced that the sun would never rise when she heard a few birds beginning to test their voices as daylight came. She noticed that she could see a little of her surroundings in the dawn as the sky took on a bluer hue and the tops of the trees revealed themselves.

Cautiously she stood up and walked a few paces up and down to bring the feeling back into her legs. There was no sign of life except for the birds and Lydia knew that she must set off now if she was to find the road that would lead her home before darkness fell again on the short winter day.

She wasn't sure which direction she'd come from, but she knew that she needed to head south to find her way home. She must avoid the village and the mill at all costs and try to find her way back to Lancaster. Though what she would do when she reached the town she hadn't decided. With no money to ride on the mail coach, she would either have to make her way home on foot or risk begging a ride on a cart – though that was dangerous in itself. What if word had spread that the constables were looking for her? The word *murderess* sprang unwanted into her mind at every opportunity.

As she walked, Lydia became aware of her hunger and thirst. The thirst was easily remedied by cupping her hand under a stream that flowed through the woods. Her hunger couldn't be resolved, but Lydia was familiar with the feeling and she put it aside as she walked on, keeping a careful watch as she left the woodland behind and came out into a clearer landscape. Here, the fields were divided by hawthorn hedges, which would break out into frothy white blossoms when Maytime came around. In some, a few sheep grazed and in others the winter barley was bravely pushing up from the warmth of the soil.

As she approached an isolated farmhouse, she wondered if she should deviate from her path to skirt around it, but her decision was made for her when she heard barking and an animal that she took for a wolf rushed at her with teeth bared, growling. Lydia screamed despite herself before she heard a man's voice calling the dog off. She thought that she was found and she stood, crying, as the man came towards her.

'No need to be affrighted. He'll not bite,' the man told her as he came near enough to grasp the dog and thread a rope through its collar to hold it back. 'Has tha lost thy way?' he asked curiously, looking her up and down. 'Is tha one o' them mill lasses?'

'No!' Lydia was alarmed, but it seemed things were not as bad as she'd first feared. This man didn't know who she was so clearly he wasn't part of a search party. Even so, she wanted to flee, but there was no clear escape and if she did run she was frightened that the man would set the dog on her again.

'What's tha doin' out here at this time o' t' mornin' then?' he asked. 'Where's tha goin'?'

'I'm on my way to Lancaster.'

'That's a fair trek.' He took off his cap to scratch his head before settling it more firmly. 'Where's tha come from?' he asked.

'Up the valley,' replied Lydia, desperately trying to think of a plausible lie. 'I'm on my way to look for work,' she added.

'There's only Fosters up there, and tha's no daughter of theirs,' said the man suspiciously. 'But tha looks weary,' he went on. 'Come up to t' cottage and wife'll happen find thee a bite o' summat. I've to take a pig into Lancaster this mornin'. Tha can ride wi' me.'

Lydia was uncertain whether to trust the man. What if it was a trap and Mr Greg from the mill was waiting there to hand her over to the magistrate? But the man seemed kindly and she realised that she had little option. If she refused he might guess that she was guilty of something and be sure to set a search party on her track. But if he'd heard nothing yet of a murderess on the run, she might be lucky enough to get to Lancaster without being caught – and from there it would be easier to head towards home.

She followed the man to his cottage where his wife looked up in surprise when Lydia was ushered in.

'Who's this?' she asked, wiping her hands on her coarse linen apron and pushing a strand of her hair from her face with the back of her hand.

They both stared at her and Lydia knew that they were expecting her to give them her name. 'I'm Violet,' she blurted out, not being able to think of anything else.

'She's on her way to Lancaster. I said she can ride with us,' explained the man.

'Well, we were about to have breakfast first,' said the wife. 'Would tha like summat?'

Lydia nodded eagerly. There was a wonderful aroma of freshly baked bread in the small kitchen and she could see a dish filled with brown eggs from the hens who were clucking around the open doorway.

'Sit down then,' said the wife, pulling out a chair.

Lydia sat, gratefully, and watched as the wife began to beat the eggs in a saucepan on her range. The man picked up a knife and began to slice hunks off the loaf. He put two on a plate and set it in front of her with a tub of butter. 'Help thyself,' he invited.

Lydia pushed the food into her mouth, thinking that she might not have to answer the inevitable awkward questions if her mouth was full.

'Where's tha come from?' asked the wife.

'Up the valley,' she repeated.

'Not from the mill then?'

Lydia felt her stomach lurch and she began to worry that these people might know more than they were saying. She wondered if she had walked into a trap after all and found herself glancing over her shoulder, expecting to see her captors approaching across the yard.

She shook her head, then forked a pile of egg into her mouth. The wife glanced at her husband and he shrugged his shoulders. 'Not our business,' he said.

The wife frowned and drew him aside to whisper in his ear. It was clear to Lydia that the woman didn't believe what she'd told her. Lydia strained to hear what they were saying but she couldn't make it out and after a moment or two the woman came back to the table and poured strong tea from her brown pot.

'If tha needs help… if tha's in some sort o' trouble then it would be best to be honest,' she said.

'I'm not in any trouble,' lied Lydia. 'I just want to go to Lancaster. I need to get work.'

The woman sat down and studied Lydia for a moment. 'I think tha's come from that mill,' she said. 'I can understand if tha doesn't want to go back there. I know they sends childer from all over the country to them and they works 'em like slaves.' She paused. 'Hast tha got any family?'

Lydia nodded. 'My father will be coming to find me in Lancaster,' she told them.

The wife looked to her husband again. It was clear she wished that her husband had never brought Lydia to their home.

'We can just let her ride with us into town,' he said. 'What harm can it do?'

The wife took a breath to speak but seemed to think better of it. 'Aye,' she said after a moment. 'Not much else we can do now. If we start makin' enquiries we'll never be in time to get a good price for yon pig. And we can't just leave her,' she added, meaning Lydia.

Lydia was thankful that the couple were more inter-ested in their own affairs than in hers. As soon as they'd finished eating she joined them on their cart. She had to sit in the back with the pig, but it was a small price to pay to be whisked down the valley towards the town and see the tall chimney of Caton mill recede into the distance. The farmer and his wife didn't say much more to her and were obviously relieved when they set her down near the marketplace. Lydia thanked them and then watched them go with slight regret. They'd been kind to her and she hoped it wouldn't get them into trouble.

–

Lancaster was busy, but Lydia kept her head down and tried to mingle amongst the crowds in the marketplace, afraid that she would be recognised. She saw a coach and horses draw up in front of a public house and some gentlemen who had been waiting inside came out and climbed aboard. Lydia wondered where it was going – not that it made any difference to her. She had no money to pay a fare and she didn't want to draw attention to herself in any case. The best thing to do, she decided, was to set off walking, but she was unsure which direction to take and was hesitant to ask in case anyone remembered speaking to her if they were questioned later.

The sun was still low in the sky. It didn't rise high at this time of the year and it was no help in getting her bearings. Lydia found herself walking in circles, setting off in what she thought was a different direction, only to find herself back in the same place. It was hopeless and her decision to walk home suddenly seemed impossible. She realised that she would have to ask the way if she was to make any progress at all, but wasn't sure who to approach. She really ought to have asked the farmer and his wife to point out the way south before she parted from them. But it was too late now.

Eventually, pulling her shawl well over her face to try to disguise herself, she went up to a man who was busy selling pies from a tray. 'Can you point out the road to the south please?' she interrupted him as he served a customer.

He turned to her in irritation. 'That way,' he told her with a nod of his head.

Lydia turned away quickly and followed the direction he'd indicated. She guessed it must be approaching midday by now and there was no chance of reaching home before nightfall. She would need to find somewhere to spend the hours of darkness, but for now, all she cared about was getting away from Lancaster and the search party she was sure must be looking for her.

Keeping to the edge of the road as she walked, she felt a ripple of fear every time she heard hooves or wheels coming up behind her, but they were only carts and the local farmers gave her a brief greeting and didn't seem much interested in her. One offered her a ride, but she refused, saying that she didn't have far to go. Lydia saw that the man disbelieved her as soon as she'd spoken, but it was too late to take the words back and she hid for a while in a ditch until she was sure he wasn't coming back with a constable.

All the people who passed her by would recall seeing her, thought Lydia as she hurried on as soon as she judged it was safe. If people came asking them if they'd seen a young woman, they would remember her and she would be in danger of being caught. She wondered if she ought to keep off the road and try to find her way through the countryside, but she was worried that she would become lost and that it might draw even more attention. At least as she walked along the road she seemed to have a purpose. If anyone saw her skulking in the hedgerows they would know that she was guilty of something.

As the afternoon came to an end and the early darkness encroached the fields, Lydia saw that she was coming to the outskirts of a small village. She wondered if there was somewhere she could safely spend the night, but hesitated until it had been dark for some time before she dared to go nearer. The candlelight spilling from the windows was just enough to light her way, even though she sometimes bumped into unexpected low walls as she fumbled her way along, trying to tread silently and keep close to the buildings.

Most people seemed to have gone inside their homes or to the inn that fronted onto the village square with its market cross. Lydia crept past like a shadow, pausing only to quench her thirst from a horse trough. She knew that there would be a stable yard around the back of the inn and she hoped that there would be no one about now that the horses had been bedded down for the night. The only danger would be if a coach came, needing fresh horses and the ostlers were roused from their beds.

The stable was lit by a single lamp, swaying gently on its hook. Lydia could hear the horses stamping their hooves and snuffling as they tore mouthfuls of hay from the racks in their stalls. They were big animals that towered over her and she didn't dare go near to them for fear of being kicked or trampled. Instead, she made her way towards an empty stall at the far end of the stables where she could just about see harness hanging, the silver of the bits glinting in the faint light. There was a pile of hay kept there and some straw and as quietly as she could, Lydia burrowed her way into it, hoping that she would be hidden from any casual glance. It was warm and dry and her intention was to rest, just for an hour or two, until she moved on again.

Chapter Eight

Lydia was woken suddenly by a bright light shining in her eyes. For a moment she couldn't remember where she was and it wasn't until a voice from behind the light spoke that she recalled her plight.

'What's tha doin' there?' the lad demanded. At least he sounded like a lad rather than a grown man because Lydia could only make out a vague outline of him behind the lantern he was holding over her.

'I was just resting for a moment,' she told him, feeling for her shawl and pulling it over her face. It shielded her eyes from the worst of the glare and she could just about make him out. He was skinny and not very tall – younger than she was, Lydia guessed.

'We don't allow no vagrants here,' he told her.

'Do I look like a vagrant?' demanded Lydia, glad that her clothing was decent and she was wearing boots. 'I just sat down for a moment because I was lost. I must have fallen asleep,' she said, cursing herself for having let her guard down.

The lad looked unsure of himself as she got to her feet, clearly an inch taller than he was.

'I ought to fetch someone,' he told her, as he stepped back.

'Why?' asked Lydia as she glanced towards the door to see the faint light of the dawn revealing a little of the yard beyond it. She must have been asleep for hours.

'Tha's not supposed to be in 'ere.'

'I've done no harm,' she told him as she brushed away some wisps of straw that were clinging to her petticoat. 'And I'm going on my way now.'

Lydia judged that it was safe to push past the lad. She doubted that he would try to stop her and she realised that she'd been lucky it was him who'd found her and not one of the burly ostlers who might have heard from a coach driver or traveller that there was a wanted lass in the area.

She ran for the door and was relieved when the lad made no attempt to restrain her. She only paused for a moment to check it was safe before hurrying out of the inn's yard and down the main street. There weren't many people about this early so she kept her head down and walked as fast as she dared. It was tempting to break into a run, but someone running would be notable, she told herself, and it was better to draw as little attention as possible.

Once she was safely clear of the village she picked up the main turnpike road again. The weather was fine and although it was cold, her eager pace kept her warm enough. After a while she began to relax and enjoy the fresh air and the freedom. Having never been so far away from home before, it was interesting to see new places as she passed by small hamlets and villages along the way.

She was hungry again. The good thing about the spinning mill had been the food. In all her life she was barely able to remember another time when she'd eaten three meals a day, and even the thick, sticky porridge would have been welcome now. Lydia found that her pace slowed as the miles passed. Her legs, unaccustomed to such walking, grew tired and heavy and she began to take rests, sitting far enough off the road to be concealed but not so far that there was a risk of getting lost. By the time the first evening star had begun to twinkle brightly in the sky, soon to be joined by the others and a growing sliver of crescent moon, she reached the outer streets of Preston and began to consider how she could find food and a place to sleep.

Even though it was dark, the town was busy. The noise that spilled out from the inns and beerhouses around the market square as the doors opened told her that they were filled inside with those who had the wages to enjoy themselves.

Lydia crept down some of the side streets, looking for a safe place. She saw another girl slip down a narrow entryway so she followed her, thinking that she might lead her to some place of safety, but by the time she'd crept down the alley, the girl, and the lantern she'd been carrying, were gone, probably into one of the cellars that led down from the street where she could hear babies crying and people shouting at one another.

She didn't want to turn back, so she went on, feeling her way cautiously with her hands and feet.

'How much, darlin'?' asked a voice and Lydia turned to see that a man had followed her. He came close, too close. She could smell the ale on his breath, mixed with the stench of decay from his rotting teeth. 'How much?' he repeated, as his face leered at her in the darkness, illuminated for a moment by a flickering candle on a nearby windowsill. She recoiled from him.

'Go away!' Lydia told him. She could see no clear way of escape. The alley was very dark and seemed to narrow even more as it wound its way around the shabby buildings.

'Tuppence,' he offered as he grasped hold of her arm.

'No! Let go!' she protested as she pulled away from him.

'Bitch!' he growled at her as he let her go. 'Think tha's too good for me, does tha?' Lydia felt his spittle land on her cheek and she wiped it on her sleeve in disgust. Thankfully, the man lurched away from her and continued on his way, and she was left alone not sure what to do. But she realised now that there was more danger in the dark narrow alleys than in the open marketplace, so she made her way back to where there were people about. And as she stood in the sanctuary of a doorway, she saw a woman come past her, leading a man by the hand and take him down the alley she'd just come out of. She'd been stupid, she realised. The man had mistaken her for a prostitute and she'd been lucky it hadn't ended badly.

It was clear that the town wasn't a safe place to be, so she decided that she'd better move on and try to find a place in the countryside to bed down for the night. She walked cautiously around the edge of the marketplace, hoping she could pass unnoticed. At least it had been too dark in the alley for the man to see what she looked like, she reassured herself.

As she walked, her eyes downcast, she caught sight of an apple that must have rolled off one the market stalls earlier in the day. She pounced on it and bit into the crisp flesh. It was tart, probably a fruit more suited to a pie than to eating raw, but Lydia was so hungry that she didn't care much and she crept away with her prize, leaving the town and its drunken revellers behind her.

As soon as it was light enough to see her way, Lydia crept out from the ditch by the roadside where she'd spent the night. She hadn't slept much and her fingers and toes were numbed with cold. Although she'd thought that the road would be deserted during the hours of darkness, she'd been surprised by several coaches that had passed her by with the horses' hooves pounding and the wheels casting up showers of mud as they passed by in the ghostly light of their swinging lanterns. Each one had made her cringe down as low as she was able, afraid of being spotted by the coachman if not the sleepy passengers. Towards morning the mail coach went by and she recognised it as the one she'd travelled north on. She knew it would be going to Bolton and she wished that could sit up there again, beside the driver and be home in time for breakfast.

It must have been much worse for her father when he was sent away, she mused as she walked along in the sharp morning air. The other side of the world was much, much further away from their home than Caton. No wonder it had taken him so long to come back.

Lydia wondered if her father had reached home yet. Would he be there waiting to greet her and hug her close? She tried to remember what it had been like when he'd hugged her before. She had a memory of him rushing into a room with a huge smile that seemed to take up his entire face. It hadn't been their home. Lydia thought it might have been their neighbour's parlour. Her father had picked her up and hugged her tightly. He'd seemed so pleased about something and she wondered if it had been the night that Rose was born. She couldn't be sure, but she knew that in that moment, she'd felt happy and loved and secure.

Maybe she would arrive home before her father, thought Lydia as her mind conjured up another scene where she was waiting at the door to greet him as he came up the fold. She knew that Thomas Holden had come back to his family like that, late one night. Folk still spoke of it like it was a miracle, to suddenly see him again after all those years. It would be the same when her father came home.

Or maybe he'd already set off to find her. She wondered if he was on his way to Caton to claim her back from the spinning mill. Perhaps he was walking in the fresh break of day, just as she was. He might even be on the same road. Lydia began to imagine that she might meet him at any moment. At every bend in the road she hurried eagerly forward, scanning the distance to see if she could spot anyone approaching. One time, her heart began to race in delight and she ran towards a figure she thought was her father, only to find that it was a peddler on his way to the market in Broughton. He gave her a strange look as if he thought she might be dangerous. She smiled at him in apology and walked briskly on, angry with herself for having drawn his attention. She must be more careful, she told herself. She must try to make herself invisible, unremarkable so that no one would recall seeing her if the constables came asking questions.

As Lydia walked on, she began to wonder whether going straight home was the right thing to do. If word reached Bolton before her, and surely it would, the first place the local constables would look for her was at Tombling Fold. She imagined turning in to the fold, filled with relief to have found her way back, only to be greeted by burly men who were waiting to take her before the magistrate and accuse her of murder.

86

Fearful for her future, she sat down at the side of the road to rest for a while before going on any further. She needed to make a plan; she had to find a way of keeping herself safe. But how? She wasn't even certain that her father would be able to protect her; he'd been found guilty and sent away to New South Wales when he'd done nothing wrong – or so her mother maintained. But her crime was far, far worse than anything her father had done. She pressed her hands over her face as she remembered the taunts of the other girls on the riverbank at Caton.

'*Tha's a murderess!*'

'*Tha'll hang for this!*'

Chapter Nine

It was over a week since Betty had written to Lydia and she still hadn't received a reply. She supposed that it would be difficult for her daughter to send a letter and she had to content herself with what both the vicar and her neighbour had told her – that if Lydia hadn't arrived at Caton, someone would have been in touch with her by now. She hoped they were right.

Neither had there been a reply to the letter that the vicar had sent to the Home Office to tell them that Betty Knowles and her children would indeed be willing to travel to New South Wales, should an opportunity arise. Betty wasn't sure that she wanted a reply to that one. She was thrilled to know that Jimmy was alive and that he wanted them to go to him, and the thought of being reunited with him filled her with a satisfied glow as she lay awake in the middle of the cold night and imagined what it would be like to see him again. But it was the part in between that worried her – the journey, the unknown sea voyage. Was she really brave enough to go through with it? Most of the time she doubted it. But she was determined that if she did go, she would take all her children with her. The idea of splitting up her family appalled her.

When Jimmy had first been convicted, she would have gone with him without hesitation if she could have sailed on the same ship. When the letters pleading for free passage had been sent she'd woken up every morning longing for a reply that told her to pack her few belongings and take her children and go. But it seemed different now. Six years was a long time and things had changed. She'd become used to being alone even if it was a struggle. And Jimmy would have changed too. His life would have been so different from hers that sometimes she doubted that they would have anything in common any more. And if she did agree to go, and travelled all that way, what would she do if she found him a changed man? She wouldn't be able to come home. She would be trapped in that strange, far away country.

But she was his wife, she reminded herself. It was true what the vicar had said. A man and wife should be together; it was a pity the government hadn't agreed on that years ago. It seemed to Betty that the only reason they were thinking differently now was because it was costing so much in relief to feed the families of those who'd been left behind. And whilst the mill owners and well-to-do gentlemen were willing to look into their purses to help the poor, they didn't like to dig too deep – or for too long – and sending families to New South Wales eased the burden on parish relief.

Betty sighed as she straightened out the clothes she'd slept in to keep warm and tidied her hair. It was the day to go before the committee again and accept with good grace their meagre handouts. Even with Lydia gone, Betty still had to find money for food and fuel and candles after the rent had been paid. The cut in what she was given was much greater than her outgoings and she regretted agreeing to send Lydia to Caton because now she'd calculated that it had left her worse off.

When it was time for Betty to go, she left Simon behind again and hoped that no more would be said about him going down the pit. It was a dismal day and the promises of spring seemed to have been false as the cold northerly wind threatened more snow to come.

Sleet stung her face as she pulled her shawl over her head and trudged towards town. Rose walked beside her without a murmur but before they reached the boardroom, Betty was wishing that she'd left her younger daughter at home as well.

The men of the committee had a fire roaring in the grate behind them, warming their backs as they sat in a line at the table. Not much of the heat reached Betty as she stood in front of them, and as she listened to the steady drip of melting ice falling from the fronds of her shawl and the folds of her skirt onto the floor, she wondered how many more weeks she could survive like this.

'Hast that lad been set on at the coal pit?' asked Mr Hamer. Betty shook her head and saw the grocer frown. 'Why not?' he demanded. 'Tha were told last week to get him set on. We'll not give relief for him if he could be working,' he told her in his booming voice. 'You can't keep coming here expectin' money for nowt!'

'You really should have made sure he was in work by now,' agreed Mr Hewitt.

'But we'll be leaving soon. It's not worth it,' Betty told them, thinking that if anything tipped the balance of her fears about sailing to the other side of the world, it was the thought of never having to be humiliated by these men again.

'Tha's talkin' nonsense,' replied Mr Lomax. 'I spoke to the Reverend Brocklehurst about it and he told me no firm offer has been made to give thee free passage.'

Betty didn't pursue the matter with him. It was clear he'd made up his mind that there was no chance of her getting a berth on a ship and she wondered whether he was right and her hopes would be dashed all over again, just like the last time.

'We can give relief for yourself and the little lass, and a token for one loaf of bread. It's the best I can do, I'm afraid,' confirmed Mr Hewitt.

'No need to sound so apologetic,' Mr Lomax reminded him.

Betty accepted what she was given, remembered to say thank you and left the warmth of the room for the freezing marketplace where the stallholders were stamping their feet and blowing on their hands to try to keep warm. The hot potato cart tempted her with its glowing coals and appetising smell, but Betty knew that if she treated herself there would be nothing left to feed them for the rest of the week.

She bought some oats and got her loaf. The candles would have to wait until another day. As long as they could gather wood to burn, it lit the parlour enough for their needs, although she knew that Simon was having to walk further and further afield to find any fallen branches. He wouldn't have time to do it if he began work, she thought. She supposed Rose would have to help, even though she was reluctant to send her young daughter out on her own.

There was no money left for such luxuries as milk and cheese and it was a long time since she'd had either tea or sugar. What she'd managed to buy would have to suffice for the time being.

Betty wondered whether to go to see the vicar again. The thought of his warm vestry was a temptation, but she hesitated to keep bothering the man. He'd promised to tell her as soon as he received a reply and she knew she must be patient.

As she walked home, she realised that her options were dwindling. They couldn't go on for more than another week or so without enough money to feed themselves and it was clear that the relief committee were adamant that Simon should be in work. Unless she could find some alternative employment for him, then he would have to begin at the pit.

'I'll go,' Simon told his mother after she repeated to him what the relief committee had said as she emptied the items she'd been able to afford from her basket and put them on the shelf in the pantry. 'I'll work in the pit.'

'I hate to ask thee,' replied Betty. 'I never thought to see the day when tha'd have to go down there.'

'It'll be all right,' he replied and Betty hugged her son to her. She felt so proud that he was being brave, but it seemed unfair that he should have to take on the responsibility of earning a wage just because they'd sent his father away. 'I'll go on Monday,' he told her, and Betty hoped that it would snow hard over the weekend and make the tracks impassable so that he would be reprieved for a while longer.

Chapter Ten

Lydia spent another freezing night huddled under some bushes at the side of the road. In the early hours, flakes of snow began to fall and as she shivered uncontrollably, she wondered whether she would be buried under them by morning. She knew that she ought to get up and move about to prevent herself becoming too cold, but she felt so very, very tired that it was impossible to rouse herself. In the end she slept a little and when she was woken by the sound of a cart going past, she was convinced that it was her father come to fetch her home. Lydia felt the pleasure envelop her as she waited to see his face, but when she'd waited and waited for what seemed either a minute or an eternity, she had a moment of clarity when she knew he hadn't really come and she wasn't even certain that there had been a cart at all.

Although she wanted to stay where she was, self-preservation made her realise that she must get up and try to warm herself if she was to survive. She knew that if she continued to lie on the ground she would probably freeze to death and despite being tempted to give in to what seemed an inevitable fate, she eventually forced herself to sit up, then kneel and eventually get to her feet. Even so, it was a struggle to flex her fingers and move her toes, as she tried to ease some feeling into them.

She stumbled as she made her way back onto the road, and when she reached it she couldn't decide which direction she should go in. She couldn't remember which way she'd been walking when she'd decided that she could go no further and crept in under the bushes in the darkness.

Lydia looked one way and then the other. The road stretched in both directions and both looked the same. If she'd had a coin she would have flipped it, but as she was penniless she took her best guess and began to walk slowly, hoping that the stiffness in her legs would soon ease.

She was hungry again. Not the hunger that comes with a missed meal, but the kind of hunger that made her feel weak and dizzy. She'd eaten nothing since the apple she'd found the previous day and she knew that she needed to find food and warmth before she would feel better, but had no idea how to achieve either.

With her head bent, she trudged on, watching her feet as she made the effort to put one in front of the other. Sometimes she was aware of carts or coaches rumbling past her, but mostly she didn't even notice them as she struggled on with no clear destination. The only thoughts in her mind were to escape the constables and somehow find a safe place to hide.

Lydia had no idea how far she'd gone when she became aware that someone was walking beside her. With difficulty, she lifted her gaze from her boots and saw an old man with a grimed and wrinkled face gazing at her.

'Is tha all right, young lass?' he asked her as she took in his bright blue eyes and cheerful yellow scarf. When Lydia didn't reply he spoke to her again. 'Tha looks weary,' he observed. 'Dost have far to go?'

'I don't know,' Lydia told him, as she swayed on her feet, wishing that she could hold on to something to help her keep her balance.

She felt him grasp her arm to steady her.

'Whoa there,' he said. 'Is tha poorly?'

'Just tired,' she told him.

'And hungry?'

Lydia nodded.

'Best sit down for a while,' he advised as he guided her off the road and, having located a stone that made a suitable seat, he brushed dirt from it with his palm before shrugging off the pack that he was carrying on his back and opening it. He took out some oatcakes and a portion of cheese, wrapped in a fancy cloth and placed them on her lap. 'Eat them,' he encouraged her. 'Don't be shy.'

Lydia was reluctant to accept his help, but her hunger overcame her fear and she broke one of the oatcakes into pieces, which she put into her mouth one by one. The man crouched beside her and cut the cheese into portions with a grubby knife he'd drawn from a sheath on his belt.

'I'm Jack,' he told her. 'Who are you?'

'I... I...'

'Surely tha knows thy name?' he teased. Then his face became serious. 'No need to tell Old Jack,' he reassured her. 'But tha need have no fears. My lips are sealed,' he said as he made a gesture of his mouth being tight closed.

He offered her some water to drink from a flagon and Lydia gulped it down thirstily and then ate up the rest of the food.

'I can't pay thee,' she told him as she picked up the last crumb from the cloth on her knee and put it into her mouth.

'Did I ask thee for money? No.' He shook his head. 'Old Jack needs no payment for a good deed,' he reassured her.

With food inside her, Lydia felt somewhat restored and she took a better look at her new companion. He looked swarthy, as if he spent all his time outdoors. She'd seen farmers with the same complexions on the market in Bolton, but this man was no farmer and she thought he must be one of the peddlers who went from town to town selling pins and needles and scraps of lace.

'Where's tha goin' all alone?' he asked. 'Dost want to walk along with me?'

'Well, where are you going?' she asked him, hoping he wasn't going to say Lancaster and prove that she'd chosen the wrong turning after all.

'I'm on my way to Blackburn, for the Easter fair,' he told her.

Lydia nodded. She'd heard of it. Some of their neighbours would walk over the moors to visit it and come back with all manner of tales about acrobats and horse tricks as well as the sheep and cattle market and stalls selling food and drink. She'd once asked her mother if they could go, but she'd said it was too far for Rose to walk, and she was too heavy to carry, and besides they had no money to spend on fripperies.

'I've ribbons in every colour tha can imagine,' Old Jack told her, patting his pack with a gnarled hand. 'It's a pity tha's no bonnet in need of a trimming.'

Lydia reached up and tucked some stray hair back under her cap. A bonnet trimmed with ribbons would be a wonderful thing, she thought. Maybe her father would buy her one. He would take her to the fair, she was sure.

'Say tha'll walk along with Old Jack,' insisted the peddler.

Lydia was unsure, but she didn't know how to get away from the man, and he seemed kind and harmless, not like the man who'd accosted her down the back alley in Preston. Besides, she thought, if the constables were looked for a lass travelling alone, they might not notice her if she was in company with someone else.

'Just as far as Blackburn,' she agreed.

He smiled and shouldered his pack. 'Come along then,' he told her. 'No time to linger.'

—

The food had made Lydia feel much better and she fell into an easy stride next to the peddler. He burst into song every now and again as they walked and she wondered whether he was a little moonstruck, but his company reassured her and she was glad that he didn't ask too many questions.

Around the middle of the day they stopped at an inn. The innkeeper seemed to know Old Jack and invited them into the parlour where the peddler opened his pack and the innkeeper's wife and some of the other women clustered around to see what he had for sale. Lydia held back, hoping that no one would notice her. She'd been reluctant to go into the inn at all and would have preferred to keep to the road, but Old Jack had clasped her hand in his and pulled her with him.

'They feed Old Jack in here,' he'd told her and Lydia, feeling guilty that she'd eaten the old man's food, followed him through the door that was barely high enough to admit them.

Lydia sat on a stool in a corner of the room and watched as the women held up ribbons and lace for each other to see and exclaimed over them as if they were priceless, before bargaining eagerly with Old Jack to buy as cheaply as they could. The peddler took their protestations of his greed in good humour as if he knew they would part with their money in the end. An aroma of meat and potatoes filled the parlour and Lydia would have loved to eat again but when a maidservant glanced in her direction, she shook her head. She had no money to buy herself any dinner and she turned her face away, hoping that the other lass wouldn't remember her.

Before long, Old Jack had eaten his dinner, packed up his wares and bid his customers goodbye. Lydia followed him out of the door without a word and they began to walk again.

As it grew dark, they approached the outskirts of a town that Lydia thought must be Blackburn. She'd begun to worry about where Old Jack was planning to spend the night and where she could sleep if he went into another inn. She was wondering if she should ask him about his plans when he paused at the head of a track that led downhill towards a farm nestled in the lee of the hillside to shelter it from the worst of the weather.

'Old Jack knows a barn where we can rest up,' he told her as he adjusted the weight of the pack on his back. His pace had slowed over the past hour or two and Lydia realised that he was tired. She couldn't guess at his age, except that he was old and, forgetting her own troubles for a moment, she realised that his life wasn't easy for him, tramping the roads day after day, and she felt sorry that he had no easier job, no home to go to at night with a comfortable bed and maybe a wife. He'd said nothing about his circumstances but as she followed him down the track, she pondered on what had led him to become a peddler.

The barn was a good distance from the farmhouse and Lydia was glad. She didn't want to be discovered.

'We'll be well enough in here,' Jack said as he eased the big door open just wide enough for them to get in. The scent of straw and hay was strong and there was just enough light left to see the huge timber frame that held up the roof and the sheaves and crooks piled up all around them.

Old Jack let his pack fall to the floor with a sigh and sat down on a pile of loose straw. Lydia settled herself some distance from him, glad to rest, but still alert to anyone coming and finding them.

Before many minutes had passed, she heard snoring. Old Jack had fallen asleep almost immediately and as she lay and stared into the dark night, Lydia wished that she could sleep so easily, but her conscience wouldn't allow it. The image of Violet disappearing under the water wouldn't leave her and she was afraid that if she did sleep the girl's ghost would come to haunt her. She shivered.

The night seemed endless and Lydia woke with every sound of rustling in the straw. She knew it was probably only mice but even that made her afraid and she was thankful when morning finally came.

Old Jack was still sleeping and she was just about to shake his arm to wake him when she heard someone coming. Terrified, she ducked down and tried to pull loose straw over herself, hoping that she wouldn't be seen. As she peered out from her hiding place, she saw a woman come in. She was carrying something and didn't seem surprised to see Old Jack sleeping on the hay. As she put her jug and dish down, Jack woke and stared at the woman for a moment, rubbing his eyes.

'I thought I saw thee arrive last night,' said the woman. 'There's a bite of breakfast there. But make sure my husband doesn't see thee,' she warned. She glanced at the peddler's pack, lying beside him and instinctively Old Jack knew her purpose.

'Ribbons or lace?' he asked as he opened it up for her inspection.

The woman chose quickly and crept out again with her gifts clutched to her bosom. From the way she looked all around before she slipped out, Lydia knew that her visit was a secret one and that the farmer would not be friendly if he found them there. The thought made her afraid and she was keen to leave, but Old Jack laughed when she told him of her fears.

'Farmer Bristow'll be along in a while and he'll tell me not to let his wife know that he's slipping me a few eggs whilst her back is turned.' He laughed. 'Come,' he said, 'Old Jack will share his breakfast with thee.'

The jug was filled with milk, still warm from the cow, and the basin held freshly baked bread and butter. Jack divided the food into two equal portions and they took turns to drink from the jug. The milk was creamy and tasted of meadowlands and wild flowers and for a moment Lydia felt content until Jack stood up, brushed the crumbs from his moleskin breeches and declared that they must be on their way.

The road that had been almost deserted when they left it the night before was busy now, with flocks of sheep and geese and herds of cows being taken to the market. Carts came up behind them, sometimes too fast, and made the birds and animals scatter, resulting in the driver being the recipient of a torrent of abuse from the farmers who struggled to get their animals back under control. Lydia hoped that the mail coach wasn't due or the mayhem would be complete.

It became busier still as they reached Blackburn and on a stretch of moorland just outside the town she saw not only row upon row of pens where the animals were for sale, but stalls piled high with vegetables and cheeses and hardware for sale. There was a band playing somewhere and the music was being carried on the clear air because the mill chimneys stood stark and smokeless on the skyline as people gathered in a holiday mood to shop and dance and drink.

Old Jack found a place for himself between a stall selling pies and the entrance to a ring where two men had stripped down to just their breeches and were preparing to fight one another. The peddler opened his pack and crowds of young lasses about Lydia's age began to gather, pushing against each other for a better look at his wares. Lydia mingled amongst them, trying to seem invisible, but she couldn't relax. She continuously scanned the crowd, watching out for anyone who might be coming to arrest her.

After a while, the fighting in the boxing ring began to repel her even though many of the other lasses seemed to find it exciting, cheering on their favourite as the men took bets on who would win. The boxers were hitting one another hard, with no respite, and their chests had become slick with blood and sweat. It made Lydia queasy and she wandered away to see if there was any more wholesome entertainment on offer.

As she threaded her way through the stalls she was startled by a sudden shout.

'Stop! Stop that lass!'

Lydia spun around, trying to see who was shouting. She was certain that she'd been found and expected the weight of a heavy hand to land on her shoulder at any moment as a constable dragged her away to a lock-up. The crowd seemed to erupt into a frenzy of excitement as people turned and looked to see what was happening. A young woman with her skirts grasped in her hands and the ribbons on her bonnet flying loose was careering through the crowd. Rather than trying to prevent her, fairgoers parted to let her through and even when she knocked a small child to its back and it let out a wail that pierced the air above the general tumult, no one seemed willing to stop her except the one man who had given chase. Lydia watched with the rest. Her heart was still racing and her legs were trembling even though she knew she wasn't the one being pursued.

'What's she got?' asked someone.

'She took a pie from the baker's stall.'

'Poor lass. She must be hungry.'

'No excuse for stealin'!'

Lydia listened to the conversations around her and was thankful that she wasn't the one being chased. No one would have helped her. She would have been just one more attraction like the lass who was fleeing with the pie.

'He'll have lost a dozen more whilst his back's turned,' observed a woman close by as they watched the baker give up and stand panting with his head down, his hands on his knees. And as the crowd closed around him, curtaining him from sight, the momentary distraction was forgotten and Lydia could only think about getting away to a place where she would feel safer.

Not knowing what else to do, she began to walk out of the town, still heading south towards her home as if drawn there by instinct. By the time the afternoon was over, she'd walked through Darwen and crossed the moors where the fierce wind brought tears to her eyes and had reached Egerton. She knew that she didn't have much further to go to reach Tombling Fold, but she was afraid of going on.

Lydia hurried down the main street, trying not to be noticed. At the end of the terraces, she came to a path that led off to the valley below and she turned and began to follow it, tracking the progress of a brook that flowed faster as it approached some buildings in the distance. As she walked, Lydia heard a bell being rung and as she watched, workers began to stream towards her, their shawls around their heads and their caps pulled well down with their jacket collars turned up against the cold. She froze for a moment, not knowing what to do, then she turned back, pulled her shawl over her own head and walked slowly until the mill workers caught up with her and began to overtake her. She hoped that nobody would notice her in the gloom.

Back on the main street, the workers called out 'Good-night!' to one another and dispersed to their homes. Lydia hesitated, not knowing what was the best thing to do next. Should she go back towards the mill? Or should she continue away from the village and hope to find a ditch or hedge where she could rest until daylight came?

'What's to do, lass?' called a voice from behind her. 'Got no home to go to?' teased the man. 'Do I know thee?' he asked as he came nearer. 'I can't say as I've seen thee afore, and I'm sure I'd remember such a pretty face.'

'I'm just on my way home.'

'Dost tha want me to walk with thee?' he offered. 'It's not always safe for a lass to be out on her own at this time of night.'

'There's no need,' she told him. She couldn't help but be reminded once more of the man in the alleyway and she was frightened.

'Well, if tha's sure. But I'd get straight home if I were thee.'

Lydia hurried up the village street, hoping that the man hadn't seen her face too clearly in the dark. She had no idea where she was going. She just knew that she had to find a place to spend the night. She hurried on, glancing over her shoulder to make sure she wasn't being followed, and didn't notice the uneven cobbles until she felt her foot suddenly trapped and she fell headlong onto the stones. Cursing herself for being so careless, she got up to go on, but found that as soon as she tried to put any weight on her left foot, a searing pain shot through her ankle. She stumbled to the ground again with a cry of agony.

Weeping with panic, she got up once more and tried to walk, but it was clear to her that she'd either broken or twisted her ankle badly and there was no possibility of her walking anywhere. She hopped towards the nearest windowsill and leaned on it whilst she explored her swelling ankle with her fingers.

She was rubbing at the joint, hoping it might ease up soon, when the door to the cottage whose sill she was using for support was opened and a woman with a candle held aloft peered out at her.

'I saw thee fall,' she said. 'Hast tha hurt thyself?'

'I think I've sprained my ankle,' explained Lydia, trying to keep her face turned away from the light. 'I'll be all right in a moment.'

'Come inside,' invited the woman. 'I'll see if I've a bit of rag tha can bind it with.'

'No. I'll be all right,' said Lydia as she put her foot to the ground and made another attempt at walking. The pain made her gasp and she clutched at the sill again.

'Tha's hurt it badly,' said the woman. 'Best come inside.'

Not knowing what else to do, Lydia managed to hop her way to the door where the woman was waiting.

'Can tha get over the doorstep?'

'I think so,' said Lydia as she made a jump on her good leg, landing awkwardly and reaching out for something to help her balance. The woman caught her arm and helped her across to a chair by the hearth.

'Sit thee down there and let's take a look,' she said as she closed the door and put the candle on the shelf by the fireplace.

As the woman crouched down to examine her ankle, Lydia saw that she was expecting a child – quite soon by the shape of her.

'I don't want to be a nuisance,' Lydia said, still holding her shawl around her face. It was such bad luck, she thought, to have to accept help when she was trying to avoid being seen. 'I'm sure I'll be all right in a minute or two.'

'You don't live in Egerton, do you?' said the woman, glancing up at Lydia. 'Where were tha goin' at this time?'

'I'm on my way home,' said Lydia.

'Is it far? This looks very swollen,' she added when she'd eased off Lydia's boot. 'If tha takes off thy stocking I'll fetch a bowl of water and tha can soak it in some knitbone. I've some on the shelf that I keep by me,' she said, leaning heavily on the arm of the chair to get up. 'Tha's taken a nasty tumble,' the woman added as she went to find the herb she'd mentioned. 'It would be better if tha could keep the weight off it for a while. Where did tha say tha lived?' she asked as she came back with the bowl and added some hot water from the kettle.

'Down Bolton way,' Lydia told her, watching as she stirred the shredded leaves into the water, releasing a pleasing aroma.

'Whereabouts?'

Lydia wished the woman wouldn't pry. 'Near th' hall in t' wood,' she told her, hoping it might throw any pursuers off track if they came here asking about her.

'Well, I can't see thee walkin' that far tonight. Put thy foot in here. It's not too hot is it?' she asked as Lydia lowered her foot into the water until it lapped around her swollen ankle. It felt good after all the walking she'd done and she wished she could soak her other foot as well.

'I'll see if I can find a bit o' rag to bind it,' said the woman. 'I'm May, by the way. What's thy name?'

'Violet,' said Lydia not wanting to give her own name but regretting her choice of the alternative as soon as it had passed her lips. If anyone made an enquiry they might put two and two together and make a link. 'But they call me Lettie,' she added quickly.

'Well, Lettie, I think that foot's soaked for long enough,' said May when she came back with the length of rag she'd found. 'Let's get it dried and strapped up and then we'll see how tha feels.'

'I think it'll be fine. It feels much better now,' Lydia told her as May knelt down and wrapped the rag in a figure of eight around her foot and ankle.

'Well, tha's welcome to stay,' May told her. 'I'd be worried about thee if I let thee go.'

'I couldn't impose,' Lydia told her, wondering how to manage her escape. She was sure she'd be able to walk now, even if it meant slow going.

'It's no trouble,' May told her. 'Tha could snuggle down on that chair with a blanket and tomorrow we could go up to the stable yard and see if any carriers are going thy way. If tha can get a lift it'll be much easier than tryin' to walk.'

Lydia was tempted. It would be so easy to stay here, she thought. The cottage was warm and cosy and she could see a stew bubbling in a cauldron above the fire. It made her stomach rumble.

'What about thy husband?' she asked.

'Oh, Joseph'll not mind,' May reassured her. 'He should be home any minute. Tha can ask him thyself. But he'll not turn a young lass like thee out at this time of night. I know him well enough to be sure o' that.'

As May finished speaking, the door was opened and her husband came in. Lydia recognised him as the man she'd spoken to earlier.

'What's happened?' he asked.

'This here's Lettie,' explained May. 'She taken a right tumble, just outside, and hurt her ankle. She were on her way to her home, down Bolton way, but she can't put weight on it.'

The man stared at Lydia and she pulled her shawl further over her face. She knew that he was suspicious.

'Tha weren't headin' for Bolton when I saw thee last,' he remarked. 'She were comin' away from t' mill,' he told his wife. 'I spoke to her earlier on t' road to ask if she were all right. I offered to walk her home, but she said no. She didn't say she were goin' to Bolton.'

'I think I'd got lost, in the dark,' Lydia told him. 'I thought I were on the right road for Bolton until I saw the mill workers comin' out.'

'Where's tha come from?' asked Joseph, sitting down on the opposite side of the hearth and watching her.

'Preston,' she replied. It was true in a way, she thought.

'And what were tha doin' there?' he asked her.

Lydia tried to think quickly. She needed to tell him something that was credible and would satisfy his questions.

'I had work,' she began, trying to concoct a plausible reason for her journey. 'But I got word my father had sent for me.'

'What work?' asked Joseph.

'Let the lass be,' May told him. 'She doesn't want an inquisition. I've said she can stay here for tonight and we'll try to get her a lift home in t' mornin'.'

Joseph frowned and May saw his doubts as well. 'We can't turn her out now,' she told him. 'Go and wash thy hands and face and I'll put thy tea on the table. Would tha like summat t' eat?' she asked Lydia.

'Perhaps I should get on my way,' Lydia said.

'Nonsense!' replied May. 'Take no notice of our Joseph. He doesn't mean to make thee unwelcome. He's just curious.' She reached for her basins and a ladle and began to share out the stew. 'Will thy family be expectin' thee tonight?' she asked. 'I hope they won't be worried. I'm not sure there's any way we could send a message.'

'No. They won't be lookin' out for me. I were goin' to surprise 'em,' said Lydia.

'Perhaps it would be easier for thee to hold this on thy lap,' mused May as she filled a basin for Lydia. 'I'll fetch a cloth. The basins are hot.'

May went into the scullery where Joseph was getting washed and Lydia heard them speaking in low voices. It was clear that Joseph didn't want her here and Lydia wished that she could just get up and run out. But when she put her foot to the floor the pain shot through her ankle again and she began to fear that a bone was broken.

After a few minutes, May came back with a cloth and lifted the basin onto her lap and handed her a spoon. 'Be careful now,' she warned. 'Don't burn thy tongue.'

Lydia kept her head down when Joseph came in and sat down at the table. She felt slightly foolish with her shawl still over her head, but she was reluctant to take it off. The less they saw of her face the better, she thought.

'What did tha say tha were called?' he asked her as he stirred his stew to cool it.

'Lettie.'

'Lettie what?' he persisted.

'Lettie… Smith.'

'Oh, aye,' he commented, clearly not believing her. 'And whereabout dost tha live in Bolton?'

'Leave her alone, Joe,' said May. 'Let her eat her tea.'

'If folk are to spend the night under my roof I likes to know who they are,' he grumbled to his wife. 'And why's she sittin' there all wrapped up in her shawl? It's warm enough by t' fire.'

'Happen she's chilled. She's been out in t' cold all day and she's had a shock. Leave her be.'

Out of the corner of her eye, Lydia saw him turn his attention to his food. She ate her own stew quickly in case he decided to turn her out despite May telling her she could stay. But when he'd finished, and May had brewed some tea, he lit his pipe and sat opposite her, smoking. Lydia kept her gaze fixed on the fire and was glad when

May came back in with a stool for her to put her painful foot on.

'There's another cushion here, to put behind thy head and tha can wrap this blanket around thyself,' she told her. 'I'll have to bank up the fire when we go up to bed, but it should stay warm for a while. Is there owt else tha needs? Dost tha need to go down the yard?'

'No,' said Lydia. She didn't want to try walking again. 'I'm right till morning. I'm sure I'll be much better by then and I'll be on my way. I'm very grateful,' she added, glancing at Joseph.

'Aye,' he said, non-committally. 'I'll check as t' doors are locked.'

Lydia was glad when May and Joseph eventually went up the narrow, winding stairs to their bedroom. She listened to the squeaking of the floorboards above her as they moved about for a while, then heard them talking quietly. She was cosy in the chair by the remaining warmth of the fire, but the pain in her ankle throbbed and she could have cried with frustration. What a stupid thing to do, she thought. She shouldn't have been so careless. And even though she'd tried to cover her tracks, it was clear that Joseph hadn't believed anything she'd said. If the constables came here asking about her, he would give her away for certain, and she couldn't even run from them when she was injured like this.

The night passed slowly. Lydia dozed now and then, but most of the time she sat awake worrying about how she could get away safely and where she could go if she didn't dare go back to her home.

As the day dawned she gingerly tried to put weight on the ankle, but, if anything, it was more painful than it had been the night before and it was obvious to her that she wasn't going anywhere without assistance.

At last May came down the stairs and after she'd revived the fire, she helped Lydia to the privy at the bottom of the yard. It was tough going and Lydia had to lean on May as she hopped along.

When they got back inside, Joseph had come down dressed to go to work.

'I expect tha'll be gone afore I comes back,' he told Lydia.

'I will,' she promised him because she wanted to leave just as much as he wanted rid of her. 'I must go,' she told May, when he'd left. 'I'm really grateful, but I mustn't outstay my welcome.'

'Have some bread and tea,' May told her. 'Then I'll go and see if I can get thee a lift into Bolton.'

Chapter Eleven

A while later, Lydia heard the sound of a horse and cart drawing up outside the cottage door and then May came in with a smile on her face.

'Mr Haslam is just setting off for Bolton,' she told her, 'and he says tha's welcome to ride with him.'

Thankful to leave, but unsure about being seen by yet another person, Lydia struggled to her feet and wrapped her shawl around her.

May offered her arm as Lydia hobbled, grimacing with pain towards the door. Outside, there was a medium-sized cart being pulled by a brown and white horse.

'This is Lettie,' May told the man, who was sitting on the seat at the front and holding the horse's reins. He was well wrapped up against the cold with a scarf that covered his mouth and nose and almost met the cap that was pulled low on his head. Only a pair of eyes peered out and Lydia found it impossible to judge his age.

'Mornin',' he said, looking at her curiously. 'Tha can sit up here beside me if tha likes, or there's room in t' back if tha prefers,' he told her, nodding his head towards the piled-up boxes and sacks.

Lydia would have preferred to ride in the back where Mr Haslam wouldn't be able to get a good look at her, but May took the decision into her own hands.

'She'd best ride with thee. She'll not manage in the back with her bad ankle.'

Lydia looked at the bench seat where Mr Haslam was waiting and doubted that she'd be able to climb up there.

'I think she'll need help to get up, though,' said May.

Lydia thought she heard Mr Haslam give a slight sigh as he put down the reins and clambered down.

'Can she not use it at all?' he asked.

'She can't bear any weight on it,' May answered for her. 'I'm worried it might be broken.'

'She'd best get it tended to then,' he replied.

'I've bathed it and strapped it up as best I can,' said May. 'But I suppose she could go to the dispensary in Bolton and let the doctor examine it.'

'Nay, she doesn't want to go there,' said Mr Haslam. 'Them quacks know nowt. She'd be better off going to Mrs Malpass.'

'Who's that?' asked May.

'Dost tha not know her?' replied Mr Haslam, sounding surprised. 'She a bone-setter. She'd have her walkin' again in no time.' He turned to Lydia. 'Come on, lass,' he told her as he picked her up easily and deposited her on the seat. The horse tossed its head and Lydia was afraid it would move off before Mr Haslam took up the reins again, but it merely stamped a foot in annoyance.

Mr Haslam rubbed the horse's nose as he walked back round the front of the cart and hauled himself up again.

'Thanks for thy help,' said Lydia to May as he picked up the reins and clicked his tongue at the horse. 'I'm very grateful.'

'Take care of thyself,' replied May and stepped back as the cart moved off.

Mr Haslam set the horse to an eager trot as they rolled down the lane out of Egerton. It was a bumpy ride and every jolt sent a fresh shockwave through Lydia's ankle. But she knew that it would have been much more painful if she'd tried to walk.

Beside her, Mr Haslam didn't seem inclined to talk and Lydia was glad. The less he knew the better, she thought as she pulled her shawl forward, to shield her face both from him and the weather.

As the road began to drop down towards Bolton, Mr Haslam cleared his throat and spoke. 'Mrs Malpass lives just there,' he said, pointing towards an isolated cottage set back from the road in the shelter of a ring of hawthorn that would hide it from sight once the leaves were out. 'I could drop thee off here,' he offered.

Lydia was unsure what to do. It was tempting to think that the woman could treat her ankle and get her walking again, but what would she do if she failed? At least if she stayed on the cart she could reach Bolton and try to contact her mother to ask if it was safe to go home.

Mr Haslam stopped the cart. 'Dost want me to go and fetch her?' he asked. 'Wait there,' he went on, without waiting for an answer. He handed the reins to Lydia and clambered down, then walked to the cottage. He had a pronounced limp that she hadn't noticed before and she wondered whether he'd had an injury that this Mrs Malpass had cured. He seemed to think highly of the woman.

Lydia watched as he knocked on the door and waited for it to be opened. She could see him speaking to someone, but couldn't see Mrs Malpass. A minute later he was on his way back and Lydia thought the woman must have refused, but he was grinning as he approached, his scarf pulled down under his chin.

'She says to tek thee down,' he told Lydia as he fastened the reins to a nearby gate before he reached up to lift her from the cart. He seemed strong, despite his limp, and he carried her easily. Lydia held on with an arm around his shoulders, but she was anxious about being so close to him and kept her face turned away, watching as they neared the cottage door, until Mr Haslam bent his head under the low lintel and carried her right inside.

'Sit her there,' said a voice and when Lydia was on the chair by the hearth she saw Mrs Malpass standing in the shadows. Her hair was long and grey, and loose about her shoulders. The sight shocked Lydia. She'd never seen an older woman not wearing a cap before.

'I'll leave thee to it, then,' said Mr Haslam. 'I'd best be on my way.'

'Oh!' Lydia cried out in alarm as a black cat leapt softly into her lap and began to circle round and round.

'Get down, Malkin,' said Mrs Malpass. 'I know that this lass needs our help.' She came across the small room and lifted the cat, setting him down softly on the floor. 'He knows when anyone is hurt,' she told Lydia. 'He senses it. Now,' she went on as she drew out a three-legged stool and sat at Lydia's feet. 'Is it this one?'

Mrs Malpass reached down and carefully lifted Lydia's ankle onto her lap. 'Who bound it for thee?' she asked once she'd gently removed the boot.

Lydia explained what had happened as Mrs Malpass moved her ankle this way and that. 'I'm sorry if it hurts,' she said as Lydia gasped in sudden pain, 'but I don't think the bone is broken. It's badly sprained and swollen but nothing that won't heal with rest. We'll soak it again,' she said. 'Thy friend was right about the knitbone. It's a useful herb.'

Mrs Malpass put Lydia's foot on the stool and went to the other side of the room where bunches of herbs hung drying on strings fastened to the beams. She selected the one she wanted and added some of the shredded leaves to warm water. The same aroma that Lydia had smelled in May's cottage filled the room and the woman brought the basin across to Lydia's chair and eased her foot into it.

'I'll get thee summat for the pain,' she said, reaching down more herbs before adding boiling water from her kettle that had been singing on a hook over the fire. Mrs Malpass allowed the tea to brew before pouring it through a sieve and bringing a cup of it to Lydia. 'Let it cool a moment,' she advised.

When she'd drunk the liquid, Lydia relaxed back into the chair. She felt a strange warmth flood through her body, radiating from her stomach, down her arms and legs to her fingertips and toes. The throbbing in her ankle eased and she felt slightly disengaged from her body. She was only vaguely aware of the cat on her lap again, kneading with its paws before settling down – a warm and welcome weight that reassured her with its rhythmic purring. She closed her eyes and felt as if she was floating. For the first time since she'd left her home she felt safe and at ease.

When Lydia woke, she wasn't sure of the time or the day or even where she was. She stared around and couldn't place anything that she saw. It was all strange to her and for a moment she wondered if she was still dreaming.

Gradually, she became aware of a heavy weight lying on her chest and it sounded as if it was rattling. She wondered if she was ill. But when her eyes focussed in the gloom she saw a black cat sleeping on her, purring quietly.

She reached out a hand and tentatively stroked its head. The creature woke and looked up at her with wide green eyes, but it seemed friendly and not inclined to bite. Malkin, the woman had called it, she recalled, as the events of the previous day came back to her.

It must be early morning, thought Lydia. She eased herself up on the straw mattress that Mrs Malpass had put near the hearth for her to sleep on. The cat protested with an irritated miaow and strolled off to sit some distance away where it began to wash itself. In the loft above her, she heard a creak of floorboards and before long Mrs Malpass came down the ladder. She was wearing the same plain dress that she had the day before. Lydia suspected it was sewn from sacking. On her feet she wore slippers. They must have been beautiful once, thought Lydia, but they were faded now and the embroidery was hanging in loose threads.

Mrs Malpass paused to stroke the cat, which twined itself around her legs, asking for food.

'In a minute, Malkin,' she told it. 'We have a guest to attend to first.'

Lydia sat up as Mrs Malpass bent to poke at the fire. 'There's some embers,' she said. 'Let's see if it'll light without me having to clear it out and re-lay it.' Lydia watched as the woman added kindling, twig by twig, until the flames took hold and she was able to place some bigger logs on top. 'I'll fill the kettle,' she told Lydia, 'and we'll have some tea.'

Lydia wondered if it would be the same tea she'd been given the day before. It had been unlike any other tea she'd ever drunk. It had made her sleepy but also content and had dulled the pain in her ankle to the point that she almost forgot she'd hurt it.

'How does it feel this morning?' asked Mrs Malpass when she came back with the water and hung the kettle on its hook.

Lydia flexed her ankle as far as it would move in the heavy strapping. It didn't feel too bad so she rolled onto her knees and stood up. She took her weight on her good foot and put the sprained ankle carefully to the ground.

'It feels better,' she said as she found that she could bear some weight on it. She tried to walk a few steps but it was still very painful. Realising that she wouldn't be able to walk far, Lydia wondered if Mr Haslam might be passing by with his cart again to give her a lift.

'Come and sit down,' said Mrs Malpass. 'It's best if tha rests it for a few days. It'll only make it worse if tha tries to walk on it too soon.'

'Maybe I could get a lift again,' said Lydia. 'Does Mr Haslam come by every day?'

'No. It'll be Monday next week before he passes again,' Mrs Malpass told her. 'But he'll call in when he does. He calls in every time, to see if I'm needing anything. I appreciate it. Not many others come now. Yon preacher at t' chapel has put it into their heads that I do the devil's work.'

Lydia didn't need to ask why. She'd been uneasy herself since Mr Haslam had brought her here. It was the sort of cottage that children would whisper about and run past in case the witch came out to catch them. And although

Mrs Malpass had shown her nothing but kindness, Lydia was keen to leave.

When the tea came, Lydia was glad that it tasted as tea should and she sipped it gratefully and ate a plate of bread and butter.

'I make it all myself,' Mrs Malpass told her. 'Mr Haslam is kind enough to drop off supplies of oats and corn for me. I don't like going to t' market.'

'Did tha help him?' asked Lydia.

'Aye. He were kicked by a horse and it broke his leg, but I were able to mend it. He'll always have a limp, but the doctors wanted to take his leg off.'

Lydia felt shocked. She wondered if the doctors at the dispensary would have wanted to chop off her leg. She shivered at the thought.

After she'd eaten, Lydia asked to use the privy. Mrs Malpass brought a stick for her to lean on and showed her to a shack at the back of the cottage where there was a deep hole in the ground.

'Use that, then throw a handful of straw down,' the woman told her. 'I'll come back for thee in a few minutes.'

It was a struggle for Lydia without a board to sit on, but the hole didn't smell as bad as the privy they shared with their neighbours at Tombling Fold, and when she was done, she leaned on the stick and made her own way slowly back to the cottage.

'I'm sure I could walk home,' she told Mrs Malpass when she went in.

'What's the rush?' she asked.

'They'll be worried about me,' said Lydia.

'Did tha not send a message with Mr Haslam?' she asked. 'He told me tha lived at th' hall in th' wood. I'm sure he'll call in and let them know.'

Lydia didn't reply. May must have told him where he was to take her and she imagined the carter calling at the big hall where space was let out to tenants and asking if anyone had a daughter named Lettie. He was bound to be suspicious when nobody had heard of her, and if the constables stopped him and questioned him about a young girl on the run he was sure to put two and two together and send them here to look for her. It became clear to Lydia that she wasn't safe in Mrs Malpass's cottage. She must find a way to leave sooner rather than later.

'I'm sure he won't forget to call and tell them,' Mrs Malpass said in an attempt to reassure her, not knowing the true cause of Lydia's anxiety. 'Come and sit down and take the weight off that ankle.'

Lydia sat down in the chair by the hearth and wondered if the real reason Mrs Malpass didn't want to let her go was because she was lonely. It was a remote spot and Lydia couldn't imagine how hard it must be to spend day after day here without anyone to talk to except the cat. But she didn't know if she could trust the woman to hide her if the constables came. She considered confiding in Mrs Malpass, telling her what had happened to Violet on the riverbank and explaining that it wasn't her fault. But she thought it was safer not to. The less the woman knew the better. She would wait until nightfall, decided Lydia. Then, when Mrs Malpass had gone up to her bed, she would slip out of the door and somehow find her way home. If she got there in the night-time she would throw a stone at the upstairs window to rouse her mother, who would come down to let her in. Surely there would be no constables there in the night? And if her father had come home, then she would be safe. He would hide her.

Lydia felt better as soon as she'd decided on a plan. She sat in the chair and rested with the cat on her lap and watched as Mrs Malpass went about her chores. They ate a broth in the middle of the day and some oatcakes that Mrs Malpass flipped on a griddle over the fire at teatime.

When Mrs Malpass offered her the special tea again, she refused it.

'It'll help thy pain,' Mrs Malpass told her.

'I'm not in pain,' lied Lydia even though her ankle throbbed incessantly. She didn't want to fall asleep and miss her chance of escape.

At last, Mrs Malpass shook down the straw mattress for Lydia to sleep on, then locked her door, drew the bolt and said goodnight before climbing the ladder to her own bed up above.

Lydia lay awake and listened to her moving about. Eventually silence fell and Lydia thought Mrs Malpass must be asleep, so she pushed back the blanket and got to her feet. She didn't need to get dressed because she'd taken nothing off since she left Caton except her boots, which she pulled onto her feet, almost crying out in pain as she was forced to bend her sprained ankle to get her foot into the left one. Then she stood, cautiously, all the while listening in case she disturbed Mrs Malpass.

Leaning on the stick, she limped across to the door, careful not to kick or fall over anything. She was lucky, thought Lydia, because a moon was rising and cast an eerie light in through the window that helped her to find her way. She reached for the bolt and carefully eased it back. She was terrified that it would squeak and give her away, but Mrs Malpass must have kept it well-oiled because it slid back easily. Then Lydia reached to turn the key in the lock.

But there was no key. They always kept the key in the lock at home and it had never occurred to Lydia that Mrs Malpass might remove it. She fumbled around in the half-light, feeling along the windowsill and then the shelf and finally the mantelpiece, but it was nowhere to be found. Lydia wondered if Mrs Malpass had taken it with her to bed. Perhaps it was in her pocket – if she had a pocket in her sacking gown.

Close to tears, Lydia sat down on the edge of the chair and leaned on the stick. There would be no escape for her tonight and she realised that she was trembling with fear as she thought of the constables coming for her as soon as the new day dawned.

Chapter Twelve

Monday morning was unexpectedly fine and bright and Betty fussed over her son as he washed his face and neck. She left Rose with Ann and, as the sun rose, she and her son set off for the pit head at Ladyshore.

There was a blackbird singing an early song as they went down the lane, trying out its voice in preparation for the new season. It was a sound that normally would have brought joy to Betty but this morning she could think of nothing but the ordeal that lay ahead for Simon.

Their pace slowed as they approached the ramshackle wooden huts that stood beside the gin where a horse was standing, eagerly eating hay from a nosebag. Betty approached the largest of the huts and knocked. A voice called her to come in and she saw a man sitting at a shabby desk, obviously infected with woodworm. He glanced up at her and shuffled the papers in front of him.

'Can I help thee?'

'I'm lookin' to set our Simon on as a pit lad,' she told him.

The man frowned. 'Is his father not a pit worker?'

'No. He's a weaver. But he's not here. I've to find the lad work.'

'How old is he?'

'Ten years.'

'Has he ever been down afore?'

Betty shook her head. 'No.'

'So he knows nowt about it?' She shook her head again. 'Lads usually go down wi' their fathers, to learn t' job,' explained the man.

'So tha can't set him on?' asked Betty hopefully.

'I didn't say that. Thing is, I can only take him on as a trapper and it's usually younger lads who do that. I can only pay a penny a day.'

Betty quickly calculated that with the extra sixpence, they wouldn't be much better off than if Simon didn't work at all. She wondered if it was worthwhile him taking the job, but she knew that if he didn't, Mr Lomax would insist that her money was stopped completely.

'What dost tha think?' she asked Simon, hating to press the decision onto him but thinking that if he refused she wouldn't force him. It had been bad enough with Lydia. She didn't want another of her children to hate her.

'What would I have to do?' he asked.

'It's simple,' explained the man, 'just a matter of opening and shutting t' doors for t' miners and t' tubs to go through. It's to do with t' ventilation, but I don't need to trouble thee wi' details. It's easy work,' he said to Betty. 'They mostly sit about all day.'

'Simon?' she asked, looking at her son's face. He looked determined and serious and she swelled with pride.

'I'll do it,' he said.

'Aye. Well, it'll be night shift, so tha needs to come back at six o'clock. Send 'im wi' a bit o' tackle,' he told Betty. 'He'll eat on t' job.'

'Aye. Thanks,' she said, pushing Simon out through the door ahead of her and wondering whether she'd done the right thing. Whilst they'd been in the office, the night shift had finished and the miners were being winched up from the pit in a bucket. They were filthy and looked weary, most of them bent and stiff as if they'd lost the ability to stand up straight. They bade one another quiet farewells and walked off towards their homes, blinking in the morning light. One or two glanced curiously at Betty and Simon but most seemed too tired to care. There were women amongst them too, some heavy with pregnancy, and children much younger than Simon, covered in dust, their faces and hands blackened with it and their clothes coated. Betty almost wept at the prospect of seeing her son in that state, but she remembered the vicar's words – she wouldn't refuse a bucket of coal and somebody had to fetch it up from under the ground.

'Best go home for a few hours,' she told Simon. 'Dost think tha'll be able to find thine own way back again later?'

'Aye. Of course I can,' he replied, but she saw that he too was staring at the underground workers who were wiping their eyes as they surfaced from the shaft and she knew that he must be dreading going down into the pit.

That evening, Betty wrapped all the oatcakes she could spare in a piece of rag and put them into Simon's pocket. She didn't want him to be hungry.

'Take good care of thyself,' she urged him, trying to kiss his cheek as he turned away from her.

'I'll be all right. Stop fussing,' he said.

'Come straight home after. I'll have summat t' eat waitin' for thee,' she promised him.

Betty stood at the door of her cottage and watched her son walk down the fold. He looked so young. At the corner she hoped he would turn back and wave to her, but he didn't, he just kept on walking determinedly.

Betty went back inside. She prayed that Simon would come home safely, the next day and every day that followed. She'd heard too many stories about roof falls and floods and explosions to have any peace of mind until he was back.

–

It was mid-morning the following day when Simon arrived back at Tombling Fold. Betty had been awake all night fretting and ever since it had come light she'd been watching out for him every few minutes. She was shocked when she saw her son in the doorway. The whites of his eyes stood out from the rest of his face that was black with coal dust. He was filthy and looked tired out.

'Come to the fire,' he said. 'I'll fetch thee summat t' eat.'

Betty had nothing to offer but oats made into a gruel. She'd made it as thick as she could afford even though she knew that she would have to go without herself. But it was only right that Simon should be fed after he'd worked all night. He sat down without a word and lifted the bowl to his mouth.

'How was it?' she asked as she watched him anxiously. He hardly had the strength to eat and swayed alarmingly, as if he would keel over and fall asleep at any moment. He didn't answer straight away, but concentrated on finishing the food, licking the dregs from a filthy finger so as to leave nothing behind.

'It were all right,' he said after a moment. 'There weren't that much to do except open and shut a trap. The rest of the time I just sat there in the dark. It was hard to stay awake.'

'Was there no light? Not even a candle or a rushlight?' asked Betty.

Simon shook his head. 'It were pitch black except for when the miners came through,' he told her. 'The work weren't that bad, but it were a long way underground. It took an age to walk down to where I was to sit and a long time to walk back. Then I had to walk home.'

'Well, tha's back now,' Betty comforted him, reaching out to push a lock of his hair out of his eyes. 'I'll fetch some water and tha can have a wash.'

'Not now,' he told her. 'Just let me sleep.'

Betty could see that Simon was exhausted. Even though he'd rested for a few hours before he went to the pit, she realised that it was as if he'd missed a full night's sleep and she didn't press him to wash. It wasn't as if she had any clean white linen sheets that would be spoiled.

'It won't be for long,' she reassured him. 'I'm sure the letter about our passage will come soon.'

Despite his tiredness, Simon's face creased into a smile. 'But I'll work for my keep until then,' he told her determinedly as she unrolled a straw mattress for him to lie on.

Betty let Simon sleep for as long as he could. She told Rose that she must keep very quiet so as not to wake her brother, but the daylight disturbed Simon and he only dozed from mid-morning even though she kept the curtains drawn across the window to shut out the light.

He roused himself late in the afternoon so that he could eat something before he returned to the pit. Betty watched as he washed the worst of the grime off his face, neck and hands with a rag at the kitchen sink. The water was cold and there was no soap, but it took the worst of it off. She wished that he could have a proper bath, with soap and hot water, but she knew that there wouldn't be much point when he would arrive home just as dirty again after his next shift.

Betty brewed tea and put a spoonful of sugar into Simon's. She spread a little lard on the oatcakes she'd made for his tea and wrapped more up for him to take in his pocket. It wasn't much and she wished that she could give him more.

'Tha doesn't have to go,' she said as he wrapped a scarf around his face and pulled on a cap that was too small for him and only sat on the back of his head. 'We'll manage,' she told him.

He shook his head. 'There's plenty of other lads down there – some a lot younger than me,' he told her. 'I'll be all right. It's not for ever.'

'No, it isn't,' she agreed as she gave him a quick hug. 'We'll soon be on our way to join thy father.'

–

Betty woke in the dead of the night with a feeling of unease. Maybe it was because there was only her and Rose at home, she thought, as she lay awake, her heart racing and her ears straining for any sound that would portend danger. It was probably just a bad dream, she told herself, nothing more. She raised herself on an elbow and stared into the blackness. It must be the early hours of the morning, she thought. Beside her, she could tell by the sound of Rose's breathing that her daughter was asleep. Everything else was silent. There wasn't even the sound of wind or rain on the window.

Betty lay back down and closed her eyes. She tried to relax and go back to sleep, but something that she couldn't explain still troubled her. As she waited for the dawn to come, she tried to calm herself with rational responses to the ideas that were plaguing her mind. It was no wonder she was anxious. With Lydia at Caton and Simon working in the pit, she was bound to find it strange. It was nothing more than her imagination and a normal mother's worries for her children.

When the square of the window grew paler than the walls, despite the thin curtain that covered it, Betty gave up trying to sleep. The fire had gone out and it was so cold she could barely move. She rubbed her hands together, rubbed her arms and flexed her legs. Then, with her shawl around her she crept out of the door without waking Rose to go to look for some wood to burn on the fire.

The first rosy rays of sunlight were peeping over the horizon to the south-east and Betty thought it was going to be a nice day. There were a few daffodils opening along the sides of the path and the sight cheered her. As she walked she picked up a stick or two here and there. They were only flimsy and would soon be burned, but they were better than nothing and would suffice until Simon carried home the bucket of coal he'd been promised at the end of the week. It was worth more than the paltry pennies he would be paid.

As she walked, watching the sun rise, Betty heard what she thought was distant thunder. It puzzled her because there didn't appear to be a cloud in the sky and she wondered where the noise had come from. Then she saw that there was a plume of smoke rising from the valley beyond Tonge. She'd never noticed it before and wondered if there was a new mill there that was running on steam power. She'd heard no talk of it. She stood and watched for a while as the smoke thickened and grew darker, spreading into the pristine morning sky like a black cloud. Suddenly, she realised where it was coming from. Dropping the sticks she'd collected at her feet, she turned and ran back to the cottage to get Rose. It was the pit, she thought. Oh dear God, it was the pit!

Rose woke with a startled cry as her mother burst into the cottage.

'Get up! We have to go!' Betty told her as the child rubbed her eyes and yawned. 'Come on!' she repeated, finding Rose's clogs and pushing them towards her feet.

Rose began to cry and Betty felt guilty to have alarmed the child, but her concern was mostly for her son. She needed to know that Simon was safe.

'Come on,' she repeated, feeling irritated that Rose was being so slow. 'We need to go.'

'Where are we going?' asked Rose as Betty bundled her into a shawl. 'Are we going to get on the ship to go to find my daddy?'

'No. No, not today. We have to find thy brother. I think there may be something wrong at the pit.'

Betty didn't want to frighten her daughter, but she needed to make Rose understand the urgency.

'Is everything all right? I heard thee shouting,' said Ann, who'd come hurrying round from next door. 'Is there owt I can do?'

'Will tha mind Rose for a while?' asked Betty. 'It'll be quicker without her.'

'What will? Where's tha going?' asked Ann.

'The pit,' replied Betty as if it was obvious. 'Hast tha not seen the smoke?'

Ann's eyes widened in horror and without a word she went out and ran to the end of the fold and looked towards Tonge.

'Dear God,' she said when Betty caught up with her. 'Tha doesn't think...' Ann glanced at Rose and said no more, but her meaning was clear.

'I need to go,' said Betty.

'Aye, of course tha does. Leave Rose with me. I don't mind.'

Betty thanked her friend and began to run towards the track that would lead her down to the pit, following in the footsteps that Simon had taken the previous evening and praying out loud as she gasped for breath that no harm had come to him.

Before long she had to stop for a moment. She bent almost double to try to ease the pain from the stitch in her side, then she walked on, crying as she went. Others had seen the smoke too and as she neared the pit head and saw the gaping hole in the earth where the gin had stood the last time she'd been there, she was joined by other distraught women, all asking one another if there was a chance that anyone had survived.

Men from the surrounding houses and those who'd already been on their way to begin the day shift gathered around. A man seemed to be taking charge, directing those who were able to bring ropes and ladders to begin a rescue.

The women held and hugged one another, whispering encouragement and hope as a man was lowered on a rope to see if there were any survivors. An anxious silence fell as they waited, until a shout was heard and the men at the top of the shaft began to lower more ropes and a large bucket that had held coal. A dozen men hauled on the rope, hand over hand, as the burden was gradually lifted. Betty heard the man coughing before his head appeared above ground and people rushed forwards to pull him to safety, beleaguering him with questions all the while, each asking if their husband or son was still alive down below.

'It were the firedamp,' he said. 'A candle must have set it off.' He told them there were many injured and he thought some must be dead. He wasn't sure. It had been hard to see anything.

Betty sat on the ground and watched as the ropes and buckets were lowered and brought up again time after time. Some of the rescued were gasping for their breath. Others were bleeding. One child was still, badly burned, and Betty could see that he was dead as they laid his body on the ground.

She watched as the bucket was lowered back down the shaft. She couldn't bear to think about what she would do if Simon was brought up like that – and she knew she wasn't the only one. The faces of the women around her betrayed their own hopes and fears as each new miner was brought out – relief that it was not the body of their relative, but still fearful that the next time it might be.

It must have been nearing midday when Betty watched the bucket come up yet again and she saw Simon. She couldn't tell if he was dead or alive. He wasn't moving and his eyes were closed. For a moment she turned away, not wanting to face the possibility that it was only his body that was being returned to her. But when she turned back she saw that he was standing upright, his face ashen with dirt and shock as he stared around at the crowd and the incongruous sunshine.

Betty rushed across the grass, pushing through the crowd to reach him. 'Simon!'

He turned at the familiar sound of her voice and she ran to him and hugged him close to her, not caring that the filth from his clothes was dirtying hers. He clung to her and she could feel him sobbing. She shushed him and pulled his face against her as the other men who had been brought up with him formed a circle around her and their eyes glared out from their blackened faces.

'He's to blame,' said one starkly, pointing an accusatory finger at Simon. 'There's good men lost their lives today because of him.'

The quiet anger in the man's voice made Betty afraid. She didn't understand what he was saying.

'Why?' was all she managed to reply as the man spat on the ground at her feet and then turned away to his own family.

There was talk that Betty couldn't quite hear. Simon was still sobbing in her arms and she moved away from the crowd who were turning their backs on her and her son, casting furious glances over their shoulders.

'Come on,' she told Simon. 'Let's go home.'

The women who had been her friends and companions only moments before were now gathered in total rejection of her. Betty had no idea what had happened down there, but it was clear that Simon was being made the scapegoat and she knew she needed to get him away before things turned even uglier.

She put her arm around his shoulders and asked him if he could walk. He nodded, but began to cough again as they made their way down the track. He was gasping for his breath and Betty was alarmed.

'It's the gas,' he wheezed after he'd sat down for a moment. 'I breathed in the firedamp.'

'What happened?' Betty asked him once she was sure the miners and their families were not going to come after them, not now at least.

'I fell asleep. I must have done. I don't really remember. I was so tired and it was so dark down there.'

'That wasn't thy fault,' Betty told him. 'I should never have agreed to thee goin' down there in t' first place. Tha weren't to blame,' she reassured him, wondering what had made the men so angry. Surely a young lad falling asleep in the dark didn't deserve the hatred that she'd seen in their faces.

She urged him to his feet and they made their way home. People came out of their cottages as they passed by to ask what had happened and Betty explained there had been an explosion underground. Many crossed themselves and said they would pray. Others said how glad they were they had no family in the pit, or that they'd been spared by being on the day shift. They sympathised with Simon, told him he was a lucky lad and wished him well. But Betty worried they would change their minds when they heard he was being held responsible.

When they reached home, Ann was looking out for them. The relief was clear on her face when she saw Simon.

'I'll not let him go down again,' vowed Betty.

'They'll not have me,' whispered Simon. 'They've told me never to show my face down there again.'

'I'm sure they didn't mean it,' Ann replied, but Betty shook her head.

'There were a lot of bad feeling,' she told her friend. 'I'm not sure why, but I were glad to get away.'

'It'll be all right,' Ann tried to reassure her. 'Get the lad inside and put him to bed. I'll lend thee a bucket o' coal for the fire so tha can heat some water to wash him,' she told Betty, 'and I'll not hear no for an answer.'

Inside the cottage, Simon dropped to the floor with exhaustion. Betty wrung out a cloth in cold water and wiped the dirt from his face and hands as best she could.

He asked for a drink and she told him she'd brew some tea as soon as she got the fire going.

'They kept saying it was my fault,' Simon told her, tears welling up in his eyes again. 'They were all saying so. They said that because I was asleep I wasn't opening and shutting the trap, and that's what made the gas build up.'

'No,' said Betty, trying to soothe him. She knew little about mining and wasn't sure whether such a thing might cause an explosion or not. 'It's more likely one of 'em was careless with a light and they were just looking for someone to blame, and because tha's new there tha's an easy target. Take no notice,' she told him. 'Tha's not goin' back so it doesn't matter.'

'But how will we manage?' he asked forlornly. Betty hugged him again. He looked so young and vulnerable and she was proud of the way he'd tried his best to earn some money to help keep them.

'It won't be long before the letter comes,' she reassured him. 'We'll manage until then,' she said, even though she had no idea how. 'Don't tha worry.'

Chapter Thirteen

Simon slept for twelve hours straight the night after the accident. He was shocked and exhausted and as Betty sat and watched over him she wished that there was a way she could turn back time so that he had never been down that pit when the explosion occurred. She'd never let him go back; he'd never be exposed to the dangers of mining for coal ever again.

Yet she felt guilty as she threw a few more cobs onto her fire and filled the kettle with water. Others had been down under the ground to bring it up and now some of them were dead. Even though she was thankful that Simon had survived, she knew there were other wives and mothers who would be grieving this morning.

Once the water was hot, she filled a small bowl from the back kitchen so that Simon could have a proper wash down when he woke. She'd wanted him to wash the night before. She'd wanted to scrub every remnant of coal dust from his face and his hair and his body. His clothes too, though she didn't know how she could get them clean. He had nothing else to wear whilst they were washed and dried and the best that she could do would be to shake them outside and brush them down as he got washed.

He stirred at last and sat up on the straw mattress. Betty poured some of the tea that she'd kept warm in the pot and handed it to him. There was no milk or sugar left; it was the best she could provide.

'Get thee washed,' she told him, 'and then we'll go down to speak to yon chaps about our relief payments.'

Surely they wouldn't allow her and her children to starve, she thought, although the image of Mr Lomax in particular made her doubt her faith in their charity and compassion.

–

As soon as they reached the marketplace, Betty could sense the hostility. Women glanced in their direction, then turned away and whispered behind their hands, and when she stood in line at the baker's stall to try to claim her allowance of bread, the man ignored her and kept serving other customers until at last he had to acknowledge her.

'A loaf please,' she said, showing him her token.

'I've none left,' he told her and turned away even though it was clear that there were still plenty.

Betty felt bewildered and upset. She began to despair of getting any food at all if none of the stallholders would serve her.

It wasn't until a clod of mud hit her with force on her shoulder that she realised how serious the situation was.

'Leave us alone!' she shouted at the woman who'd thrown it, egged on by her friends. 'We've done nowt wrong.'

'Dost tha know how many are dead because of thy lad?' demanded the woman. 'Tha should be ashamed! I don't know how tha dare show thy face here after what was done yesterday!'

'The lad's done nowt wrong,' Betty told them as she put protective arms around her son and daughter. She could see that they were both scared as the crowd came closer and gathered around them in a circle.

'It were him that caused the explosion!' accused another. 'Ten dead, and all because of him!'

'Mam?' Simon looked at her, confused and afraid. 'Was it my fault?' he asked her, his bottom lip trembling.

'No. Of course it wasn't,' she reassured him as she tightened her hold on him. 'These folk are just upset, that's all. They're talkin' nonsense.'

'It's all right for thee,' called out another woman. 'Thy son came home, but Peggy Greenhalgh at Little Lever has a son to bury tomorrow.'

'Aye and Mrs Holt lost a lad and her husband. Both were at the coalface and they were so badly burned when they brought 'em out that she couldn't even recognise 'em at first.'

'I'm sorry,' replied Betty, not knowing what else to say. The women were coming ever closer and had been joined now by some men, probably miners, she thought. Their faces were filled with anger and hatred and she began to fear their purpose.

She glanced about in alarm to see if there was anyone who would help her, but all she saw was hostility on every side. Another clod of mud struck her, narrowly missing her face. She pulled Rose and Simon close to her, trying to protect them with her shawl, although it was clear that they stood no chance against this mob and her heart raced with fear as she wondered if they were set on killing them in their desire for vengeance.

Another missile was thrown and this time it was a stone. It struck Rose on the thigh and the child cried out in shock and sobbed in pain.

'Please,' Betty begged. 'Please leave us alone. The child's done nothing wrong,' she pleaded as she tried to comfort her daughter.

One or two people on the outskirts of the crowd were calling for calm.

'It'll do no good. It'll not bring back the dead to hurt a woman and her childer,' they argued. But the crowd was fired up. Another stone was thrown, followed by another, which struck Betty on the head. Pain seared through her and she felt warm blood flow down her cheek and drip from her chin. She sank to the ground, gathering Rose beneath her to protect her daughter with her own body. She hoped that the crowd would stop now that they'd made their point. But she felt the hard toecap of a clog on her ribs and the crowd began to jeer and encourage those who were brave enough to strike her.

'That's it! Show 'em what for!'

The words hurt Betty more than the blows. How could these people say such things? She'd always thought of the townsfolk as her friends and neighbours. Why would they suddenly turn on her and her children like this?

Then, she became aware of a change in the atmosphere. The blows stopped and people began to move away from her. There were raised voices, berating the crowd and telling them to move away. She felt a hand under her arm.

'Can you get up? Are you hurt?'

Betty recognised the Reverend Brocklehurst's voice and she replied shakily. 'I'm all right,' she told him, not wanting to make a fuss.

Her legs felt weak as she stood up and she accepted the handkerchief that was thrust at her to stem the bleeding from her head. She kept her other arm around Rose, who was clinging to her and still sobbing.

'Simon?' She turned to look for her son. He seemed unscathed, but was trembling and white-faced as he gazed at the retreating crowd, who were being ushered away by some gentlemen who'd come out of a nearby inn to see what the commotion was.

'You'd better come down to the vestry,' the vicar told her as he cut a path between the curious bystanders. 'I was on my way to see you anyway. The letter has come,' he told her.

Betty limped down Churchgate beside the vicar, clutching Rose's hand with one of hers, whilst using the other to keep the handkerchief pressed to her head. Simon walked beside her and kept glancing back, nervously, to check they weren't being followed.

'Shall I send for the doctor?' the vicar asked when he had them safely inside and the door closed.

Betty took the handkerchief away from her head and was shocked to see how red it was with blood, but she was more concerned about her children. She wanted to check on Rose's leg but didn't want to raise her daughter's skirt up in front of the vicar.

'No,' she replied after a moment's hesitation. 'I think we're all right. I'm grateful to you for coming along,' she added. 'It was getting nasty.'

'There were others coming out to see what was going on,' he told her. 'I don't think you were in any real danger.'

Betty was inclined to disagree. She was shocked to her soul by what had happened. She'd never had experience of a crowd turning on someone as the townsfolk had just turned on her.

'They were blaming Simon for the accident,' she said, reaching out to caress her son's head.

'People often look for someone to blame in circumstances like these,' said the vicar. 'It's wrong, but it's human nature I suppose. Are you sure you don't want the doctor? It looks a nasty cut. I'll fetch some water,' he said. 'You can at least bathe it.'

Whilst the vicar was out of the vestry, Betty took a look at Rose's leg. Although the skin wasn't broken, it looked very red and she knew there would a huge bruise by tomorrow. But Rose had stopped crying and she said that she could bear weight on the leg and walk, so Betty thought there wasn't too much damage done. Simon hadn't been physically hurt, but he was still shaking and pale-faced, and he visibly jumped on his stool when the vicar pushed open the door and came back in with a bowl of water and a rag.

'It's cold, I'm afraid,' he apologised, 'but at least you can wash away the worst of it.'

'Thank you,' said Betty as she squeezed out the cloth and dabbed at her temple. 'Did you say the letter had come?' she reminded him. 'Is it good news?' she asked, hopeful that it would be. Her doubts about leaving home had been quashed by her encounter in the marketplace. Now she thought that getting away from this place and these people would be the most appealing thing to do.

'Indeed it is!' The vicar beamed. 'The Home Office has written to offer you passage on a ship.'

Sitting on the chair by the fire, with Rose on her lap, Betty waited as the Reverend Brocklehurst unfolded the letter and smoothed it out on his desk.

'"The ship *Maria* being appointed to convey the persons named in the margin hereof to Port Jackson, New South Wales, they are desired to be on board the said ship, which is lying at Deptford on or before the seventh day of April if their health be of such as to allow of their undertaking the voyage,"' read the vicar aloud as Betty tried to take in all the details.

'Which persons are named?' Betty asked, praying that both Simon and Lydia had been included.

The vicar glanced down the page and nodded. 'You, Lydia, Simon and Rose,' he confirmed.

'Thank God!' replied Betty. 'But the seventh of April is less than two weeks off!' she exclaimed, suddenly alarmed at the prospect of making the arrangements necessary to go. 'How will we get to Deptford?' she asked as she began to worry that one more opportunity might be snatched from her simply because it was impossible to reach the ship in time.

'There must surely be some provision,' replied the vicar. 'I'll speak to the parish guardians about it, to see if there are funds for your travel expenses. And the letter also mentions adequate clothing,' he added, with a glance at Betty and Rose's threadbare apparel. 'I'll see what can be arranged about that too.'

'And Lydia?' asked Betty. 'You did write to Caton, didn't you? I can't leave without her.'

'I'll send word again to Caton,' said the vicar. 'I'll appeal personally to Mr Greg if necessary. Don't worry, Mrs Knowles. I'll do everything in my power to get you and your family safely aboard that ship,' he promised her. 'Come to see me again tomorrow morning at eleven o'clock and I'll let you know what arrangements have been put in place.'

—

By the time they came out of the church, most of the stallholders had packed up and left, and the crowd of shoppers had either gone home or into the public houses. A few stragglers cast them curious looks and hurried by, but Betty decided not to try to make any purchases. It would be better to go hungry than risk another assault.

'Where is Deptford? Is it a long way?' Simon asked after they'd arrived home and were drinking tea in place of the meal that Betty had been unable to buy.

'I'm not sure,' admitted Betty. 'It must be down south somewhere, on the coast. But we'll know more after we've spoken to the vicar again tomorrow.'

'When will we go?' Simon asked.

'We'll go as soon as our Lydia gets home,' Betty told him. 'It's probably for the best if we don't stay here,' she added. 'And it's not like we've much to pack,' she went on, glancing about the near empty room and wondering how she would bear leaving her home behind. It was all the security she had in a challenging world, this little cottage that had once been such a happy place when Jimmy was in it. But they would be happy again, she told herself. It would be a different cottage in a different place, but after all these years they would be together again, and they would be happy with a husband and father to protect them.

–

When Betty woke the next morning, she struggled to get up from her mattress on the floor because she was so sore and bruised from the day before. Her head had stopped bleeding, but it throbbed and she couldn't bear to touch it with her fingers to check how much damage had been done. She wasn't sure if she was glad or sorry that she had no mirror to see herself in. She felt as if she looked a mess and when Rose woke and looked at her and asked why her eye was all swollen and funny colours, she knew that she was right.

Her ribs were sore too and hurt every time she breathed. She hoped that nothing was broken and wondered whether she'd been too quick to refuse the vicar's offer of a doctor. But her first thought had been her inability to pay and she didn't want to be shamed or forced into debt if the doctor had attended and then demanded money from her.

She would heal, she thought. She didn't have much other option.

'Never mind my face, how's thy leg?' she asked her daughter. Rose had been limping by the time they'd arrived home the day before.

Rose pulled up her skirt with a grimace. 'It still hurts,' she told her mother and Betty saw that the bruise had spread right across her thigh, as black as thunder and swollen.

'Canst tha walk?' asked Betty. 'We've to see the Reverend Brocklehurst again this morning, but tha can stay with Ann if tha'd rather not go.'

'I'll come,' said Rose. 'I don't like being left behind.' Then she hesitated. 'Those people won't be there again, will they?' she asked.

'No. Not today,' Betty reassured her. 'It's not a market day.'

Simon was still quiet when he woke. And although he said nothing, Betty knew that he'd been having bad dreams all night. She'd felt him turning restlessly in his sleep and heard him mumbling incoherent words to himself. She knew that he'd dreamt about being trapped in the mine.

They'd run out of sticks for a fire so Betty decided that they might as well get on their way. They would be able to warm themselves at the vicar's fire for a while and she'd send Simon out to look for fuel when they came back.

They had a drink of cold water and set off. There was a sprinkling of late frost glistening on the grass as they went down the lane, walking slowly because their injuries dictated their speed. Betty noticed a few people glance at her and then look quickly away. They probably thought she'd been on the receiving end of a husband's fists, and it made her angry and defensive because Jimmy was a gentle man and would never have laid a finger on her. She pulled her shawl around her face and hoped that when they eventually saw one another again, he would still be the man she remembered and that his experiences would not have spoiled him.

Bolton was thankfully quiet as they made their way down Churchgate towards the vicar's vestry at the far end of the church. As Betty approached the door she heard two voices and she hesitated, thinking that she'd better wait outside if the vicar was meeting with someone else. She sat down in the front pew and Rose and Simon sat quietly beside her, Rose leaning against her for comfort and Simon tapping the floor with his foot, giving away his anxiety.

After a while the door opened and Betty stood up expectantly.

'There you are!' exclaimed the vicar. 'I didn't realise you were waiting. Come in.'

He stepped back into the warm room and Betty ushered her children ahead of her, wondering who else was in there. She'd seen no one come out and she knew there was no other door.

She was disappointed when she saw that it was Mr Lomax taking up the chair by the fire. If one of the parish guardians had to be present she would have preferred it to be Mr Hewitt, who had shown her some compassion.

'You're late!' accused Mr Lomax.

'We were waiting outside. I didn't want to intrude,' explained Betty, but she could see that he dismissed it as a flimsy excuse.

'Mr Lomax and I have been discussing what can be done for you,' explained the vicar as he found another chair for Betty, leaving Simon and Rose to stand at the back of the room. Betty sat down and tried to turn her face from Mr Lomax, who was frowning at her black eye. 'How are you this morning?' went on the vicar.

'Not too bad.'

'Your eye looks sore. How is Rose's leg?'

'It hurts her, but she's managed to walk down,' replied Betty.

The vicar smiled at Rose. 'I'm glad to hear that,' he said, before turning to Mr Lomax. 'Mrs Knowles and her children were subject to a vicious assault in the market-place yesterday,' he explained.

'Aye, so I believe,' replied the ironmonger. 'Everyone who came in my shop were talkin' of it. Seems they think the lad were the cause of the explosion at yon pit.' He glared at Simon and Betty saw her son's cheeks flush as he lowered his gaze.

'He did nothing wrong,' she said. 'He did his best.' She wanted to tell Mr Lomax that he was the one who was responsible anyway. If he hadn't insisted Simon take the pit job, the miners would have had to find someone else to blame.

'Well, let's talk about getting you to Deptford and onto that ship,' said the vicar, trying to change the subject. 'That's what we're here for this morning,' he added as he rubbed his hands together and waited until he had the attention of both Betty and Mr Lomax. 'I've been discussing the matter of your travel, Mrs Knowles, and the relief committee have agreed to pay the coach fares and to provide you with some new clothing.'

'Second hand, of course,' interrupted Mr Lomax, 'and outside seats on the coach.'

'I'm very grateful,' Betty told him. It was more than she'd hoped for. 'Have you heard back from Caton yet?' she asked the vicar. 'Is Lydia coming home?'

'Lydia can't go with you,' Mr Lomax told her bluntly. 'She has her apprenticeship to Mr Greg.'

'But Reverend Brocklehurst said it might be arranged,' replied Betty. 'We can't go without her.'

Mr Lomax's face darkened. 'It's beyond me how you can be so ungrateful still,' he told Betty, 'after everything we've done for you.'

'I'm not ungrateful,' protested Betty. 'I appreciate the help, I do. But I can't go off to the other side of the world and leave my daughter here.'

'Well, it's your choice,' Mr Lomax told her. 'The committee have made a generous offer, but it's up to you whether you take it or not.' He turned to the vicar. 'There's some families just won't be helped,' he complained. 'And there's a limit to our patience. If she won't accept this offer then we'll strike her from the books. She'll have to fend for herself in the future.'

'Don't be hasty,' implored the vicar. 'Surely you can understand Mrs Knowles wanting to keep her family together. And I did promise to do what I could. I wrote to Caton to ask if Lydia could be released from the agreement.'

'It wasn't your place, vicar,' Mr Lomax told him. 'The apprenticeship was arranged by the guardians.'

'I know. But surely you can see that these are exceptional circumstances?'

Mr Lomax retreated a little at the vicar's words. 'Well, we'll see what Mr Greg says, but I'll not push for it,' he said. 'And we'll not pay fare or clothing for her. We've been generous enough I think.'

'But how will Lydia travel with us?' asked Betty. She had no money to pay for the fare.

'Don't worry about that for now,' the vicar told her with a look of exasperation. 'I'm sure something can be sorted out.'

'Not with parish money,' Mr Lomax told him. 'I'll not be accused of misusing what people have donated in good faith.'

'Well, let's leave it for now,' said the vicar as he reached to pass Mr Lomax his hat. 'We'll not keep you any longer. I know your time is valuable.'

'Aye.' The ironmonger stood up, realising he was dismissed but determined to hold on to his dignity. 'I'd best get back to my business,' he agreed.

'I won't go without Lydia!' Betty repeated to the vicar after Mr Lomax had gone.

'Well, let's wait until we hear back from Caton,' the vicar told her. 'I'm sure it will be all right. And in the meantime, you'll have your fares and some clothing to take. That's good news.'

Betty knew that it was true. Some decent clothes to travel in and a way to get to Deptford before the seventh of April would have solved all her immediate problems if only they'd included Lydia.

She thanked the vicar and he told her to pack what possessions she needed to take with her so she would be ready to leave as soon as she had her tickets. She just hoped that Lydia would be home in time to go with them and that a way would be found to pay her fare.

Back on the street in the cold wind, Betty decided to try her luck at the baker's shop. Surely the man wouldn't turn her away again when she had her token to spend.

She left Simon and Rose waiting outside with instructions not to move and she pushed open the shop door, to be met by warmth and the aroma of freshly baked bread. It made her mouth water.

The baker glared at her when he saw who it was, but Betty refused to be cowed by him.

'A loaf, please,' she said, proffering the crumpled token from her pocket.

Without a word, the baker took one from the pile on his counter and thrust it at her as he snatched the token without a word. He seemed chastened and she wondered if the vicar had had a word with him.

'Thank you,' said Betty as she made a dash for the door before he could change his mind. 'Come on,' she told the children. 'Let's get home and get a fire lit, then we can eat this with a bit of lard. It'll be tasty.'

Chapter Fourteen

The next morning, Betty was busy filling a box with the few serviceable possessions she intended to take with her to Deptford when there was a knock on her cottage door. Although she knew it couldn't be Lydia, because her daughter would have come straight in, Betty hoped it was news that she was on her way and her hopes surged when she saw the Reverend Brocklehurst standing there.

'May I step inside?' he asked as he took off his hat.

'Aye. Come in,' said Betty. His solemn face worried her. He was always a serious man, not given much to smiling, but there was something about his demeanour that made him seem sterner than ever this morning. She was worried that he'd come to say that there was a problem with the arrangements for her travel.

'I think you'd best sit down,' he told her.

'Why? What's wrong?' she asked. 'They haven't changed their minds about our passage on the ship, have they?'

'No.' The vicar shook his head. 'Sit down, Mrs Knowles,' he repeated. 'It isn't about the passage, but I do have some bad news.'

Betty felt herself becoming increasingly alarmed. She knew that it wasn't about Simon or Rose. They were out gathering wood for the fire and had only been gone for ten minutes at the most.

'Lydia?' she asked. 'Will they not let her go from Caton?'

The Reverend Brocklehurst took her elbow and looked around for a seat, but finding none, he let his hand drop and allowed her to continue to stand.

'I have had a letter from Mr Greg at Caton,' he told her, 'but it wasn't what I was expecting.' He paused, obviously finding it difficult to find the right words and, as Betty watched him, her fears grew.

'What's happened?' she asked, hearing the quaver in her own voice.

'It seems that on the Sunday before last, after church, the children were allowed to go down to the riverbank to play. It was a common occurrence and there had never been any question of it being dangerous,' he added. Betty found she was struggling to breathe as panic gripped her. 'There was an accident,' went on the vicar. 'There was some argument, some horseplay – as children are inclined to after a week spent working inside. It seems that one girl was pulled from the water. But Lydia is still missing. Despite a long and thorough search, she hasn't been found.'

Betty stared at the vicar, trying to make sense of what he was telling her. 'So she's not at Caton?' she asked after a moment. She must be somewhere, thought Betty. People didn't just disappear. They must not have looked hard enough.

'Nothing is certain, Mrs Knowles,' the vicar told her. 'I'm assured that they have not stopped looking for her. But...' He hesitated. 'The river runs fast in the wet weather,' he went on. 'It comes down from the hills. The other children raised the alarm immediately and they were lucky to rescue one girl. But your daughter... Lydia...'

'No!' screamed Betty as the implication of what she was being told hit her with its full force. 'She's not drowned! She can't be drowned!'

She could feel her heart pounding in her chest and for a moment Betty was sure that she was going to die too. She turned around and around, wishing that all her chairs hadn't been burned, and eventually she slumped down next to the box that she'd been packing and held her head in her hands as she sobbed. It couldn't be true. It just couldn't. Not Lydia. She had more life in her than most people. She was young and strong.

The blackness and disbelief were still swirling around her when she felt a hand on her arm and heard her name being called.

'Betty? Betty?' It was a moment before she realised it was her neighbour, Ann. 'Get up,' she encouraged her. 'Come on. Let's go into my cottage and tha can sit by my fire. Tha's had a shock,' she told her.

Not fully aware of her surroundings, Betty allowed Ann to put an arm around her and take her to a chair by a warm fire. Her friend put a cup of tea in her hands and when Betty took a sip, she found it was hot and sweet.

Betty looked up to see that the vicar had followed them in. He was sitting at Ann's table with his own cup of tea untouched beside him.

'There's more, I'm afraid,' he said as if the weight of the news he'd brought was crushing him. 'The tickets for the coach to Deptford have been purchased and you're to go on Monday. There'll be an overnight stop at Birmingham and the coach will take you on to London the next day. From there it's just a short walk down the river…' He stumbled over the word and then cleared his throat.

'A short walk down the Thames to where the *Maria* is anchored.'

'Monday?' repeated Betty. 'But we can't possibly go on Monday. We can't go until they find Lydia!'

'It has to be Monday, I'm afraid,' he told her. 'The parish guardians insist.' He reached into the inside of his coat and produced the tickets and a small purse. 'The guardians have agreed to give you five pounds for your expenses,' he told her. 'I think it's very generous. I'd advise you to go down to the market today to see what clothing you can purchase so that you'll be ready to leave. But remember you'll need to keep some back for your overnight stay in Birmingham and to pay for your food. Everything will be provided for you once you reach the ship. Midday Monday,' he instructed her. 'The coach will leave from outside the Old Man and Scythe. Be there in good time.'

'I can't go without Lydia.'

'You must go, Mrs Knowles,' the vicar told her. 'This is your only chance to be reunited with your husband. You can't give it up.'

'But, Lydia…' she persisted.

'Your daughter is in God's hands now,' replied the vicar. 'I will pray that she is found safe,' he told her. 'And if not, I will pray that you are given the strength to accept His will. Go to your husband, Mrs Knowles.'

The Reverend Brocklehurst bid them good day and, having put his hat back on, he retreated to the door and left.

'He thinks she's dead. But I'll not believe it. I'll not give up hope,' Betty told Ann. Her daughter wasn't gone. It wasn't possible. She must be out there somewhere, in the cold, thought Betty, hearing a burst of rain drum against the window. 'I bet they've hardly looked for her at Caton at all,' she said. 'I should never have let her go there. I should never have trusted them to take care of her. And now she's lost. Out there somewhere in this weather and probably not even knowing her way home. I can't leave on Monday! Not if she hasn't come home. I can't go without her!'

Betty's eyes were blurred with tears as she watched Ann crouch down beside her and take hold of her hand.

'I don't really want thee to go,' she told Betty. 'I'll miss thy company. That's for sure. But…' She paused a moment before going on. 'I think it might be for the best,' she added.

'No.' Betty was shaking her head. Why was everyone against her? Even her friend was turning on her now. It wasn't fair.

'Think about it,' implored Ann as her grip on Betty's hand tightened. 'Think about what will happen if tha doesn't go. The parish won't keep paying thy rent,' she told her. 'They're only payin' for thee to go to that ship because they think tha's already too much of a burden on their funds. And what'll happen to thy Simon? Dost tha want him forced to go back down a pit – and happen Rose as well if there's no other work.'

As Betty wondered how to reply, she heard her children coming up the fold with the wood they'd collected. They came to Ann's door and peered in anxiously.

'What's the matter now?' asked Simon.

'It's nothing,' Ann told him. 'Go and get the fire going in thine own place. Thy mother'll be home in a minute when she's drunk her tea.'

Betty saw that her children knew something was amiss, but she couldn't face explaining it to them just yet. 'I'll be home in a minute,' she said, trying to sound normal, but she knew she'd failed when Simon and Rose exchanged a worried glance before slowly turning away.

Ann closed the door and came back to her. 'Tha must think of Simon and Rose now,' she told her. 'Tha must do what's right for them, and that's takin' them to be with their father. Go down to the market now,' Ann advised, 'and get some clothes to travel in. And if Lydia hasn't come home by Monday morning then tha must go anyway. Tha must do what's best for the two tha has left. And tha must explain it to them,' she told Betty. 'It has to be faced.'

-

Betty clutched the purse in her hand. Five pounds was a huge amount of money and she was terrified that she might lose it, because she realised that if she could buy some clothes cheaply, there would be enough left over to pay the fare for Lydia to travel with them – if only she would come home before Monday.

Betty wouldn't believe that it was true – what the vicar had implied about Lydia being drowned. She would have known if her child was dead. A mother always knew, she told herself.

She was fearful about going down to the market again and had left Simon and Rose behind in the cottage to wait for her. They'd looked alarmed when she'd come home from Ann's, but she had quickly reassured them that there was nothing to worry about and that Lydia had got into a bit of trouble at Caton, but would soon be home and they would all leave together on Monday.

Betty prayed it was true. She hoped that her own prayers would be heard directly without the need for the intervention of the vicar. Although she knew he meant well, he didn't know Lydia like she did. Her daughter would never be foolish enough to fall into a river.

The market wasn't so busy at this time of the day, and Betty hoped that her tormentors had already made their purchases and gone on their way. Even so, she glanced about for any sign of trouble as she wove her way through the stalls towards where Mrs Holt sold her second-hand garments.

'I were just about to start packin' away,' she grumbled when Betty approached and began to look at the gowns and petticoats she had hung up on display. 'What's tha after?' she asked. 'I keep a few things by for special customers,' she told Betty with a wink.

Betty ignored her. It was a long time since she'd had any money to buy from the stall, but she knew that Mrs Holt said the same thing to everyone.

'I just want some serviceable things. Not too fancy,' she said as she fingered a brown jacket and wondered how much Mrs Holt was asking for it.

'For thissen?' she asked.

'Aye. And summat for my childer an all – if tha's got owt at the right price.'

Betty knew that Mrs Holt loved to haggle and would name an exorbitant price for any garment when first asked, but Betty was sure that she could beat her down and get some good bargains, especially so late in the day. Anything she bought would be less for Mrs Holt to pack up and cart away with her.

'Look at this lovely shawl. Paisley,' tempted Mrs Holt, strewing the garment across her stall for Betty's inspection. 'Tha'll not get owt nicer than that. Why not treat thissen?'

It was beautiful, finely woven wool. But Betty shook her head. She would have loved it, but this was no time to be extravagant.

'This jacket's more to my liking,' she replied, 'and that petticoat maybe.'

Under the watchful eye of Mrs Holt, Betty carefully chose what she thought would wear the best. She pushed aside the expensive items that Mrs Holt insisted on showing her and settled on the plain brown jacket and the petticoat. She chose some similar garments for Rose, adding a new shift and a bright red scarf that she knew her daughter would delight in. For Simon, she chose a jacket and trousers to replace the ones ruined in the pit and two plain shirts.

'How much?' she asked hesitantly as her purchases piled up. She knew she mustn't spend all the money.

'Three pounds, three shillings and fourpence!' announced Mrs Holt. Betty knew it was too much. She needed to keep money back for their lodgings on the journey and she was determined to give Ann something to pay her back for all the coal and candles and food that she and Peter had helped her out with over the years. She didn't want to leave feeling that she owed her friends a debt.

'I can't afford that!' she replied in horror that was barely a sham. Mrs Holt rolled her eyes and began her usual ritual of bargaining until they reached a price Betty thought more reasonable.

'Will tha throw that gown in as well? For nowt?' asked Betty in a final bid. She'd had her eye on the flowered gown all the time. It looked too small for her, but she knew it would fit Lydia like a dream and her daughter would love it. For just a moment, she questioned the wisdom of buying clothes for a child she might never see again, but Betty quickly pushed her doubts aside and smiled in triumph as Mrs Holt nodded and began to fold the items ready to be wrapped in paper for Betty to take home.

As Betty walked back to Tombling Fold, she thought that she might not be that sad to leave after all her recent troubles. The thought of seeing Jimmy again spurred her on, but she didn't know how she would ever go without all her children.

'Come back, Lydia,' she said out loud as she walked. 'Please come back before Monday morning.'

When she arrived back at the cottage, Simon and Rose examined the clothing in delight. It was a long time since they'd had anything new to wear.

'We'll get ourselves washed all over in some hot water,' Betty promised them, 'then we can dress ourselves in the new clothes before we set off.'

'Will Lydia be home by then?' asked Rose. Betty could see that her younger daughter still felt anxious and wasn't quite sure whether to believe her reassurances that nothing was wrong.

'I'm sure she will,' Betty replied. 'And she'll love this gown. Isn't it pretty?'

'I wish tha'd got one for me,' said Rose.

'But I got thee this beautiful scarf! Tha likes it, doesn't thee?'

'Aye. Of course I do!' replied Rose as she lifted the square of fine cotton to her cheek to feel its softness. Betty smiled at her and wished that she could have afforded to buy her a gown as well, and a scarf for Lydia, and lots of other things that she knew her children deserved.

'Just wait until we get to New South Wales,' she told them. 'Your father'll be waitin' for us and he says as he can provide for us, and we'll never be hungry or have to go without anything again.'

Betty forced a smile. She hoped it was true. She had to believe that they were going to a better life. And she had to believe that Lydia would go with them.

–

The following morning, Betty took the children down to the morning service in the parish church. It would be their last opportunity to worship there and she felt that she owed the Reverend Brocklehurst the courtesy of their presence for one last time before they left. She would never see him again, she realised, and the thought made tears threaten to overwhelm her as the last hymn was sung and the congregation stood up to leave.

Betty lingered near the porch as the vicar greeted his parishioners at the door until, at last, he noticed her.

'I'm glad you came,' he said. 'Are you feeling better?'

'I wanted to thank thee properly,' said Betty.

'I'm pleased to help you,' he told her. 'It's always sad to see parishioners leave, but you're going to your husband and that's as it should be.' He paused. 'But I'm sorry about Lydia. I wish you could have gone with all your children.'

Betty nodded. His sympathy was welcome, as was his kindness, but she still couldn't accept that Lydia wouldn't come home. She would have to come soon, though, thought Betty as she glanced around at the worshippers leaving to get their dinners. There wasn't much time left.

She walked home with Simon and Rose and they ate some oatmeal made with boiled water. The money in

Betty's purse would have provided them with a better meal, but she'd been loath to spend more when there was a sack of perfectly good oats to eat up before they left. They would have the same for their tea and their breakfast the next day. It would fill their bellies and that was all that mattered.

As the afternoon wore on, they did little but sit around the fire. Every time Betty heard footsteps outside in the fold, she hurried to the window to see if it was Lydia, but every time she felt a wave of disappointment as someone else passed by. She felt more afraid as each minute went by. Each one reduced the hours that were left before they had to go, and the time in which Lydia might come home. Simon and Rose said nothing as Betty got up and went to the window again and again, watching, waiting, hoping. She knew that her worries were making them anxious, but she didn't know what she would do if morning arrived and Lydia still hadn't come.

After a while Betty picked up her purse and told the children that she was going next door. They asked to come, but she told them to stay by the fire and that they could say goodbye to Ann and Peter the next morning. What she wanted to tell her friend was not for their ears.

She knocked briefly on the door and went in. Ann and Peter were resting by their hearth, Ann sewing and Peter reading a book and sucking on his pipe – the aromatic smoke rising and mingling with the smoke that was rising from their coals.

Ann put her sewing aside and stood up to offer her chair to Betty, but Betty refused and drew up a stool.

'I came to give thee this,' she told Ann, holding out five florins in her hand.

'No! I can't take that. It's for thee, for the journey. Tha'll need it,' Ann warned Betty. 'I've heard it's not cheap to travel on them coaches even if tha's got a ticket. There'll be food and lodgings to pay for afore tha gets there.'

'I know. I've kept some back,' Betty reassured her. 'But I want thee to have summat. Tha's helped me out so much in t' past that I feel I owes it to thee.'

'Don't talk nonsense, Betty,' interrupted Peter. He waved his pipe at her. 'We've done nowt any friend or neighbour wouldn't do. We'd not see thee and the childer go cold and hungry when we had a bit to spare. Put that money back in thy purse.'

'There were another reason I wanted ye to have it,' Betty told them. She took a breath to steady herself to say more. 'If our Lydia's not home by mornin'…'

Ann reached out and put a hand on her arm as Betty was unable to continue. 'If Lydia does come back then we'll care for her, of course we will,' she said, but Betty saw the glance she exchanged with her husband and she knew that neither of them believed that Lydia would come.

'I want thee to have this money so that she can use some of it to come to us,' insisted Betty as she thrust the coins at Ann. 'I want thee to promise that tha'll do everything tha can to get her on a coach to Deptford before the seventh. I can't bear to think of her being left behind. Please,' she added. 'Please take it.'

Ann reluctantly took the money. 'As long as tha's not leavin' thyself short,' she said.

'I'm not,' replied Betty. 'I have enough left, but this is for thy help, and for Lydia. Please, keep it. I don't know as I'll be able to leave tomorrow if I've not made provision for her.'

'Tha must go!' Ann told her sternly. 'Tha mustn't give up this opportunity. It'll not come again,' she warned her. 'Tha must think of Simon and Rose and do what's right for them. I'll miss thee. Tha knows I will, but tha must go,' she repeated as she looked to Peter in an appeal for him to back her up.

'Aye,' he added. 'It'll be a hard thing to do, but think of thy Jimmy waitin' for thee to come. Tha doesn't want to leave him disappointed, does tha?'

'No, of course not,' said Betty. She knew that what they were saying made sense to them, but they didn't have to endure the agony of wondering where their missing child was.

After a while Betty went back home and began to check that everything was ready for the morning. The new clothes were laid out and all their other service-able garments were folded and packed along with a few household implements – a knife, basins, spoons, as well as a needle and some threads, a ball of string, a few rags, a hairbrush and some pins and the packets of seeds she'd harvested from the few crops she'd grown in the little garden by her door. Everything else would be left behind, although there wasn't much apart from the straw mattresses and a few tallow candles.

Betty heated some water over the fire and cooked the remaining oatmeal. They ate some and she put the rest on the hearth. They would eat it cold in the morning before they left. Then she poured what was left of the hot water into a basin and they took turns to wash themselves, beginning with Rose, then Simon and finally herself. Betty washed herself down as best she could considering the cold and the lack of privacy. Then she let the fire go out. There was no more coal or logs and she didn't want to send the children out again. Instead, they huddled together on their mattresses and listened to the rising wind blowing through the gaps in the stone walls. It would rain again before morning, thought Betty. She hoped Lydia was safe somewhere and would come before they had to set off for the coach.

–

Betty thought that she hadn't slept, but she must have dozed, as she woke several times during the dark night. Twice she thought she heard footsteps approaching, but it was just the wind rattling the door and windows. As the sky lightened from the east and the sun rose, even if wasn't visible behind the grey overcast sky, Betty abandoned all thought of rest and got up. She dressed in the new clothes and carefully folded the things she had taken off. They were shabby, over-mended and fraying. They weren't clean either, but she decided she would have to take them with her anyway. There had been no chance to launder them when there was nothing to change into, but they were too good to leave behind when garments were so expensive to buy.

She woke Simon and Rose and they ate in silence, in the cold, not knowing what the future held for them. Only knowing that they had hardly any time left in the sanctuary of their home and must shortly embark on a journey that Betty thought could only hold terror and anguish – especially as she was now being forced to admit to herself that Lydia was not coming.

Betty wondered if they should just stay put. But Peter's words about Jimmy waiting expectantly for them repeated themselves in her head. And she couldn't let Simon go down that mine again. It was an impossible decision, but Ann was right when she'd said that she must think of her two younger children – and she knew that Ann would care for Lydia if she came home too late to reach Deptford in time.

She turned away from the children on the pretext of checking the box because she didn't want them to see her crying. Betty tried to cry quietly and not give in to the raucous sobs that were threatening to overwhelm her whenever she thought about Lydia. She knew they must leave soon to catch the coach and she had to face the truth: that perhaps the vicar and Ann were right when they believed that Lydia was lost to her for ever and she would never see her elder daughter again in this world.

'We'd best go,' she said at last as she looked around the room, trying to remember its every detail to help her remain strong. Her children were ready, their faces scrubbed and their hair brushed. They looked smart in their new clothes – Simon with his cap at a jaunty angle and Rose with her red neckerchief brightening the dismal morning. Their faces, though, betrayed their own apprehension.

'Are we not going to wait for our Lydia?' asked Rose, her bottom lip trembling with emotion.

'We must catch the midday coach that we have tickets for,' explained Betty. 'Lydia will follow us on a later one.'

Then Betty opened the door and breathed in the familiar air, slightly damp and mixed with the smell of smoke from the chimneys. She would never see this place again, she thought, choking back fresh tears.

She brushed her face with the heel of her hand as she heard Ann come out. She turned to her, forcing a smile.

'I've made these, for thy journey,' said her friend, holding out a package. 'It's only bread and dripping, but it'll save thee from hunger along the way.'

Betty took the package gratefully and Ann hugged her tightly. 'Go safe,' she told her. 'God bless thee and the childer.'

'I'll miss thee,' said Betty as she saw Peter come to the door to see them off. 'I'll send thee a letter when we get there,' she promised.

'Aye, do that. It'll be good to know that tha's arrived safely.'

'It'll give thee an address to write to.'

'I'll write back. I promise,' Ann told her. 'Now, get on thy way or tha'll be missin' that coach. It'll not wait for thee.' She did her best to summon a smile, but Betty could see the anguish on her face.

'If Lydia comes home…'

'We'll care for her.'

'And tha'll send her on to us?'

'Aye. We will.'

There was an awkward silence for a moment as Betty made no move to leave. She stared down the fold, willing her daughter to appear, just in time. But the horizon remained empty except for a few sheep moving towards the shelter of a dry-stone wall because it had begun to drizzle again.

'We'd best be off,' she said at last, looking at Simon and Rose, carrying the box of belongings between them. They were waiting for her, relying on her to do the right thing even though Betty still wasn't sure what that was.

'Aye, tha'd best go,' replied Ann sadly.

Betty nodded and began to walk slowly down the fold with her children beside her. At the corner they turned back for one last look. Ann was still standing on her door-step, drying her eyes on a corner of her apron with one hand and waving a farewell with the other. Betty waved back and after one last hopeful look up the track for Lydia, she turned away, defeated, and they began to walk towards Bolton.

Chapter Fifteen

As the days had passed, Lydia had begun to wonder if she would ever escape from Mrs Malpass. She became convinced that the woman was keeping her prisoner deliberately and she began to fear what Mr Haslam had told her. He'd seemed amiable enough, but he had been so insistent that she came here. Lydia began to wonder if suspicions had been raised by May in Egerton when she went to ask him about a lift. Perhaps they'd plotted this together. Maybe May had heard that Lydia was wanted for murder and, rather than keep her in her own cottage, she'd agreed with Mr Haslam to bring her here until the constables came to arrest her.

The thoughts chased themselves around in Lydia's head as she sat by Mrs Malpass's hearth with her foot on the stool and her ears straining for any sound that might betray the approach of men coming to take her away to prison.

Mrs Malpass wasn't unkind. She fed Lydia and bathed and bound her ankle every day. She made sure she was comfortable and warm, but she never left her alone for more than a moment. And whenever Lydia mentioned leaving and tried to demonstrate that she could walk perfectly well, Mrs Malpass told her she must rest and ushered her back to the chair.

'But I can walk,' insisted Lydia in exasperation. 'It won't trouble me to walk the rest of the way home from here.'

'No, tha mustn't put weight on it until it's properly healed,' the woman replied. 'What dost tha need to rush off for? Another day or two won't make any difference.'

'But my family will be expecting me.'

'I'm sure Mr Haslam will have told them that tha's here. They'll not be worrying,' she replied.

Lydia gazed out of the small window, trying to see the track that led from Bolton to Egerton. What if her father was walking along it? What if the figure she could see hurrying along was her father, setting out to look for her and not knowing she was so close by. Lydia wanted to call out, to shout *I'm here!* But she didn't dare. She knew from experience that the herbs hanging from their hooks on the far side of the parlour were potent and she feared that Mrs Malpass might try to poison her if she made a fuss.

She wondered if Mrs Malpass might go out to market, but her captor never left the cottage and no one came by, even though Lydia saw people on the track. They seemed to hurry past as if they were afraid, and Lydia didn't blame them.

As day dawned on the Monday morning, revealing a grey overcast sky and rain that came and went in squalls on the wind that swept down from the moorland, Lydia hoped that it was the day Mr Haslam would come. She felt so afraid and sick that she couldn't eat the breakfast Mrs Malpass put down on the little table beside her. The oatmeal, smothered in treacle, would normally have been a special treat, but this morning it stuck in her throat and she found it impossible to swallow.

She set the spoon down in the bowl and put it aside. Mrs Malpass was watching her from the other side of the room and she came across and laid a hand on Lydia's forehead.

'Tha's not burnin' up. That's a good thing,' she announced. 'But summat's not right with thee.'

'I just want to go home,' replied Lydia, thinking of the cottage where she'd spent all her life at Tombling Fold. Her mother would be there now, kindling a fire, boiling water for tea, and making oatmeal for Simon and Rose to eat before she sent them out to collect wood for the fire. Then she'd tidy round what few belongings they had, wash the bowls and sweep the floor. Lydia tried to imagine what it would be like with her father there. If he hadn't set out to search for her, he might be busy threading up his loom in the cellar in the way she remembered from all those years ago. She ached to be with them.

Lydia sat and fidgeted as the time passed slowly. She kept watch out of the window, dreading what was going to happen to her. She'd heard people talk about the prison, that it was dark with no windows and only damp straw on the floor. She'd heard that they chained prisoners to an iron ring on the wall so they couldn't escape and that they didn't feed them. And as for what would happen after her trial… She couldn't even begin to imagine what that might be like. She knew full well the penalty for murder and she wished now that she'd flung herself into the river after Violet.

Then she saw Mr Haslam coming down the track and her stomach lurched with fear, even though he appeared to be alone and was carrying two sacks – one over his shoulders and another in his arms.

Mrs Malpass heard her gasp and went to look out of the window. 'Here he is now,' she told Lydia in an encouraging voice, though she seemed puzzled when she saw the terror on Lydia's face.

As Mrs Malpass opened the door, Lydia cringed back in the chair, trying to make herself small and invisible.

'Here tha goes,' said Mr Haslam as he stepped inside and allowed the heavy sacks to slide to the floor with a thud and a puff of dust. 'One of flour and one of oats. That should keep thee goin' for a while.'

'Thanks. Put them over there will thee, up on the box,' she instructed. 'It makes it a bit harder for the mice.'

'Old Malkin not doin' his job?' asked Mr Haslam as he fondled the ears of the cat that was twining itself around his legs.

'He's gettin' on,' replied Mrs Malpass. 'I don't think he sees as well these days. I should replace him with a kitten but I'll not part with the old chap.'

Mr Haslam dusted flour off his breeches and turned to Lydia. 'How's the ankle?' he asked her. 'Canst tha walk on it now?'

Lydia nodded, too frightened to speak. She was still watching the door, expecting the constables to burst through it at any moment. Mr Haslam followed her gaze and turned to close it.

'It's cold out there. We don't want thee in a draught,' he said. 'How is she?' he asked Mrs Malpass, having had no reply from Lydia.

'Her ankle's much improved. She seems a bit off colour this morning, though.'

'Is she well enough for me to take her into Bolton?'

'Would it be a trouble to take her all the way home?'

'Well, that's the thing,' said Mr Haslam. 'I went to enquire at th' hall in th' wood and none of the families there had ever heard of a lass called Lettie.'

Both Mr Haslam and Mrs Malpass turned to study Lydia and she felt her cheeks flush a bright red.

'Is Lettie not thy real name?' asked Mrs Malpass. She sounded disappointed and Lydia didn't know what to say. 'If tha's in some sort of trouble and needs help, tha's only to say so,' she went on.

Lydia just shook her head and kept her gaze down, looking at her hands.

'I suppose it's none of our business,' said Mr Haslam as he sat down in the chair opposite to her and watched as Mrs Malpass poured tea from her pot on the hearth and buttered him a thick slice of bread to eat with it. She offered some to Lydia, but she shook her head, still unable to face food.

'Hast tha got somewhere to go?' Mrs Malpass asked her. 'Tha's been keen to leave all week. Is someone expectin' thee?'

'I want to go home,' whispered Lydia.

'And where is home?' asked Mrs Malpass. Lydia didn't reply. 'Where did tha come from?' she pressed her. 'Hast tha run away from somewhere?'

Lydia nodded but didn't tell them where. She was wondering if perhaps she could trust these people after all. Mr Haslam had not brought the constables as she'd expected, even though he knew she'd lied to him. But how would they react if she told them that she'd killed a girl? She was sure they wouldn't be so sympathetic then.

Mrs Malpass handed her a cup of tea and Lydia sipped at it, wondering what would happen to her now. She hoped they wouldn't insist on her answering their questions and that Mr Haslam would take her into Bolton with nothing more being said.

'I wish tha'd confide in me,' Mrs Malpass told her. 'But if tha doesn't want to I'll not press thee. Mr Haslam will take thee to Bolton if it's what tha wants.'

'It is,' Lydia told her.

'All right then. Take the stick with thee to lean on, and try not to walk more than tha needs. It'll only set that ankle back if it takes too much stress.'

Mr Haslam stood up and Lydia followed him to the door, with her shawl clutched around her shoulders and the stick in her hand. She turned to thank Mrs Malpass.

'Tha's welcome here any time,' the woman told her. 'If tha's nowhere else to go, or if thy troubles are too much for thee, I can help. I've herbs for many an ailment,' she added and Lydia realised the woman was suspicious that she might be running away because she was with child.

She nodded and limped up the track behind Mr Haslam. When she turned back Mrs Malpass had gone inside and closed the door and Lydia wondered if she'd misjudged the woman.

'Can tha climb up or does tha need a lift?' asked Mr Haslam when they reached the cart.

'I'll manage,' said Lydia. 'I'll get in the back.'

Her ankle hurt as she struggled, but Mr Haslam made no comment as he watched her. Once she was settled, he unfastened the horse's reins from the low branch of the tree where he'd secured them, got up at the front and clicked his tongue. The cart rolled off towards Bolton and Lydia felt hopeful for the first time in days. These people had not given her away after all and there was now a chance that she could reach home.

The drizzle soaked through her clothing as they drove on. Mr Haslam spoke only to the horse as they travelled and Lydia watched the landmarks became familiar as they dropped into Bolton.

When they approached the town, the roads became busier and Mr Haslam had to guide the horse around groups of people walking or pushing carts along, and near the town centre he was forced to pull into the side of the road to let a coach through. Lydia watched as it passed by, the four horses galloping as the coachman drove them on at speed. It looked packed with passengers and luggage, both inside and on top. Lydia wondered where it was going.

'London coach,' remarked Mr Haslam, turning back to speak to her for the first time. 'They've a timetable to keep and they drive like imbeciles. No wonder there's accidents,' he said with a shake of his head as he encouraged his own horse back onto the road. 'I'll drop thee off outside the Old Man and Scythe,' he told her. 'Tha can make thine own way from there.'

Once he'd stopped, Lydia clambered down.

'Think on what Mrs Malpass told thee,' he advised before continuing on his way. 'She's a good woman, despite what folks say, and she'll help thee if tha's in trouble.'

'I'll be all right,' Lydia told him, as she pulled her shawl over her head and around her face.

Mr Haslam nodded and Lydia watched as the cart rolled on before turning towards the street that would lead her towards her home. She'd been lucky so far, she thought, but this was no place to linger. She might be recognised and apprehended at any moment. Her only hope was to get home where her parents would hide her.

Lydia's ankle blazed with pain as she walked and she found that she had to sit and rest more and more often as she climbed the incline towards Tombling Fold. But she pressed on despite her agony, determined to be back in time for tea.

At last, she reached the familiar corner that led into the fold. Her desire was to hurry on, but fear made her hesitate. She pressed herself against the wall of the nearest cottage and looked cautiously around the end of it. She couldn't see anyone loitering or watching so, leaning on the stick, she hobbled towards her home, relief flooding through her to have made it all this way without being caught.

She reached the front door, lifted the sneck in her hand and pushed. The door didn't yield. Lydia pushed against it again, not understanding. They never locked their door in the daytime. They had nothing to steal. She knocked on it, impatiently, expecting to hear footsteps from within, but there was only silence. Perplexed, she peered in through the window, shielding her eyes to block the reflection from a watery sun that was attempting to shine through the clouds. The cottage looked empty. The fire was out. The mattresses were piled neatly in the corner. And slowly the realisation dawned. They must all be out looking for her.

She couldn't walk any further on her ankle, so she sat down on the doorstep to wait, wondering how long it would be before they came back. There was always the danger that the constables would come and she was thinking about finding a place to hide when she heard her name being called.

'Lydia!'

She looked up to see their neighbour Ann at her door.

'Lydia. Wherever hast tha been?' she asked as she came towards her. 'Tha's missed 'em. They went this morning.'

Lydia got to her feet, helped by the stick. 'Are they looking for me?' she asked.

Ann's expression changed to one of consternation. 'No,' she said. 'We thought tha were...' She hesitated. 'Tha'd best come inside,' she told her.

Lydia limped after her and hopped over the doorstep with a grimace. Inside, Peter was sitting at his loom, but he stopped work and stared at her for a moment before getting up to help her to a chair by the hearth.

'Tea?' asked Ann. 'Tha looks like tha could use it.'

Lydia watched as she poured it out and handed her a cup before turning back to the table to cut a slice from the loaf of bread that was there.

'We thought that tha were dead,' Ann said, without looking up. Lydia didn't reply. She wondered if Ann meant herself and her husband or if her mother thought that she was dead as well. The thought alarmed her. 'Reverend Brocklehurst came with a letter from Mr Greg at Caton,' she explained as she handed the food to Lydia. 'He said there'd been an accident and that tha were missing.'

'Accident?' repeated Lydia. 'He said it were an accident?'

'Aye. He seemed to think tha'd fallen in t' river like t' other lass, except they couldn't find thee.'

'I saw them pull her out,' admitted Lydia. 'I didn't intend her to drown,' she protested.

'What's tha talkin' about?' asked Ann. 'He never said t' other lass were drowned. It were thee that concerned them. They searched for thee, but in the end had to admit that tha were probably under t' water. Thy mother were hopin' and hopin' that tha would come home, but I told her I didn't think it were likely. So they went this mornin'.'

'Went where?' asked Lydia, not following what Ann was telling her.

'Went on the coach. To Deptford. For the ship. The *Maria*.' She saw that Lydia was puzzled. 'Did tha not know that thy father wrote and sent for thee all?' she asked.

'My mam sent a letter to say she'd had word from him,' said Lydia, feeling thoroughly confused by what was happening. 'I thought he was coming home, like Thomas Holden did and Jack Fisher.'

'No.' Ann was shaking her head. 'It were to say he'd asked for all of thee to go to him. Thy mother agreed and word came that there were places on a ship.'

'But…' Lydia couldn't believe what she was being told. 'They've not gone to New South Wales without me?' she whispered.

'Hush. Hush, don't cry,' said Ann, leaning to take the cup and plate from Lydia and grasp her hands as the tears began to flow. 'Thy mam were adamant she'd not leave without thee, but the coach tickets were for today and there were nowt else she could do. She waited and waited 'til the very last moment and it were me that persuaded her she must leave. I'm sorry,' she added as she still clasped Lydia's hands. 'I really didn't think tha would come.'

'They went just this mornin'?' asked Lydia.

'Aye. Tha's only missed 'em by a few hours.'

It was less than that, thought Lydia as she remembered the coach rushing past her and recalled Mr Haslam's words. Her mother and Simon and Rose must have been the passengers huddled up top, wrapped against the weather. She'd passed by them so closely and she hadn't even recognised them.

'What am I going to do?' she asked, feeling bereft. She'd thought that if she could get home she would be safe. She'd never expected this. She'd believed her father was coming to them.

'Don't fret. Don't fret,' Ann told her, patting her hand. 'Thy mam didn't abandon thee. She left some money and asked me to make sure tha followed on if tha came home in time. Let me fetch it.'

Lydia watched through the blur of her tears as Ann opened a drawer and took out her purse. From it she counted five florins and placed them in Lydia's hand, folding her fingers over them so she was grasping them tightly. It seemed a huge amount of money to Lydia – more than she'd ever seen before.

'But how?' she asked. 'How will I find them?'

'Tha'll have to make thy way to Deptford,' said Peter. 'Tha'll have to ask about a ticket for the coach when tha gets back to Bolton.'

'I must go,' Lydia said, standing up, keen to be on her way. But as soon as she tried to put any weight on her ankle it was clear that she couldn't manage to walk all the way back into town.

'Tha can't go now,' said Peter. 'Tha can barely walk. What happened to thee?'

'I fell,' she explained. 'It isn't a broken bone, just twisted. It'll be all right if I rest it for a while.'

'Tha'd best stop here for tonight,' suggested Ann, glancing at her husband for confirmation. 'Tha can go first thing tomorrow. Tha'll not find a coach at this time of day anyway.'

And even though Lydia wanted to leave straight away to find her mother she knew that what Ann was saying made sense. It would be dark soon and it wouldn't be safe for her in Bolton with nowhere to spend the night. Besides, it was cosy and familiar by Ann's fire and she was tired.

Chapter Sixteen

Betty's spirits had sunk when she'd seen the coach, with its fresh horses, ready to leave. Climbing aboard had been an admission that she had failed her elder daughter, but she didn't know what else she could do.

Simon and Rose had climbed the ladder to the seats up top and when she'd seen their box stowed on the luggage rack, she'd climbed up to join them, then pulled her shawl around Rose as well as herself to shield them from the rain.

The bugle had sounded and the coachman had cracked his whip. They'd galloped away, making people and dogs leap back out of danger, and as they'd sped down the road the lesser carts, pulled by oxen or heavy horses, had been forced to move off to the side to let them through.

Once out of town, the coachman let fly and they raced along, occasionally almost thrown from their seats as the wheels hit holes in the road and the driver cursed in words that brought a blush to Betty's cheeks. The wind was whipping strands of loose hair against her face and her knuckles were white as she clung to the rail, afraid of falling. She could see from Simon's face that he found it exciting and exhilarating, but beside her she sensed Rose's fear and her own emotions prompted tears of regret and despair.

They galloped south towards Manchester, the notes of the bugle sounding in every village and hamlet that they passed through to warn of their approach. The rain intensified and before long Betty could feel that the water had soaked through her jacket and her petticoat, wetting her to the skin. It was uncomfortable and cold and she was glad when they reached their next stop and were allowed a few minutes at an inn to warm themselves near a roaring fire.

Some of the inside passengers tried to order a breakfast and the aroma of fresh fried bacon made Betty feel hungry, but before the meal was served, the coachman was calling them out again to continue on their way. The passengers grumbled but came out unfed and the inn owner grinned. He'd had his payment and knew he could sell the meals again. Betty thought he'd been tardy deliberately and wondered at the misdeeds that people got away with when Jimmy had been sentenced to seven years over the seas for merely attending a meeting.

On they went with their heads bowed to prevent the rain falling straight onto their faces. Rose was leaning against Betty and whimpering now and again in fear, and even Simon seemed to have lost his enthusiasm for the journey as the hours passed and they were jolted this way and that in the cold and the wet.

By the time they reached the Hen and Chickens in Birmingham, long after darkness had fallen, they were exhausted, hungry and soaked through. Once the inside passengers had alighted, Betty climbed stiffly down, thankful to feel solid ground beneath her feet. She reached up a hand to help Rose whilst Simon retrieved their box.

The inn looked warm and well-lit but it was crowded when Betty led the children inside. All around the tables and on the long benches in the bar, men were drinking and talking and laughing. They paid her little attention as she squeezed through the mass to ask about a bed for the night and some food.

'Ask the porter,' the barman told her irritably as if it was something she ought to have known. Betty wasn't sure where to find him and went wearily back out into the yard where she saw a well-dressed man instructing a lad to carry some baggage up an outer staircase to the accommodation above.

'I need a room for the night,' she said once he'd turned towards her. He looked doubtfully at her bedraggled appearance.

'It's two and six each for supper and bed,' he told her, 'plus tips.'

Betty had no idea what he meant. She wasn't even sure what a tip was, but she had enough in her purse to give the man seven shillings and sixpence and he led them up the stairs to a small room with two beds. It looked clean enough and Betty sank down onto the soft mattress with relief and closed her eyes for a moment.

'Supper is served downstairs in the dining room. Potluck at that price. Or pay more if you'd like something more extravagant.'

Betty knew that the man was sneering at her but she was too tired to care and she simply nodded, not understanding why he was still standing in the doorway rather than going away. He cleared his throat a couple of times before making himself clear.

'My tip,' he reminded her. 'You need to pay me sixpence for my trouble,' he told her outright when it became clear that Betty didn't understand. Embarrassed at her ignorance, Betty felt about in her purse for a coin. 'And another shilling for candles,' said the porter. 'Would you like a fire?' he asked, indicating the cold fireplace.

Betty knew he would ask for more money so she shook her head.

'No thank you,' she replied with as much dignity as she could. 'We've no need of that.'

'As you wish.'

The moment the porter was gone, Betty regretted her decision. Another shilling might have seen them able to warm themselves and dry their clothing before morning, but pride made her hesitate to call the man back and say she'd changed her mind.

'Let's get something to eat,' she said to the children, hoping that the dining room would be warm and that afterwards they could get straight into bed, and that the blankets would be sufficient and the sheets clean.

The potluck turned out to be mutton chops served with potatoes and cabbage. It was hot and plentiful and Betty and the children ate well even though they were all so tired it was a struggle to lift the forks to their mouths. As they were leaving, Betty saw that it was required that she should give another sixpence to the girl who had served them and she began to become anxious about the amount of money she was having to take from her purse to pay these incessant small charges that were demanded of her. The five pounds had seemed like a fortune when she'd received it but after buying the clothes and giving ten shillings to Ann, she was now beginning to worry that she wouldn't have enough left over to get them to Deptford, especially if she had to find accommodation again the next night.

The beds were comfortable and they slept well. In the morning Betty was relieved to find only a few bites from the bugs on her legs, and her jacket, although still damp, had dried sufficiently overnight for it not to feel too uncomfortable when she put it on.

It wasn't until she went back to the bed to wake Rose that she noticed her daughter seemed unwell. Her cheeks were flushed and when Betty put a hand to her forehead she felt hot and clammy. She must have caught a chill the day before and it was obvious that she was running a temperature.

Betty was unsure what to do. If they'd been at home she would have left her daughter to sleep and maybe tried to find the money to purchase a draught from the chemist, but here, in this strange place, she had no one to turn to and she was afraid that if they missed the coach they would be stuck in this town because the tickets were not transferrable.

'Tha must get up,' she urged Rose. 'We have to go.'

'My head hurts and my throat,' mumbled her daughter.

'I know. But tha must get up. Tha'll feel better soon,' Betty urged her. She turned to Simon. 'Gather our things,' she told him. 'Then run down and find out what time the coach leaves and if we've time for breakfast.' She was about to add that he should ask the cost as well, but she didn't want to worry him. 'Come on,' she told Rose, once he'd gone. 'Tha must get up!'

Betty had to drag her reluctant daughter from the bed. Rose sat on the edge of the mattress, her teeth chattering together as Betty tried to get her damp clothes onto her. If she could just get her onto the coach, thought Betty, she could let her rest against her and sleep, then hopefully she would feel better before long. For just a moment, Betty considered stealing one of the blankets from the bed to wrap her daughter in to keep her warm and stop her from shivering, but she knew that the penalty for such a theft was severe and she mustn't risk it.

Simon came back up the steps to say breakfast was sixpence each and the coach would leave in twenty minutes. Betty could see that he was hungry but decided that it was too expensive and that they would probably be forced to leave before the food appeared, so she told her disappointed son that they would wait until later to eat.

'Tha'll have to bring our things on thine own,' she told him. 'Tha sister's not feelin' too good.'

Betty helped her shivering daughter into the yard, whilst Simon followed them with the box, dragging it down the steps. It was fine at least, although a cold wind was blowing. They struggled up onto the top seats of the coach and Betty put her arm and her shawl around her daughter and held her close as the other passengers got on board. Soon they were on their way and Rose seemed to drift in and out of sleep as they drove along through the grey morning.

Rose seemed a little better at the next stop, but didn't want to eat anything, still complaining that her throat was sore. She managed to drink some tea but that was all and there was little time to do anything more before they were hurried back onto the coach to continue their journey.

As the day passed, Betty began to worry about what they would do when they reached London. It would be too late to find their way to Deptford and in any case Rose wasn't fit to walk all that way. She would have to pay for another room in another inn, she decided, even if it meant all her money would be spent. She would just have to hope that they really would be provided with all their needs when they reached the ship, otherwise they might starve to death on the long voyage. She almost regretted giving

Ann the ten shillings. It would have come in handy now, and maybe her friend had been right when she'd said that Lydia might not come back. Betty pushed the thought from her mind. Lydia must come. She had to believe that she would somehow find her way to them before it was too late and that the ten shillings might just make all the difference.

It was late when they approached London. Rose was asleep on Betty's shoulder; her breathing was quick and sounded laboured. Simon looked concerned as well, even though Betty had tried to make light of the situation and said that it was only a cold.

Betty had never seen anything like the city. The streets seemed to go on for ever and there were more inns and taverns than she could count. The buildings seemed huge and the streets were crowded with every class of person from gentry to beggars on the street corners and everywhere there seemed to be someone trying to sell something.

Even though darkness had fallen, everything seemed to be lit up, from the lamps that lined the streets to the light pouring from shops and doorways and boys holding lanterns aloft as they guided pedestrians along. Simon was staring about him, this way and that, from their vantage point on top of the coach. His excitement had been kindled once more as they passed by a stall selling something that smelled like fish and another selling coffee. The sounds and smells and sights made it seem as if they'd come to some exotic foreign place and Betty thought that if London was so different from anything she'd seen before then how strange would she find the new country they were bound for.

At last they pulled into the yard of an inn named the Swan with Two Necks and the weary horses were led away by the ostlers as the stiff and equally weary passengers got down from their seats.

'Wake up,' said Betty to her daughter, shaking her gently. 'Wake up. We're here.'

Rose stirred uneasily and Betty, with help from Simon, managed to get her down the ladder. Her daughter was shivering again. She was obviously poorly and needed to be in bed. As Simon collected their box, Betty looked in her purse, even though she was reluctant to take her money out in such a crowded place for fear of having it stolen from her. She had seven shillings left. It wasn't much but she knew she must enquire about a room.

Being much wiser than when she'd left Bolton just the day before, Betty looked about for the porter and told him she needed two beds for the night. He asked her for five shillings, plus his tip and took them up two flights of stairs to a garret in the attic where they had to duck their heads to get in through the door. The two beds were so close together that there was no space to stand between them or on either side. They completely filled the room, but Betty nodded her thanks, gave the porter his sixpence and helped Rose undress so that she could lie down.

Betty knew that her daughter needed a doctor, but she had no idea where to find one or how much they might charge. She would just have to let Rose sleep and hope that by morning she was feeling better.

Betty couldn't leave Rose alone to take Simon to the dining room so she told him to stay with his sister and she ventured out to buy food from one of the many stalls that lined the streets. Spoiled for choice and slightly bewildered by all the calls around her, Betty bought some pies and hurried back to the inn where she climbed the narrow steps and stooped into the room. Simon's eyes brightened in the light of the solitary candle Betty had been able to afford when he smelled the food and he bit into the pie she passed to him hungrily.

'It's good!' he exclaimed as if he'd been fed manna from heaven above.

Betty took a bite from hers and agreed with him. It was hot and tasty. She offered some to Rose, but her daughter shook her head, still complaining that her throat was sore. After the chills of the day she was hot and burning again and Betty went to beg a bowl of water and a cloth to try to cool her so she could sleep.

After Betty had washed Rose in tepid water and Simon had fallen asleep, she settled herself under the blankets. But her mind was still whirling with thoughts of the journey, of Lydia and of the ordeal to come. They must get to the ship tomorrow, she knew, because she had no more money to pay for another night at the inn. But she recalled the words that the Reverend Brocklehurst had read out to her from the letter she'd been sent. *If their health be of such as to allow of their undertaking the voyage.* And Betty began to worry that if Rose didn't improve soon, they might not even be allowed to board the *Maria*.

Chapter Seventeen

Lydia had slept fitfully on a mattress on the floor of Ann and Peter's house. Even though she was warm and comfortable, she still yearned to be in her own home. It had seemed strange to be so near and not be able to go in there. She knew it hadn't been as well-furnished as their neighbours' house for a long time now, but she still craved the familiarity. If only her mother and sister and brother were there and her father had come back, they could have made it cosy, like it was in her memories. But now it seemed that it would never be her home again. The thought of the long journey ahead of her frightened Lydia, but she knew she must be brave if she was to be reunited with her family.

Ann and Peter were kind to her, as they had been for as long as Lydia could remember. Ann made sure that Lydia had plenty to eat and she packed her a parcel of food to take with her. She even gave her an old cloak to wear to help keep her warm and dry. She couldn't have done more and Lydia was tearful as she said her goodbyes and set off to walk back to Bolton.

She'd made light of her ankle to Ann and Peter, saying that it was much better today, but the truth was that every step was torture as she hobbled down the track in torrential rain. The only thing that made it easier was the news that Violet was not drowned after all and had been pulled from the river alive. At least I'm not a murderess, thought Lydia with relief. But whether she was free was less clear. Ann had told her that they were still looking for her at Caton and she feared that she could still be caught and taken back as a runaway. She would need to have her wits about her as she travelled if she was to make it to Deptford in time. Ann had told her that she thought the ship would sail on the seventh and that was only a week away.

When she reached Bolton she went straight to the Old Man and Scythe in the hope of finding a coach that was going to London. She had to wait a while, but when one came in and the horses were being changed she approached the driver and asked him where he was going.

'Manchester,' he told her.

'I need to get to London,' she replied. 'Is there a coach that will take me there?'

'I could take thee into Manchester and tha could change there. Or tha could wait for the mail coach,' he said. 'I think it comes through about four o'clock. Tha'll need to get a ticket, though,' he warned her. 'It's often full.'

'How much will it cost?' she asked.

'I couldn't rightly say. But it'll be more than a stage-coach. I think they charge sixpence a mile.'

'How many miles is it to London?'

'Over two hundred.' The driver looked Lydia up and down. 'Tha'll need five pounds,' he warned her, 'plus money for food and tips and an overnight stay in Birm-ingham. It's a long journey.'

Lydia watched as he nodded to the ostlers and turned to mount the coach. She realised that the ten shillings she had in her purse was nowhere near enough to travel by coach and that she had better set off walking straight away if she was to have any chance of catching up with her mother and brother and sister.

As she walked disconsolately and began to head along the street that would take her towards Manchester, she saw a horse and cart coming towards her and recognised the skewbald coat of Patch with Mr Haslam driving. The carter reined in as he reached her, the rain dripping from the brim of his hat and seeping through the sacking that he'd thrown over his shoulders to help keep him dry.

'Where's tha off to now?' he asked her.

'I've to get to Deptford,' she told him, wondering if he might be of any help.

'Deptford. Where's that?' he asked. 'I can't say as I've heard of it.'

'It's in London,' she told him.

He whistled. 'That's a long way,' he observed. 'Why dost tha need to go there?'

Lydia hesitated. She wasn't sure how much to reveal to him. He seemed trustworthy but she was still reluctant to confide too much in him.

'My mother's there,' she said at last, hoping that it was enough of the truth to satisfy him.

'Well, tha'll struggle to walk all that road with thy gammy leg,' he said. 'And I doubt tha's got money for a stagecoach, but there might be a carrier goin' thy way. I know Mr Bailey takes goods as far as London. Hop up,' he instructed her. 'Let's go to see if he's at home or if his wife knows when he's due. Happen tha could ride with him.'

'I don't want to put thee to any trouble,' replied Lydia. She was conflicted between the thought of getting a lift and her reluctance to throw her lot in with yet one more unknown person.

'It's on my way,' Mr Haslam told her. 'Hop up,' he repeated and Lydia hauled herself onto the back of the cart once more, hoping that she was making the right decision.

They headed out, past Tonge as the rain finally cleared away to the east. They drove through the countryside until they came to a smallholding where a woman was throwing corn for a flock of chickens that were scrabbling and arguing around her feet, pecking one another furiously. The woman came across to the gate when she saw them and greeted Mr Haslam.

'How do?' she said. 'Is tha lookin' for our Zachariah?'

'Aye. Is he about?'

The woman shook her head. 'He's gone to pick up a load, but he should be back soon if tha'd care to step inside and wait.'

'I'm a bit stretched for time, to tell t' truth,' Mr Haslam told her. 'But it's about this lass.' Lydia returned the woman's curious gaze.

'What about her?' asked the woman.

'She's after gettin' to Deptford. It's London way.'

'Aye. I've heard of it.'

'Thing is, she's taken a bit of a tumble and hurt her ankle so I were wonderin' if there were any chance of her ridin' wi' Zach.'

'Who is she to thee?' asked the woman inquisitively. 'I didn't think tha had family here.'

'She's not kin,' replied Mr Haslam. 'I'm just doin' a young lass a favour.'

The woman looked doubtful. 'It'd have to be up to my husband,' she said.

'Best get down and wait here then,' said Mr Haslam to Lydia. It was clear that he'd done his best and didn't want to waste any more of his time, so she climbed down, thanked him and watched as he clicked his tongue and the cart began to roll away from her. She was grateful for his help, but unsure if he'd done her a favour or not.

The woman looked at her suspiciously. 'Tha'd best step inside,' she said, sounding less than welcoming.

Lydia followed her across the yard, where the chickens were still pecking in the mud and squabbling. A dog barked and Lydia hesitated until she saw it was tied with a stout rope through its collar.

'Take no notice of Bounty,' said the woman. 'He's all bark and no bite. Has no teeth left anyroad.'

She led the way to a door where the green paint was flaking off to show the bare wood beneath. 'Come in,' she said. 'Sit thee down.' Lydia limped to the chair that the woman had drawn out from under a table that was piled high with pots and pans and vegetables waiting to be prepared. 'I suppose tha'll be wantin' tea,' she grumbled but didn't wait for Lydia's reply before she poured a strong brew and set it on the table in front of her.

Lydia sipped the tea as she watched the woman go about her tasks, setting her kitchen in order.

'It's a long way to be goin' to London,' she remarked. 'What takes thee there?'

'I'm goin' to find my mother,' said Lydia.

'Thy mother is it? I thought tha might be on the run.'

'No,' said Lydia, shaking her head and wondering why everyone presumed she was fleeing from trouble. She must look guilty, she thought, hoping this woman wouldn't send her pursuers after her. She wondered whether she should just leave and take her chances elsewhere, but the tea was good and it was a relief to rest her ankle for a while.

'My husband shouldn't be long,' the woman told her. 'He's gone to pick up some chests of goods from the big house. They're sendin' some stuff to their townhouse. There might be room for thee,' she said. Lydia nodded and watched as she picked up a broom and began to sweep the floor. 'Tha's only young,' she commented after a moment. 'Tha'll have to watch thyself if tha doesn't want to get into trouble. Don't be flauntin' thyself,' she advised.

'I won't,' replied Lydia not entirely sure what the woman was getting at. All she wanted to do was get to get to her mother in Deptford before the ship sailed. Nothing else was important.

—

It must have been nearly an hour before they heard the wagon turn in to the yard. It was much larger than the cart that Mr Haslam drove, and rather than being open was covered by a canvas awning and pulled by two horses, both black – one with a white blaze.

'Here he is now,' said the woman as Lydia saw a stout-looking man with a rosy red face jump down, whistling as he tied up the horses.

He came into the kitchen, first stamping the mud from his boots at the threshold, and looked surprised when he saw Lydia.

'Who's this then?' he asked his wife as he rubbed his hands together to warm them.

'She's lookin' for a lift.'

'Oh, aye.' He turned to Lydia and gave her a lingering look that went from her face to her feet and back again.

He seemed pleased with what he saw. 'What's thy name then?' he asked.

'Lydia,' she told him, deciding it was simpler to be truthful.

'Right. And where's tha going, Lydia?'

'I've to get to Deptford. It's near London.'

'Aye, I know it,' he said. 'I've taken goods to the ships there before now. Why Deptford?' he asked, his eyes still on Lydia and an unnerving smile lingering around his lips, which he licked with his tongue, as if they were dry.

'She says she's goin' to her mother,' interrupted his wife.

'I can pay,' offered Lydia. 'How much would it cost?'

The woman looked back at her, obviously doubtful that she could afford to pay much.

'I'd not be takin' money off such a bonny lass,' said Mr Bailey.

'Tha'll ask her for five shillings!' said his wife.

'Does she have that much?' he asked her, although his gaze never left Lydia.

'I can pay five shillings,' said Lydia.

'There, tha sees?' said his wife with a sly smile. 'Best pay it to me,' she told Lydia, coming across to the table. 'He'll only squander it on drink if tha gives it to him.'

The woman stood over her with a palm outstretched and, not knowing what else to do, Lydia reached into her purse and took out the florins. She placed three on the woman's palm, hoping for some change, but the woman tipped them into her own purse with a look of satisfaction that made Lydia realise she had paid far too much. 'Tha can eat some dinner with us,' she said as if she was bestowing a great favour.

The dinner was stew and bread and Lydia ate as much as she could stomach. She knew that once the food Ann had packed for her was gone she would need to buy more and she wasn't sure how long the four shillings she had left would last.

'How long will it take us to get there?' she asked Mr Bailey as they ate.

'A week to ten days,' he told her.

'I have to be there by the seventh of the month.'

He gave her a quizzical look. 'Why's that?'

'I have to reach a ship before she sails. My mother has gone ahead, but I need to get there in time.'

She knew she sounded desperate when the carrier and his wife exchanged a quizzical glance.

'I'll do what I can,' promised Mr Bailey, 'but I can make no promises. Tha'd have been better paying for a coach ticket if tha was in such a rush.'

'Don't say that,' said his wife. 'Lass'll be askin' for her money back. Besides, it would have cost her much more and I doubt she has it.'

-

Once the meal was finished, Mr Bailey said goodbye to his wife and he and Lydia got up onto the cart. There was no room in the back with the two huge chests that were secured there, so Lydia was obliged to sit beside him up front, an arrangement he seemed happy enough with as she felt his hand brush her thigh as he gathered the reins.

'Think on what I said and don't flaunt thyself,' his wife reminded her as Mr Bailey turned the wagon around in the narrow yard.

'I won't,' said Lydia, pulling the hood of the cloak over her head and moving as far from the carrier as she dared without risking sliding off the seat at every bend in the road.

Mr Bailey called to the horses to 'gee up' and with a creaking of harness, the animals strained against their collars and they were on their way. The rain of the morning had given way to a cloudy but dry afternoon and Lydia was thankful that it had come fine.

Mr Bailey had little conversation as they travelled, but with the reins in one hand, his free hand continued to brush against Lydia's thigh. It made her feel uncomfortable, but she couldn't shift any further away and she didn't like to say anything in case it was accidental and she made herself seem foolish. Besides, if she fell out with this man she didn't know how she would reach Deptford in time.

Soon after darkness had closed in, Mr Bailey guided the horses into the small yard of a roadside inn.

'This is our bed for t' night!' He grinned as he turned to Lydia and winked. She didn't reply, but she had an uneasy feeling about travelling with this man and wondered if it had been a mistake. They hadn't travelled any faster than a walking pace and she thought that if only her ankle was less painful she would have been better striking out on her own, on foot.

She jumped down from the seat, wincing as the pain shot through her. A man had come out to help unharness the horses and stable them for the night and Mr Bailey told her to go inside and warm herself by the fire.

Lydia was aware of the momentary silence that greeted her entrance to the bar. The customers sitting around the stove at the centre of the room were mostly men and she could feel their eyes on her, assessing her, as she looked around for someone to ask the price of a room for the night.

'What can I do for thee?' asked a woman coming in from what Lydia took to be the kitchen with two bowls of food in her hands.

'I need a room for the night,' Lydia told her.

The woman put the bowls down in front of two customers and turned to study her more closely. 'Is tha travellin' alone?' she asked curiously.

'I've had a lift with a carrier,' Lydia told her. 'He's just outside, sorting out the horse.'

'I've a couple of rooms upstairs,' the woman told her. 'It's tenpence a night. Other than that tha'll have to share.'

'Does it include a meal?'

'Aye. Tha can have some of the hotpot,' said the woman as Lydia felt inside her purse for the money. At this rate, she thought, she would have nothing left long before she reached Deptford and she had no idea what she would do then, but a safe place to sleep for tonight was all that concerned her for the moment.

Lydia was sitting at the table furthest away from the stove, waiting for her bowl of hotpot, when Mr Bailey came in. He was rubbing his hands together against the cold and the men at the table by the stove greeted him as if they knew him and made space for him to sit down near the fire.

The woman innkeeper greeted him by name as well. 'Is that lass come with thee, Mr Bailey?' she asked, with a nod of her head towards Lydia.

'Aye. She's ridin' to London with me. What's tha doin' over there in t' shadows,' he called to her. 'Make room for the lady,' he encouraged his friends and the men shifted up on the benches again to make a space beside the carrier who patted the seat beside him. 'Come and sit 'ere!' he called to her.

Reluctantly, Lydia got up and went to sit beside him.

'That's better!' he declared, patting her knee with his hand. 'Now, what's tha drinkin'?'

'Just some water please,' said Lydia and blushed as the men around her roared with laughter.

'Tha doesn't want to be drinkin' t' water,' Mr Bailey warned her. 'It's not healthy, is it?' he asked his companions with an exaggerated wink. 'Tha needs a proper drink. Now what'll it be? Ale? Or gin?'

'Tha knows we've no spirits here,' the innkeeper told him. 'I'll not lose my licence by servin' 'em.'

'Never stopped thee before,' Mr Bailey reminded her.

'I've beer,' she offered.

'Beer it is then. Bring a jug and a cup for the lady.'

'I can't afford beer or ale,' protested Lydia.

'My treat,' Mr Bailey told her, bringing his face much too close to hers for Lydia's comfort. She could smell the stale tobacco on his breath and for one moment she feared he was going to try to kiss her, but he drew back with a grin and filled her cup with beer, making it froth over the edges as he poured it from a height. 'Now, get that down thee. It'll do thee a power of good,' he announced.

Lydia was aware of all the men watching her as she raised the cup to her lips and took a sip. It tasted bitter — worse than the tea that Mrs Malpass had given her. But she minded her manners and gave a slight smile as she placed the cup back on the table.

'Very nice,' she said and couldn't understand why the men erupted into more howls of laughter at her expense.

'That's a good lass. Tha'll grow to like it,' Mr Bailey told her as he patted her knee again.

He poured himself a full cup and drank it down in a series of long gulps, slammed the empty cup onto the board table and wiped his mouth on the back of his hand before filling it up again.

Mr Bailey seemed to be a different person now, thought Lydia as she listened to him talk loudly. Earlier he'd seemed quiet, but now he was putting the world to rights, telling everyone that the government and the gentry were wrong about everything and that if only they would listen to the working man then the country would be a much improved place.

The hotpot came and Lydia ate it. It was mostly potatoes but there were one or two bits of gristly meat that added to the taste and she mopped up the gravy with a crust of brown bread. In between she took a few sips of the beer. She hated the taste of it, but didn't want to seem ungrateful. She'd never had anything like it before. At home all they'd drunk was water or tea, occasionally some milk, but never anything like this. She'd sometimes seen men in the street when her mother had taken her to Bolton, men who seemed unable to stand up or walk steadily. They'd often been singing or shouting words at her mother that Lydia hadn't understood, and her mother had hurried past them muttering that they were drunkards and it was a word Lydia had come to fear. The men sitting around her now seemed to be drunkards. As time passed their voices grew louder and their laughter more raucous, and Mr Bailey seemed less worried about putting his hand on her leg or his lips to her cheek. She wanted to push him away, but she was afraid of offending him.

At last, she decided that she would go upstairs to bed. The men didn't seem to want to go home and she was tired. She began to stand up, but Mr Bailey grasped her arm and pulled her back down onto the bench beside him.

'Where's tha off to?' he asked.

'I'm going to bed,' she told him and one or two of the men sitting near enough to hear her began to laugh again and nudge one another. 'I'm tired,' she protested.

'She's tired of waitin' for thee, Zach!' one of them told Mr Bailey. 'Best get upstairs!'

They all laughed and Lydia felt confused and slightly afraid. She stood up again and shook the carrier's hand away. She glanced across at the innkeeper in an appeal for help and the woman nodded.

'I'll show thee up,' she said.

When Lydia tried to follow her towards the steep stairs that led to the upper floor, she felt the room tilting around her and the boards beneath her feet didn't seem firm any more. It was as if they were moving. She reached out to steady herself as she walked and clung to the banister rail to prevent herself falling. The innkeeper lit her way down a short corridor with a candle and opened a door for her. Inside she saw a bed and a small table with a bowl and a jug. The woman set the candle down on the table and went across to the window to draw the curtains.

'I'll fetch some hot water in the morning,' she told Lydia as she went out. 'I'd lock the door,' she advised her before she left her. 'Unless tha wants thy fancy man in here.'

With a slight sniff she moved away into the darkness and Lydia closed the door behind her and turned the key in the lock before sitting down on the bed and wishing that the room would stop spinning. She wasn't sure what was wrong with her, but she suspected that Mr Bailey had done it deliberately. The thought alarmed her. How could she continue to travel with this man if he seemed set on taking advantage of her?

Lydia wasn't completely naïve. Her mother had talked to her about men and how she must be careful of them before she had left to go to the mill at Caton. She'd hardly listened at the time. Her grief at being sent away had pushed all other considerations from her mind, but now she realised that her mother's warnings were not without substance and she wished she'd listened more carefully and asked more questions.

Lydia undressed and lay down in the bed. It seemed clean and she was grateful for that and the fact that she was on her way to join her family, but the room still spun every time she closed her eyes and she could hear the voices of the men downstairs growing ever louder.

At last she heard them begin to call out some farewells and the stout outer door slammed shut a time or two as they went on their way. As the silence crept through the inn she was able to hear the quieter sounds and before long there were footsteps in the corridor outside her door, making the floorboards squeak and groan as the person approached. She knew it was Mr Bailey before she heard the sneck on the door raised as he tried it to see if she'd left it unlocked. Lydia found that she was holding her breath as she lay and prayed that he would leave. After what seemed to be a long time she heard him move away and the door of the adjacent room was opened and closed. She heard the springs of his bed, but it was some time before he seemed to settle and Lydia felt safe enough to pull the covers up around her neck and allow herself to drift off to sleep.

When she woke in the morning, she thought for a moment that she was still at Caton and was alarmed that she was alone, thinking that the other girls had gone and she would be punished for being late for her work. Then, slowly, she recalled where she was and what had happened. Her head throbbed when she sat up and she felt sickly. She hoped that she wasn't going to be poorly because it was urgent that she continued on her way if she was to reach Deptford in time. She was plagued by an image of reaching the port only to see the ship on the horizon, missing them only by hours as she had missed them leaving Bolton.

She swung her legs over the edge of the bed and prodded at her ankle. The swelling was hardly noticeable, she thought as she tightened the bandaging around it. She was sure that she would be able to walk some distance on it soon and she considered leaving before Mr Bailey woke so she wouldn't have to ride with him. But the man, or at least his wife, had taken most of her money, she reminded herself, and it would be a waste if she left now. She would give him another chance, she decided. But she must be more careful in future and keep out of his way at the next place they stopped.

Lydia heard a gentle knock on her door and her stomach lurched.

'Who is it?' she called. She heard the tremor in her voice.

'Hot water!' called back the innkeeper.

Relieved, Lydia turned the key in the door and accepted the freshly filled jug. Then she washed herself all over and got dressed before going down the stairs to find a simple breakfast laid out on the table. She ate some bread and bacon then sat with her cloak around her shoulders and the small bag of provisions that Ann had given her on her lap as she waited for Mr Bailey to come down so that they could resume their journey.

Every time she heard a board above her move, Lydia expected him to come down but it seemed like many hours later when he did eventually stumble down the stairs, swearing as he banged his head on a low beam and calling for ale.

He glared at her when he saw her. 'What's tha starin' at?' he demanded as he scratched at the back of his britches.

'I was just waiting,' she replied.

'Aye. And judgin',' he complained as he took a deep drink from the cup the innkeeper put in front of him. 'Just let a chap fill 'is belly and we'll be on our way soon enough.'

Lydia thought that it must be approaching noon before the horses were harnessed up and backed into the shafts of the cart. She couldn't help but wonder how far she could have got if she'd set off walking rather than waiting for Mr Bailey and the frustratingly slow progress of the horses as they pulled the weight of the creaking cart.

They didn't stop for their dinner. Lydia was hungry because it was a while since she'd eaten her breakfast. She had the oatcakes and cheese that Ann had packed for her, but she was reluctant to get them out in front of Mr Bailey in case he expected her to share them with him.

After his conviviality of the night before, he seemed to have sunk into a lower mood. He said little to her other than to complain that he had a headache and the sunshine was hurting his eyes. Lydia was glad of the sun. Even though the spring hadn't taken hold yet, she felt some warmth in it and it comforted her as she sat on the hard seat and tried to keep out of the reach of the odious man beside her.

Their progress was unhurried as Mr Bailey allowed the horses to plod along at their own pace.

'No point spoilin' 'em,' he told Lydia when she asked if they could go any faster. 'Not like them coach horses,' he remarked. 'They drive them to death, but I can't afford to buy more if I lose these.'

Exasperated as she was by their lack of speed, Lydia had to agree that Mr Bailey was right. As they'd travelled, they'd been obliged more than once to pull into the side of the road to allow a mail coach or heavily laden carriage to race past them, with the insistent blowing of their bugles to warn them of their presence. The horses she'd seen had been panting and covered in sweat. The spittle from their mouths had been carried backwards on the wind as they raced past, with the driver cracking his whip and urging them on. She knew that if Mr Bailey treated his horses like that they would probably expire long before they reached London.

'Slow and steady,' he said. 'Besides, we've some valuable things in them boxes,' he added with a nod of his head towards their cargo. 'The Claughtons won't be pleased if anything's broken when I get there – and I've my reputation to consider.'

There was nothing more Lydia could do except resign herself to the slow progress and pray that she would reach Deptford before the ship bound for New South Wales set sail.

Chapter Eighteen

Used to the quiet nights at Tombling Fold, disturbed only by the hooting of owls or an early morning cockerel, Betty found it impossible to sleep for the countless noises that assaulted her ears in London. At first, she'd thought that they would quieten down after a while, but folk here seemed to never go to bed and the arrivals and departures, the shutting and opening of doors, the ringing of bells and the calling out for porters lasted until the early hours.

She slept on and off for a while, but as dawn approached, she was woken by the sound of a bugle as the mail coach raced into the yard below so quickly that it made the building shake. Betty sat up in bed, knowing that even though it was early there would be no more rest for her. Beside her Rose was still asleep. Her breathing seemed easier and Betty hoped that she was getting better. Simon was still sleeping too. The noises of the night seemed not to have disturbed him at all and she had to call his name twice before he opened his bleary eyes, looking around in surprise as he found himself in a strange place.

She told him to wash his face in what was left of the water from the previous evening. It was cold now, but she knew she would have to pay extra for hot. They got dressed and Betty woke Rose.

'How dost tha feel this mornin'?' she asked her hopefully.

Her daughter still looked pale, but she was no longer shivering and as Betty bathed her face and helped her into her petticoat and jacket, she hoped that she was well enough to get to the ship. Although she would have preferred to stay put for another night, she knew that she couldn't afford it and that they must vacate the room promptly before they were charged for another day.

They were already on their way down the steep steps from the galleries when Betty saw the chambermaid coming up with her brush and cloth. The girl smiled ingratiatingly, obviously expecting a tip, but Betty hurried past her without meeting her gaze. The girl cursed and spat after them, and Betty felt sorry for her but the money in her purse was for her children and she couldn't keep giving it away like the gentry could afford to.

Betty decided to forego the dining room and buy food from the street again. She knew that it would be cheaper. Opposite the inn was a busy street market where there were several vendors with carts or baskets already calling their wares.

'What dost tha fancy?' she asked Simon as he stared around in wonder at the scene before him. There was a muffin man with freshly baked muffins and crumpets, a cart with baked potatoes, a stall selling fried fish and a young woman with shrimps and oysters. After a careful study he pointed towards the cart selling hot potatoes and they walked across to wait their turn in the queue and make their purchases.

'Canst tha tell me how to get to Deptford?' Betty asked the vendor. The man looked puzzled as if he hadn't understood her.

'Deptford?' repeated Betty and a look of comprehension passed across the stallholder's face and he gabbled out a list of twists and turns that Betty was barely able to comprehend, pointing a finger this way and that. She nodded and thanked him.

'I think we need to find the river,' she told Simon, who looked equally bewildered. It made sense that the ship would be waiting where the water was, but Betty was still no nearer knowing just how far they would have to walk to reach it.

After they'd finished eating their breakfast, Betty hurried her children away in the direction she thought was best. As they walked, the rumbling of the traders' carts gave way to the faster coaches and carriages that flew by them, throwing up dust and gravel from under their wheels. Shopkeepers were opening their doors, pulling back their shutters and laying out their goods. There were hatters and tailors, and shops piled high with fabrics of every description. Betty longed to linger and look at all that was on offer, but she had neither the time nor the money for any luxuries.

Before long they reached the river that ran through the city like an artery. Betty was amazed by how wide it was and how many boats and ships there were on it, from triple-masted sailing boats to barges and small rowing boats that wound their way in and out of the larger vessels like the pond skaters she'd seen on the slow streams around her home. In the sky, gulls whirled and called, swooping down every now and then to grab a morsel from the piles of fish that were stacked on the quayside, making the fishermen shout and wave their arms to frighten them away. It stank too, and Betty wondered how people could bear to be near it for any length of time.

Once again, she asked the way to Deptford and how long it might take them to reach it. The woman she spoke to directed them to the far side of the river. They crossed a wide, stone-built bridge that was thronged with traffic, stepping around the piles of muck that the horses left behind. Rose was still coughing and her breathing was shallow. Betty knew she wasn't fit to walk far, but she doubted there was enough in her purse to pay for a coach ride. And even if there was, she wasn't sure where she might enquire. Although the city seemed thronged with coaches, she had no idea where to catch one or how to discover which direction it might take.

They walked on for a couple of hours, stopping now and again to rest and sometimes asking their way. The townhouses of the gentry gradually gave way to the homes of the tradesmen and then the poor as they walked away from the busy centre of the city.

When they eventually reached the docks at Deptford, they found the river crowded with even more boats and ships than there had been upstream. The sailing ships were anchored in tiers from near the dockside almost to the middle of the river. Between them, rowing boats were going to and fro taking people and goods to each one. Betty was unsure what to do. She'd been given no instruction as to how to board the ship when they eventually arrived and had no idea which might be the right one. She looked around for someone to ask and cautiously approached a man who was tying up his rowing boat near to the river stairs.

'I'm looking for the *Maria*,' she explained.

The man regarded her suspiciously. 'That's a convict ship,' he said.

'I know. I have permission to sail on her. I'm going to join my husband.'

'Have you been cleared to board?'

'No. I don't know. I have a letter.'

'Go to the office over there,' said the man. 'Get a pass and I'll row you out.'

Betty left the children on the quay with the box and eventually found the correct door and went into an office that reminded of her of the boardroom in Bolton. A man in naval uniform was sitting behind a desk and she showed him her letter. He glanced at it, at her, and then banged down a stamp to make a mark on it before handing it back to her. Then she returned to the rowing boat and they clambered down the slippery steps, slick with green weed, and climbed into the little boat.

Betty wasn't a gifted reader but she knew her letters well enough to recognise the *Maria* as they approached; her name was etched in wood on the prow and on the stern. She was a barque with three masts, her canvas sails furled at the moment as she creaked sightly on the rising tide. As the rowing boat closed in on the wooden hull that seemed to tower above them, Betty wondered how on earth they were supposed to get up onto the deck. The boatman heaved on the oars and drew them in beside a rope ladder that hung down the side. Betty stared at it as the ship rose and fell on the swell, hardly believing that she was expected to grasp hold of it and climb up.

'Go first,' she told Simon, knowing he was more agile than she was. 'Then I'll pass our things up to thee.'

She watched as her son stood up in the rowing boat and found his balance. He reached out for the side of the *Maria* and grasped the ladder, springing up onto it with a confident leap that saw his legs disappear over the side of the ship in moments. With a grin on his face, he leaned down and took the rope handle of the box from his mother and hauled it up onto the deck beside him.

'Go next, Rose,' Betty said to her daughter as she helped her to stand up in the rowing boat. Simon leaned over and reached down to clasp his sister's hand and even though Rose seemed reluctant she was soon safely aboard. With both her children on the *Maria*, Betty knew she must join them. The boatman kept the rowing boat as still as he could as she inched her way to the side. She reached up a hand to grab the ladder, but it moved away from her and she let it go again.

'Be quick!' shouted the boatman. 'I can't hold her steady for ever!'

'Come on, Mam!' called Simon from above her.

Betty reached out for the rope ladder again and managed to get a foot onto one of the rungs. She pulled herself forward and felt the rowing boat plunge away from her. Suspended between the two vessels, she felt a moment of panic as the water rippled beneath her, but she looked up to see her son's face and his hand reaching out to her, so she climbed as best she could, encumbered by her skirts, and moments later she was pulled over the edge of the ship and onto the deck.

It took Betty a moment to gather her wits, she'd been so afraid. When she looked back, she saw the rowing boat was already well on its way back to shore. She was aboard the *Maria* and there was no turning back now, she thought. She glanced about her, wondering what to do next. A group of women were huddled on the deck. Although cleanly dressed, they seemed miserable as they sat around barely speaking, staring off into the middle distance as if troubled by their thoughts. Betty had no way of knowing if they were other women going to join their husbands, like her, or if they were convicts.

She was wondering whether to call out to them to ask for information when a man came up onto the deck from below and noticed them.

'Who are you?' he asked her, looking at her as if she had no business to be there.

'Betty Knowles and my children. We have free passage,' she told him, fumbling in the pocket that was tied beneath her petticoat to retrieve the crumpled letter.

The man fished a pair of wire spectacles from a small pocket in his waistcoat, and, having hooked them over his ears, he took the letter and read it carefully.

'Which children have your brought?' he asked.

'This is my son, Simon, and my younger daughter, Rose.'

He looked up and studied Simon carefully. 'How old is this boy?' he asked.

'He's ten years old,' Betty told him truthfully, hoping that the man would believe her.

'Are you sure?' he asked. He seemed doubtful. 'He appears older than that. And no boys over ten years can be taken on board,' he reminded her. 'This is a women's ship.'

Betty saw Simon give her a worried glance and she hoped that he had the good sense to say nothing. 'He's ten,' she confirmed, not admitting that Simon would be eleven in just a few days' time. She was terrified that if there was a delay and Simon's birthday came before they sailed, they might decide to put him off the ship. She couldn't possibly leave him behind. 'The parson checked the parish register and he wouldn't have signed if he thought it was wrong,' she told the man. 'There.' She pointed at the paper. 'Reverend Brocklehurst.'

'There's another name here: Lydia.'

'We had to set off without her,' explained Betty. 'She went as an apprentice and we were waiting for word that she could come with us, but she was delayed.'

The man frowned. 'If she's not come with you, I can't hold a place for her,' he said. 'The government are keen to fill every bunk.'

'She'll be here soon,' protested Betty, wondering what she would do if Lydia arrived and they wouldn't let her on board. It was unthinkable and she pushed the thought aside. Of course they would let her come aboard. They must.

'Well, we'll see,' said the man. 'I'm Mr Prosser, the surgeon and superintendent of the convicts,' he told Betty. 'If you wait here I'll tell the captain you've arrived.'

Betty and the children waited as he disappeared. The women on the deck showed little interest in her and she didn't like to stare at them. They must be convicts, she thought. She wondered what crimes they'd committed to be sentenced to transportation. Some had small babies in their arms and some had two or three children gathered around them, subjected to the same cruel fate as their mothers.

Moments later, Mr Prosser returned. 'Come this way,' he told her as he led them towards the ladder that went down below the deck.

'Are we to be housed with the convicts?' asked Betty anxiously when they reached the bottom, looking about in the gloom of a solitary lantern at the rows of narrow bunks and the long wooden tables with benches on either side.

'You're a convict wife,' he told her. 'I'm sure you didn't expect to be given a cabin?' Betty ignored his sarcastic tone. She hadn't given the matter any thought, but as a free passenger she was shocked that she was to be treated no differently from the convict women.

'Here,' he told her, indicating a tier of bunks built into the side of the ship. 'These are furthest from the latrines, so they'll get the best air, especially if the sea gets rough and we have to batten down the hatches. I take it you're all well and fit to undertake the voyage?' he went on. 'If there are any problems you can come to me in the sick bay.'

'Rose has been unwell,' ventured Betty. She hoped that the surgeon might have something that would help her daughter. 'She caught a chill on the journey.'

Mr Prosser turned to Rose. 'Show me your tongue,' he instructed as he grasped her wrist to feel her pulse. 'I'll give her a powder,' he told Betty. 'Bring her to me tomorrow if she isn't improved.'

Betty thanked him. She was grateful to him and glad that she wasn't expected to pay for his brief consultation.

She turned to the bunks and said that Simon should have the top one, Rose would sleep in the middle and she would take the bottom one. She pushed their box underneath and wondered if there was anything that could be done to make the place look a little more homely. It was nothing like she'd imagined and later, when all the convict women were sent down, it was noisy and cramped and crowded and Betty wondered how they would survive the voyage if they were to stay cooped up like this with nothing to do for months on end.

Chapter Nineteen

By nightfall on the Wednesday evening, Lydia and Mr Bailey had reached Macclesfield. Lydia had three shillings and fourpence left in her purse and she was beginning to regret ever asking to ride with the carrier. She was sure that if she'd used six shillings to buy a coach ticket, she could have got much nearer to Deptford in the two days that they'd been travelling even if she hadn't been able to afford to travel all the way by coach. It would have given her the opportunity to rest her ankle and she was sure that she could have walked the rest of the way.

Mr Bailey threw the reins to a stable lad and turned to Lydia with a sly grin.

'Here we are again,' he said. 'I hope tha might be more friendly to me tonight.'

Lydia didn't answer, but followed him in through the front door of the inn where Mr Bailey was greeted by the innkeeper, who poured him a cup of beer.

'Pour one for the lady as well,' said Mr Bailey.

The innkeeper glanced at Lydia but made no comment and poured a second cup as Mr Bailey pushed some coins towards him.

'Will tha be wantin' one room or two?' he asked.

'Two,' said Lydia firmly.

'That'll be a shilling,' said the innkeeper and Lydia took a coin from her purse and paid him.

'Can I see it?' she asked. 'The room?'

'Aye. Of course,' said the innkeeper and called a lass in from the back kitchen to show her the way. 'What about thy beer?' he asked as she turned away.

'I don't want it,' replied Lydia.

She followed the girl up the stairs to a neat room at the front of the inn. It looked clean if plainly furnished with a bed and a dresser.

'Dost tha want candles?' asked the girl. Lydia nodded. It was growing dark. 'That'll be tuppence,' she said, holding out her hand. Reluctantly, Lydia parted with more money and sat on the edge of the bed until the girl came back with two candles, a flint and a holder.

When she'd gone, Lydia turned to the door to check that it could be locked. She was pleased to see a sturdy bolt and she pushed it across before striking the flint to light one the candles. Her plan was to eat the food that Ann had given her and not go back downstairs until the morning so that she could avoid Mr Bailey. She'd learned her lesson the night before and she wasn't going to repeat her mistake.

—

Lydia slept well in the surprisingly comfortable bed and felt better in the morning when she woke with a clear head. She walked around the small room, a few paces back and forth, to test her ankle and found that she wasn't in much pain at all and the swelling had subsided. She wondered whether to leave early, before Mr Bailey made an appearance, and set off walking, but when she went downstairs he was already eating his breakfast, ready to leave.

'Get a move on,' he told her. 'I want to reach Stoke by nightfall.'

Pleased that the man seemed sober, Lydia quickly ate some bread and butter with a cup of tea and then put on her cloak and went out to the stable yard where the cart was ready. She climbed up onto the seat, optimistic that today they would make more progress than they had the day before.

The turnpike road was better surfaced than the one they'd travelled on previously and Mr Bailey eased the horses to a gentle trot now and again, keen to reach his planned destination before nightfall. It was just after a nearby church clock had rung out twelve sonorous chimes for midday that they approached the first tollhouse and Mr Bailey handed over a shilling to the woman who came out to greet them and open the gate so that they could go on their way. Beyond it, the road seemed to deteriorate and there were potholes filled with water that the carrier did his best to steer around, swearing as he did and demanding to know, of no one in particular, what he had paid his shilling for if the road couldn't be kept in better repair.

As they were negotiating a particularly rutted stretch, Lydia looked anxiously into the distance as she saw an approaching coach coming towards them at speed.

'Look out!' she cried, although Mr Bailey had seen it too and was urging the horses into the side of the road.

Lydia felt the bump of the wheels hitting the grass banking at the side of the road as the coach raced past them in the opposite direction, the furious-faced driver shouting abuse at them as he went by and the faces of the passengers peering, horrified, from the windows. There was a grinding noise followed by a crack and Lydia grabbed onto the seat, but she was already sliding. Time seemed to play out in slow motion as she felt herself part company with the cart and land with a bump that knocked the breath from her.

Gasping, she sat up in bewilderment and stared at the wreckage. One of the cart's wheels was buckled and broken and hanging off the axle. The precious load was tipping precariously and one of the horses was on its side, legs flailing in the air.

'Is tha hurt, lass?'

Lydia looked up at Mr Bailey's worried face. 'I don't think so,' she said, as she stood up.

She watched as the carrier hurried away to unfasten the fallen horse from its harness and get it to its feet. The animal had blood trickling down its hind leg but seemed otherwise unhurt. Mr Bailey soothed it and led it away from the shafts to tie it to a nearby tree. The other horse, the one with the white blaze, was whinnying in distress and he unfastened that one too and led it away to calm it.

'What will we do?' asked Lydia when he came back to survey the damage. It was clear that they could go no further and would have to get help.

Lydia sat on the banking and watched Mr Bailey pushing at the cart to try to straighten it, but it was hopeless and it was clear that it was only a matter of time before the two huge chests that were loaded onto it would tumble to the ground, probably breaking and smashing the contents he'd been so determined to keep safe.

Some agricultural workers came hurrying across the field to assist him.

'I saw that stage being driven like the devil!' announced one. 'Tha's got a right mess here,' he observed. 'Tha'll be needin' the wheelwright to put that back on.' He nodded towards the smashed wheel.

'You all right, miss?' asked the other man, looking down at Lydia.

She nodded. Still shocked. Still not knowing what she was going to do now. It was clear that travelling with Mr Bailey was no longer an option and that she would need to find another way to get to Deptford.

When the men saw that Lydia was limping, they decided that she was hurt after all and one of them went to fetch another cart to take her to a nearby inn.

'I'll go and fetch the surgeon,' said the other. 'Then I'll enquire at the wheelwright's for thee. Does tha want to come?' he asked Mr Bailey.

The carrier shook his head. 'I'd best stay and guard this load,' he said.

When Lydia arrived at the inn, the innkeeper's wife came hurrying out, fussing over Lydia and insisted that the man carry her inside despite her protests.

'Poor duck. Poor duck,' she kept saying as she fetched a basin of water and a cloth to help Lydia clean herself up.

It wasn't long before there was the sound of hooves outside and a man burst through the door with a leather bag clutched in his hand.

'Where's the patient!' he cried as if he thought it was a matter of life and death.

He was young and Lydia thought he seemed over-enthusiastic as he grasped hold of her leg to examine it.

'I'm all right,' she told him, as she pushed her petticoat down. 'It was sprained already but the fall jolted it again.'

The surgeon seemed not to be listening.

'No bones broken!' he announced after a moment. 'I'll put a better bandage on it for you and you should be fine. But no walking on it for a few days,' he warned.

'Will you be needing a room then?' the innkeeper's wife asked her. 'And maybe one for the driver? Is he your father?'

'No,' Lydia told her. 'I was just getting a ride with him. I have to get to Deptford.'

'I saw some men starting to unload the cart,' said the surgeon as he bound Lydia's ankle. 'It looks like it's going to take some time to get everything mended and back on the road.'

'I can't stay here,' said Lydia. 'I have to get there before a ship sails.'

'You'd be best getting on the coach,' the innkeeper's wife told her. 'It comes through tomorrow morning. It'll take you as far as Birmingham and you'll be able to travel on from there. You could be in London by the day after tomorrow.'

If only it was that simple, thought Lydia as the surgeon released her foot from his lap and she carefully eased her boot back on over the bulky strapping. She would need to walk at least part of the way and she had no idea what had happened to the stick that Mrs Malpass had given her.

'How much would it cost from here to Birmingham?' she asked.

'Two shillings, I think, for an outside seat,' said the innkeeper's wife. 'If they have room. They're fussy about how many they take these days.'

'It's to stop accidents,' the surgeon told her. 'Coaches are too top-heavy if they let more than a few up. Makes them turn over on the bends. That causes some nasty injuries,' he said with a slight gleam in his eye as if he enjoyed others' misfortune. 'It's a long way to fall,' he added.

A shiver ran through Lydia. It had been bad enough falling from Mr Bailey's cart. If she fell from the top of a coach she would surely be killed, but what choice did she have other than to take the risk? If she could get as far as Birmingham then maybe she could continue on foot the rest of the way to Deptford, though whether she would be left with enough money to feed herself she had no idea. She supposed she would have to depend on people's kindness.

'Do I owe you anything?' she asked the surgeon, hoping that he would be kind now. Thankfully he shook his head.

'I was passing this way anyway,' he told her before ordering up a plate of meat pie and boiled potatoes.

'Would you like some?' the innkeeper's wife asked Lydia. 'Potluck. Only tuppence.'

Lydia nodded. Although it was all she had apart from her fare to Birmingham, she was hungry and it smelled good.

A few minutes later she heard a commotion in the yard, and through the window she saw the men who'd come to help them struggling with the huge chests that had been on the back of Mr Bailey's cart. The carrier was already shouting at them to be careful when they dropped one on its side and he cursed them loudly.

Moments later, he burst red-faced into the inn. There was a gash across his forehead that he wiped from time to time on his soiled handkerchief.

'Best let the surgeon take a look at that,' advised the innkeeper's wife when she came back in with the plates of food.

'Bring me summat t' eat as well,' he replied as one of the men who'd been struggling with the chests came to the door.

'We've got them both in the barn for now,' he told Mr Bailey. 'Your horses are in the stable and the wheelwright says he'll take the wheel later for mending.'

'Aye. Thanks,' said the carrier. 'But I hope nowt's broken,' he added.

'I daresay as them chests took a good knock when the cart went over,' replied the man, tipping his cap and retreating outside before he took the blame for anything else. Lydia thought that Mr Bailey ought to show more gratitude after they'd been good enough to help him.

'Looks like we're stuck 'ere then,' Mr Bailey told Lydia.

'I'm going to get the coach tomorrow if I can,' she replied.

'Leavin' me in the lurch, then?' he said. 'I thought tha were short of money?'

'I've enough to get to Birmingham,' she said. The truth was that she would be glad to get away from the man. She thought that if he hadn't been trying to touch her leg, he might have had more control over his horses and the accident would never have happened. But in a way she wasn't sorry. It would have taken them days to get to Birmingham on the cart and now she could be there by tomorrow night.

After an hour or so, having no money to pay for a room, Lydia crept out of the inn unnoticed and found herself a dry place to spend the night behind the chests in the barn.

She was woken the next morning by the sound of the coach clattering into the yard and hurried out, brushing straw from her clothing. The ostlers had come out to change the horses whilst the passengers hurried into the inn, asking what there was to eat and demanding it straight away.

The coach driver was watching as the fresh horses were brought out and Lydia went across to him.

'Excuse me? Have you room for an outside passenger?' she asked.

The man turned his gaze on her and a smile played on his lips as it lingered.

'All on your own?' he asked.

Lydia felt her cheeks burn. She was sure it couldn't be that unusual for a woman to travel alone, but then she knew so little of the world that she wasn't sure.

'The innkeeper's wife told me that you charge two shillings,' she said, guessing that he might ask more if he thought she didn't know the price.

'That's right,' he told her, holding out an upturned palm as he watched her feel for the slit in her petticoat and reach for her purse that was tied around her waist. She got out her final florin and placed it in his hand.

'Up you go then,' he said as he grasped her elbow to steady her against the swaying of the coach as the horses were backed up and their harness secured.

Lydia gathered her petticoat and grimaced as she put her weight onto her injured ankle to climb the ladder. She pulled herself up, aware of the coachman looking at her exposed legs as he continued to assist her.

Once aloft, she settled herself into a corner where she could hold on to the rail. The top of the coach was slippery and slightly damp and the surgeon's words about nasty injuries were still clear in her head.

When the coachman had chivvied the rest of his passengers back out of the inn and onto the coach, they were ready to leave. Lydia could hear her companions grumbling that they hadn't been given enough time to eat their breakfast and had had to leave their plates half uneaten. They were lucky to have had anything, she thought as they set off, bumping out onto the turnpike road. Her stomach was growling with hunger, but at least the miles would pass quickly now and she was more optimistic that she would reach Deptford in time to sail with her family.

Chapter Twenty

Lydia arrived in Birmingham very late that night. Tired and hungry, she got down from the coach and stood in the yard of the Hen and Chickens. All around her, passengers were coming and going, calling for rooms, calling for their luggage, calling for food and drink. Lydia had never been in the midst of such a melee and she was bewildered, excited and a little afraid.

People were pushing past her, knocking into her as they did and no matter where she moved to she was always in somebody's way. As she moved further and further back she was inched out of the yard and onto the street.

Lydia wondered what to do next. With no money left in her purse, she could pay for neither food nor accommodation and there was nowhere safe for her to sleep here. She decided that she would be safer outside the town where she might be able to find a barn or hedgerow to rest until the daylight came, but she was unsure which way to go. She tried to ask which was the London road, but her voice went unheard in the busy street where people were hurrying past or rolling on their way to drink in yet another inn before falling comatose in a corner if they were lucky, or under the wheels of one of the many coaches if they were not.

Lydia thought that if she knew the destinations of the coaches that seemed to continuously clatter in and out of the inn yards she could follow in their tracks when she discovered the one that was London bound, but it seemed impossible to know. Eventually, to get away from the crush, Lydia found herself walking into narrower streets where the people seemed less well-off and the coaches were fewer. She saw people sleeping in the doorways of shops and in back alleys and she wondered how safe it would be to simply find a dry spot and rest; after all, she had nothing of value to attract a thief and her options were few.

Tired out and feeling weak, she came to a shop where the doorway was vacant. She wasn't sure what kind of shop it was because its windows were empty, but after glancing around to see if anyone was watching her, she sat down with her back to the door, pulled up her knees and crossed her arms around them. She thought that it would be safer not to sleep, but that she was less conspicuous in her chosen spot than walking with no purpose and drawing attention to herself. When the morning came, she would find the London road and set out.

The sky was overcast and even though the night was not frosty and Lydia was wrapped in her cloak, she shivered with cold and fright until her teeth chattered together uncontrollably. Now and again she dozed, but quickly woke with a feeling of panic that she had let down her guard. Even though the night had grown quieter and there seemed to be fewer people on the streets she was still afraid of what could happen if she didn't stay alert.

As the approaching dawn lit the sky with hints of pink and yellow over the high rooftops, Lydia was woken from a disturbed slumber by the sounds of people moving about on the other side of the door where she was resting. The shop would soon be opening and it was time that she was on her way. She stood up, feeling stiff and with a pain in her neck where her head had hung at an awkward angle. Putting her injured leg to the ground, she tested it and found that although it was painful again after being thrown from the cart, she was able to walk, if only slowly. Once again, she lamented losing the stick that she'd had and hoped that she might find another that would help her. She had no idea how many days' journey it was to London from here, but she imagined it would be quite a few – more if she could only make slow progress.

Her stomach ached with hunger as she retraced her steps towards the inn and saw that the marketplace beyond it was already thronged with early risers. The aroma of food and drink seemed to be everywhere to taunt her, from the enticing aroma that escaped the doors of the coffee houses to the carts and stalls selling all manner of fare.

As she stood and watched, she saw a man arrive with a huge basket of quartern loaves for sale. Customers quickly gathered around him to buy the bread that was gently steaming, fresh from the bakery, and the man was jingling change in his hand as he took payment. Lydia's mouth watered uncontrollably at the sight and smell and she couldn't resist the temptation to approach more closely.

The man had put his basket down on the ground as he served his customers and Lydia realised that she was unseen as she came up behind him. Later, she told herself that it was hunger that overcame her, that and self-preservation, because she knew that she wasn't a thief. But she couldn't stop herself reaching out and picking up one of the loaves. She stood for a moment, glancing around, planning to say that she was intending to pay for it if she was challenged, but no one saw her and a moment later, the bread was clutched under her arm, hidden by her cloak. Head down, she hurried away, unaware of the pain in her ankle as she rushed to get well clear before the loaf was missed.

Moments later she heard a cry.

'I'm one short! Someone's stolen one! Who's taken it? Where's the thief?'

Without glancing back, Lydia began to run. Each step sent a searing pain through her, but her only thought was to escape and to keep hold of the precious food. Behind her she could hear people calling and searching. As she turned the corner, she risked a glance back and saw the baker holding a young lad by the ear and accusing him. The boy was wailing his innocence and Lydia felt guilty, but she knew she couldn't return. She kept on going until she was forced to stop, panting for breath. She looked behind her again, but couldn't see anyone following her. She must have got away with it, she thought as she crept into an alley and pulled a chunk off the bread and pushed it into her mouth. Nothing had ever tasted so good and she ate and ate until she couldn't stomach any more.

The remains of the loaf in her hand seemed to sear her fingers as Lydia felt so guilty about what she'd done. She felt like tossing it away so that no evidence would be found on her, but she realised that she would be hungry again later and she must keep hold of it. She broke what was left into pieces and pushed them into her pocket, down her boots, and up her sleeves until nothing obvious could give her away. Then she dusted the crumbs from her hands and went to enquire about the way south.

–

As Lydia plodded on, she couldn't shake off the impulse to keep looking over her shoulder to check that she wasn't being pursued. Her feelings of shame and regret threatened to overwhelm her and she wished that she hadn't stolen the bread. She'd only just managed to shake off the guilt of believing that she'd sent Violet to her death, and now this hung over her like a dark cloud.

A few carts and wagons passed her as she walked. Some of the drivers greeted her but not all and, although she would have welcomed a lift, Lydia was wary of falling in with some other man who thought that he was entitled to some reward for the slightest kindness shown to her.

Her ankle hurt as she trudged on and she began to limp more obviously. As soon as she felt able, she ate the remains of the bread. She just wanted it to be gone so that she couldn't be accused if the constables did find her. By the time the daylight began to fade, she was close to tears of despair, wishing that she could simply go home and find her family around the hearth. But it could never be and she told herself that she had to be brave and keep going. The thought that she might be left behind and have to fend for herself like this for the rest of her life terrified her. Lydia simply wanted her mother.

Eventually she saw the light of some lamps ahead and it spurred her on towards them. As she got nearer, she saw that it was a tollhouse and the keeper was opening the gate for a coach that had just passed her to go through. He held up the lantern as he saw her approaching.

'It's late for a lass like you to be out all alone,' he observed. 'Where are you headed?'

'I'm on my way to London,' Lydia told him and when she saw him begin to shake his head, she wished she'd told him a lie.

'Do you know how far it is?' he asked, swinging the lantern around and shining it more closely towards her, dazzling her.

'A day or two's walk.'

'More than that. And you're limping badly already. Where are you staying tonight? There's no inn for miles yet,' he warned her.

Lydia wished that he would just let her through the gate. She didn't want to answer his questions. The less people knew about her the better.

'Who is it?' called a woman from the open doorway of the house. She had a baby on her hip and another child peeping out from behind her, looking curiously at Lydia.

'Young lass. Walking alone. Says she's on her way to London, but she looks exhausted and she can barely walk.'

'I'm all right,' insisted Lydia. 'Let me through.'

'You'd best come inside,' called the woman. 'This road can be dangerous at night.'

Lydia hesitated and the woman came out to speak to her. 'When the mail coach comes through they just sound their bugle and we have to run out to have the gate open before they arrive. They slow for nothing,' she warned. 'If you're walking in the dark and they don't see you, you'll be run down for certain. And then there's the robbers,' she went on. 'Best come inside. A young girl like you shouldn't be on the road all alone,' she told her.

Although Lydia was reluctant, she was tired and in pain, but she also knew that she was penniless.

'I can't,' she told the woman. 'I can't afford to pay for a bed.'

'Bless you!' cried the woman. 'We wouldn't think of asking you for money, would we, Charlie?' she said, turning to the man whom Lydia thought must be her husband. 'We're good Christian folk,' she told Lydia. 'We only want to offer rest to the weary traveller. Come inside,' she said again.

Lydia glanced at the man. He was still standing blocking the way and other than running back the way she'd just come she realised she had no choice but to follow the woman inside. They did seem good people, she told herself, and maybe all they wanted to do was help her.

Inside the tollhouse, Lydia saw that it was almost round in shape with windows, lit by lanterns on every side.

'It's so we can see the travellers coming,' the woman said as she gave the baby to another older girl, who was minding a younger boy near the fire. 'They sneak past if they can without paying,' she explained. 'And some try to go around the gate through the field, but they get bogged down mostly and have to come shame-faced asking for help.' She laughed. 'Sit down,' she told Lydia. 'Over here where it's warm,' she invited, plumping a cushion and putting it back on the chair near the hearth. 'Whatever are you doing walking to London all on your own?'

Lydia could see the woman was curious. She must suspect that Lydia was in trouble and it worried her.

'I'm not running away,' she protested. 'I'm going to find my mother.'

'Are you hungry?' asked the woman as she took up a thick cloth and lifted the lid on the cauldron that hung over her fire to stir its contents. An aroma of herbs and vegetables and the unmistakable tang of mutton wafted across the room. 'Set the bowls on the table,' she instructed one of the children, 'and set an extra place for this young lady. What's your name?' she asked Lydia.

'Lettie,' she replied, using the name that she'd given to May and Mrs Malpass back in Egerton.

'Well, Lettie, you're welcome to share our food,' she said. 'I'm Judith and my husband is Charlie.' She went on to name all her children but Lydia didn't attempt to memorise them. She'd soon be gone from here.

Charlie came inside and sat down at the head of the table. Lydia watched as all the children and Judith clasped their hands and bowed their heads, waiting for him to say grace before they ate. Judith filled a bowl with a generous portion and offered Lydia bread to go with it. Lydia accepted a small piece, wondering how she could bring herself to eat it. She thought that she never wanted to see bread again after munching her way through the huge loaf that she'd stolen that morning.

She listened to the family chatter as she spooned the broth into her mouth. She wished she was sitting around a table with her own mother and father and Simon and Rose. She longed to be a part of a close and happy family like this.

'So, what does your mother do in London?' asked Charlie after a while.

'She's arranging passage to New South Wales. She went on ahead,' said Lydia.

She saw Charlie exchange a glance with his wife and it was clear what they were thinking.

'She isn't a convict!' Lydia told them. 'We're going as free passengers.'

Lydia was glad that she didn't have to add any further explanation as the clear sound of a bugle carried to them on the stillness of the night.

'Mail coach,' declared Charlie, leaping up from his chair and hurrying to the door to open the gate. Moments later, Lydia heard the thundering beat of the hooves and through the window she glimpsed the lanterns of the coach before it raced through, rattling the windows and the pots on the table as it passed.

Charlie returned after a minute or two and resumed his meal. 'So, New South Wales,' he continued as if there had been no interruption. 'That's a long way.'

'I need to get there quickly – to Deptford that is,' Lydia told him. 'Our ship sails on the seventh.'

'You're cutting it fine if you're planning to walk all the way,' replied Charlie. 'And you were limping.'

'I sprained my ankle, but it's much better now.'

'And you say you have no money?'

Lydia shook her head.

Charlie broke off more bread and soaked up the remains of his stew with it before savouring the taste. He looked thoughtful, as if he might suggest some solution, but before he could say any more there was a commotion outside as a vehicle pulled up and someone began to bang insistently on the door.

'I'm coming!' shouted Charlie, wiping his mouth on a cloth. 'Who can it be at this time of night?' he asked as he went to open it.

'Please can you help us? We've been robbed!' wailed a woman's voice. 'Can you send for the constable?'

The word sent a wave of panic through Lydia. She couldn't stay here if they were sending for the law.

She watched as Charlie helped the sobbing woman and her companion inside. It had started to rain heavily outside and they were drenched and bedraggled. One took the chair by the fire where Lydia had been sitting and Judith fetched a stool for the other.

'What happened?' asked Charlie as Judith attended to the new arrivals, offering them stew, bread and tea.

'He was a terrible man, with a scarf covering his face, and he had a pistol that he threatened us with,' cried the first woman in a shaking voice as her companion sat in silence and trembled. 'He took my ring and my brooch and snatched Miss Bannister's purse with all her money!'

Lydia heard Charlie tell the eldest boy to run for the constable and she wondered what was the best thing to do. Should she creep away unnoticed and continue in the darkness, hoping not to come across this despicable man that the woman was describing? Or should she stay and hope that the constable would be too distracted to notice her and that she'd come too far for him to have heard about a young fugitive?

In the end it was the thick darkness of the moonless night and the worsening weather that persuaded her to stay. She went to sit in the shadows and hoped that the constable wouldn't see her.

When he came, he was a small, plump man with a florid face who listened to what the two women had to say and made some notes in a small book with a pencil, nodding as he did so.

'Sounds like Swift Stanley. He's notorious on this road. They say he's always polite, though, especially to the ladies.'

'He was not polite to us!' protested the first woman. 'And he manhandled my companion most indelicately.'

'Well, leave it to me,' the constable told her. 'I know his local haunts. He'll be under lock and key by this time tomorrow, you have my word.' He snapped his notebook shut and put away the pencil. 'Where are you ladies heading?' he asked.

'To Selly Grove. We were on our way to visit the Owens, but we were delayed. We never intended to travel in the dark.'

'You can rest here until morning,' suggested Judith, but the woman was shaking her head.

'We can't impose.'

'It's no trouble. It's not uncommon for us to take in stranded travellers,' she insisted. 'We've a room prepared. I was going to give it to our other guest, but I'm sure she won't mind a truckle bed instead.' She turned to Lydia.

'I'm more than grateful for that,' Lydia replied, relaxing now that the constable had put on his hat, picked up his lantern and gone out into the storm.

'Then it's settled,' announced Judith, and Charlie went outside to attend to the women's horse and move their gig so that it wasn't blocking the road.

–

The next morning, after eating a breakfast of bread and cheese, Lydia thanked Judith for her hospitality and stepped out into an early mist that was draping the branches of the trees on the edges of the forest, and although it had stopped raining, moisture was dripping from the eaves with a steady rhythm.

A covered wagon was drawn up outside and Charlie was chatting with the driver, an elderly man with long white whiskers who was wearing a smock.

Lydia was hesitant to interrupt them to ask Charlie to open the gate for her. She decided to wait until he opened it for the wagon and go through then. Whilst she waited, she wandered around the back and saw the array of boxes and sacks inside. They weren't packed tightly and Lydia realised that there was plenty of room to sit amongst them. If she could rest her ankle for a while longer she would have a much better chance of getting to Deptford, she realised.

Making a quick decision, she moved the flaps of the canvas covering a little further apart and put a foot to the step. The wagon was solid and held steady as she climbed up. Then she turned to arrange the canvas in place behind her. With her heart pounding in her ears, blocking out all other sounds, she squeezed herself between two of the largest boxes and sat down. The men were still talking, but it was only moments before they called their farewells and the wagon began to move. They bumped over some ruts in the road and Lydia heard the driver begin to whistle a tune as they headed away from the tollhouse. She had no idea where the wagon was heading or how long it would be before she was discovered, but for now, at least, she was on her way and moving at a faster pace than she could have kept up on foot.

They lumbered on for most of the day. Lydia couldn't see much except for the road behind them through the small slit in the canvas flap at the back. Every so often they were passed by faster vehicles but mostly they went past people on foot and she often heard the driver pause his tune to call out a greeting. When evening came, she felt the wagon turn and realised that they were stopping at an inn. She heard ostlers come out for the horses and the wagon was manoeuvred into a barn or shed and the doors were closed on her, leaving her in pitch blackness.

Lydia felt panic rise as she realised that she was trapped. She felt her way down from the back of the wagon and recognised the feel of stone under her feet, but there were no windows, only the doors where a faint slit of light revealed the way out to the yard. She felt her way carefully towards it, but when she pushed at the doors she found they were firmly locked and Lydia had no choice but to spend a cold and hungry night in the shed.

She found her way back to the wagon and lay down between the boxes, wrapped in her cloak. Although she was desperately hungry and thirsty there was nothing to eat or drink and all she could do was try to sleep until morning came and she would be released.

Chapter Twenty-One

Betty's first full day onboard the *Maria* was difficult. She woke early, restless in the strange surroundings. Betty could hear her daughter's chest wheezing as she breathed, but when she rolled out of her bunk and looked at her, she saw that Rose's face was less flushed.

There was water for them to wash before they dressed, but it was sea water. It was cold and there was no soap. Betty had never tasted sea water before, never even seen the sea, and she cupped a little of it into her palm and put it to her lips. It tasted of nothing but salt and she spat it out, wondering what they would drink after they sailed. She hoped she wouldn't have to get used to this tangy brine. Even boiled up with tea it would be unpalatable.

At eight o'clock they ate a breakfast of porridge oats, and were allowed to boil water in kettles to provide them with a drink of tea. Betty tasted it reluctantly but found that the water from the barrel was fresh and she hoped that there would be plenty of it taken on board before they left.

When the meal was finished, they were instructed to make their beds and tidy any belongings, the floors were swept and the buckets that had been used as privies in the night were taken up on deck for the contents to be thrown overboard and the buckets scrubbed out.

At nine o'clock, Mr Prosser came down the ladder to inspect that everything was clean and in order. After a perfunctory glance around, he seemed satisfied and allowed the women to go up onto the deck for fresh air and instructed those who had any ailments to visit him in the sick bay. Betty was unsure whether or not to join them. She was still worried about Rose. She'd eaten a little of the porridge, but she was listless and pale and her coughing was bringing up a nasty greenish phlegm from her lungs.

'I wouldn't be too concerned,' Mr Prosser told Betty after he'd listened to Rose's chest and looked down her throat and taken her pulse. 'It's only a cold. A trifling matter,' he told her, but he went to his bureau to make up another dose of medicine for Rose to take. 'Come back tomorrow if there's been no improvement,' he said. 'But I'm sure your daughter will be much better by then.'

That afternoon, more convicts were brought on board. A wherry came alongside the *Maria* and a ladder was let down for them. Betty watched from the deck as the women struggled to clamber up the ropes. They were heavily ironed with chains that ran from bands around their ankles to iron belts around their waists to the manacles that encompassed their wrists. Betty knew how hard the climb had been for her and she watched with growing anger as the women were subjected to a torrent of abuse as they struggled up the side of the ship, some desperately holding on to babies at the same time. No matter what they'd done, thought Betty, they didn't deserve to be treated like this.

Once on deck they were herded into a group and their names checked off against a list by Mr Prosser. Then they were taken below.

'Are they very bad people?' asked Rose, watching with anxiety on her young face.

'No, I'm sure they're not,' Betty reassured her, hoping that it was true because she didn't want her daughter to spend the whole voyage in fear. It wasn't what she'd expected, though. Betty had thought that there would be others like herself who were going to join their husbands in New South Wales, but it seemed that she and her children were the only free passengers so far except for a lady and her daughter whom she'd seen earlier, taking air on the deck. Betty had smiled at them, but they'd turned and walked in the opposite direction when they saw her approaching. They clearly thought her no better than the convicts and Betty decided not to try to engage with them again.

When they went back below deck, Betty saw that the bunks were filling up. They would sail when they were full, she realised, but she didn't know if it would give Lydia enough time to arrive. Every time she heard an order shouted or saw a sailor adjusting a rope, she feared that they were about to make sail and that her daughter would be left behind.

When she asked one of the sailors what day they would leave, he shrugged his shoulders and told her that they'd know soon enough when the orders came. Betty wondered if she could ask the captain, but the man didn't mingle with the lower decks and she thought he wouldn't welcome an approach from her even if she was a free passenger. It was only those wealthy and important enough to pay for cabins that were likely to have the captain's ear.

On the Sunday there were prayers and hymn singing on the deck in the morning, which Betty found she was obliged to attend. The captain gave a long and tedious sermon that she didn't attend to. Her gaze constantly swept the harbour, watching the comings and goings of the small boats and the distant people on the quayside. It was Lydia she was seeking. But there was no sign of her.

After the worship was finally concluded, the women went below to cook their dinner. As it was the sabbath, they had been allowed a small portion each of salted mutton, although Betty found that it was tough and needed a lot of chewing before it could be swallowed. The convicts were clearing away their bowls and mugs and handing them to their mess monitors, whose task it was to take them and wash them in the barrel of water on the upper deck, when Betty heard a shout of excitement from above them.

Not being forced to remain below until permission was granted from Mr Prosser, she and Simon and Rose climbed the steep wooden ladder onto the deck to see what was happening. Betty saw a rowing boat approaching. It was not filled with more emaciated and chained women like the ones who had arrived before, but brought a party of plainly dressed women wearing dark gowns and bonnets.

Betty wondered if they were more passengers. If so, it was surprising to see so many unaccompanied women setting out to sail so far and she wondered who they were. Curiosity drew her closer as the captain came out to meet them. It seemed they were of some importance.

The first of them was helped over the side and onto the deck by the captain himself. He smiled warmly at the woman and asked her how she was. It seemed that he was familiar with her and Betty heard him call her Mrs Fry. Soon the other three ladies had arranged themselves on the deck, adjusting their bonnets and their clothing, which had been disturbed by the climb up.

'Shall I ask for the women to be brought up on deck?' asked the captain.

'I would like to inspect the quarters below first,' Mrs Fry replied with a disarming smile.

Betty heard a noise behind her and glanced around to see the surgeon come up onto deck, looking flustered as he buttoned up his jacket.

'Ah, here is Mr Prosser,' the captain told Mrs Fry. 'He has responsibility for the convicts' welfare and is the ship's surgeon.'

'Ma'am,' said the surgeon as he bowed his head to Mrs Fry. 'Please, come this way. Do mind your step,' he told her as they reached the hatch where the steep steps went down below.

Betty heard the sound of excited voices as the ladies descended. Not from them, but from the convict women. It seemed that they also knew Mrs Fry and she was greeted as a friend.

It wasn't long before the ladies reappeared one by one on the deck and the convict women came up behind them and stood in ranks on the quarter deck before the captain. Most of them were smiling and there was a joy about them that Betty hadn't seen before. The ones who had been shackled were now released and Mrs Fry was speaking urgently with the captain and Mr Prosser, expressing some heartfelt opinions and the men, normally so self-assured, seemed slightly shame-faced under her tongue.

The nearest of the women turned to Betty with a smile. 'She came!' said the woman.

'Who is she?' asked Betty.

'Dost tha not know? She's Mrs Fry. She came to visit us in the prison at Newgate many times. She was keen to pray and read to us from the bible, but she didn't leave it at that. She made sure we were well treated, that we had clothes to cover us and that the babies were provided for. She promised she would come to say goodbye before we sailed. I don't think any of us believed she really would get on a boat and come out here. But she has. God bless her!'

'She's promised to send work for us to do on the voyage as well,' whispered another before the captain turned back to his prisoners with a frown and bid them to be silent and pay good heed to the parting words that Mrs Fry had for them.

Betty, who had found the man's sermon that morning boring and patronising, expected more of the same. But when Mrs Fry began to speak, she listened with growing interest. After a short bible reading, the visitor spoke directly to the women as if they were her equals. She bade them to take this opportunity to better themselves, to turn to God and repent of their past crimes and to live pure and useful lives in their new home.

There was palpable sorrow as she left. Betty saw several of the convict women crying as their benefactress was helped over the edge of the ship to climb down to the boat, and although the captain instructed them to return to their quarters they pleaded to be allowed to remain on deck until Mrs Fry had been rowed from their sight.

'Was she the queen?' asked Rose, gazing out across the river as the rowing boat disappeared from view.

'No,' Betty told her daughter. 'But whoever she is, she's a good woman and I'm glad that we saw her and heard her words.'

Chapter Twenty-Two

Lydia was woken by the sound of the shed doors being opened. She lay very still as she heard the horses being brought in to be put between the shafts. As the men worked, she sat up and then began to creep towards the back of the wagon where she cautiously opened the canvas. She wished that she'd woken earlier and got down whilst there was nobody there. She didn't know if she could hide in the shed, but she was desperate to escape. She knew that she couldn't spend another day hidden on the wagon with nothing to eat or drink.

Lydia put her foot on the step and lowered herself to the ground. There were two men at the front of the wagon, buckling up the horses' harness and she hoped they would be too preoccupied to notice her as she looked desperately around for a hiding place.

'Who's that?' someone asked and Lydia turned around to see the wagon driver looking straight at her. 'Where did you come from?' he demanded. 'Have you been in my wagon?' he asked as he realised that Lydia could not have come from anywhere else.

'I'm sorry,' she said. 'I've not done any harm. I haven't touched anything.' She was afraid that she would be accused of theft and the constable would be sent for again.

Ignoring her, the carter came around the back of the wagon and opened the canvas to check his load. Having satisfied himself that nothing was amiss, he fastened the covering tightly and turned to scowl at her.

'Have you been in there all night?' he demanded.

Lydia nodded. 'I was locked in. I'm sorry.'

Lydia was relieved to see the man's face soften slightly as she apologised again. 'I just needed a ride,' she confessed as she described how she'd crept aboard at the toll gate.

'Why didn't you just ask?' he replied. 'I'd have let you ride with me gladly. How far are you going?'

'I've to get to London – well, to Deptford. I must be there before the seventh.'

'I'm going that far,' he told her. 'But I doubt I'll get there by the seventh.'

Lydia felt the disappointment sweep away her moment of hope. She'd thought the man was going to let her continue with him, but what use would it be if she didn't arrive in time?

'Have you had anything to eat?' he asked her.

'Not since yesterday.'

'Go and get summat,' he told her. 'I'll be leaving in ten minutes. If you're back you can ride with me – up front.'

Lydia nodded and hurried out of the shed. She had no money for food, but she found the privy, drank from the horse trough and hurried back to where the wagon was now standing in the yard.

'Get up!' called the man and Lydia climbed up beside him and watched as he picked up the reins and the strong muscular horses heaved the heavy wagon forwards and back out onto the road.

They travelled all day at a steady pace and Lydia was at least thankful that she didn't have to walk, but whenever a stagecoach passed them, leaving sprays of wet mud in its wake as it splashed through the puddles that littered the road after the heavy rain, she wished that she was on board one of them and sure of arriving in London before her mother and sister and brother sailed away without her.

She was so hungry that her stomach was painful and when the carter opened a cloth that held some bread and boiled eggs, she gratefully accepted a small portion even though she would have liked to eat more.

By evening they came to an inn and the carter turned off the road and drew his horses to a halt.

'We'll stop here tonight,' he told Lydia. She nodded, not knowing where he expected her to sleep. 'Come inside with me,' he went on. 'I'll buy you some supper.'

Lydia waited as he gave instructions about the cart and the horses, then she followed him into the long, low building with the sign of a wheatsheaf hanging above the doorway.

The inn wasn't busy. There were a few men sitting in small groups with pints of ale in front of them, smoking their pipes, and a man who sat alone near a blazing fire, reading a newspaper.

'Lookin' for your name in there?' the carter called across to him.

The man lowered his paper and grinned. 'Not me. I've turned over a new leaf,' he replied.

'Is that so?' asked the carter. 'It's not what I've heard.'

He turned as the barmaid approached them and told her to bring them some food and pour a couple of mugs of ale. When it was done, he picked up the pint mug for himself and handed the half-pint to Lydia before going to sit opposite the man with the paper.

'What have you heard?' asked the man. Lydia thought he looked concerned and wondered why. He appeared to be well-dressed with sturdy polished boots and clean breeches, topped off with a navy-blue jacket and a silk cravat. They were the clothes of the gentry, but although he had a confident air about him, his way of speaking and general demeanour made Lydia doubt that he belonged to the upper classes.

The carter waved Lydia towards a stool beside his chair and she sat down and sipped at the ale, hoping her food would soon come and worrying about where she was going to spend the night. The carter had made no advances towards her during the day and he was a man old enough to be her grandfather, but Lydia still thought that he might want some recompense for his generosity. She couldn't afford a bed of her own and she was wondering whether she might be allowed to sleep in a barn or a loft or in the back of the cart again when she realised that the men were discussing the ladies who had been robbed near the tollhouse.

'Charlie told me that the constable had been sent for and he swore it was you from the description they gave. He said he knew all your haunts and promised he'd have you in the lock-up by now.' The carter took a long drink as the other man stared at him, obviously perturbed. 'Was it you?' he asked.

'No!' protested the man. 'I've turned to an honest living!'

'Aye,' replied the carter and wiped his mouth on the back of his hand. Lydia had the impression that he didn't believe him. 'I'm surprised he hasn't been here looking,' he went on.

The man glanced about restlessly. 'Is this the truth?' he wanted to know. 'You're not pulling my leg?'

'Cross my heart,' replied the carter.

The man suddenly seemed to notice Lydia and fixed her with a piercing stare. 'Who's this?' he asked. 'She's not your granddaughter.'

'No. Our Isobel's wed now. She doesn't come with me any more. This lass needed a lift to London, so she's riding with me. I would have welcomed the company but she's not much to say.'

Lydia hung her head, feeling uncomfortable under the scrutiny of the two men. She wished she could sit somewhere else but the inn was gradually filling up.

'What are you going to do?' the carter asked the man after the food had come. Lydia took an eager mouthful and the heat of it burned her tongue so badly she had to gulp a mouthful of the ale to lessen the pain. The man glanced at her again.

'I'd best not stay here,' he said after a moment. 'Not if the constable is looking for me.'

'You've nowt to fear if you've done nowt wrong,' pointed out the carter.

'You know that's not true. If they've already decided it was me, no jury will find otherwise. I'll be the first to admit I've got a history, but it wasn't me this time, I swear it.'

'Not my concern,' the carter told him. 'I've given you warning, but I'll not judge.'

'Aye. And I'm grateful for it,' said the man as he stood up and reached for the coat he'd tossed across the back of his chair. As he did, Lydia saw the pistol thrust into his belt and she felt a ripple of shock.

'Where will you go?' asked the carter.

Lydia saw the man hesitate as he seemed to weigh up whether or not the carter was trying to trick him.

'I'll probably go London way,' he said after a moment. 'Folk think the open countryside is safer but there are more places to hide in the streets of the city — at least until the hunt is called off or they find some other soul to swing for it.'

He was fastening up his coat now and as he picked up his hat, he looked at Lydia again.

'You're going to London?'

She nodded, wondering what was on his mind.

'I think I'll take you with me.'

Lydia stared at him, not sure that she'd understood.

'Why would you do that?' asked the carter.

'They'll not shoot me with a maid in my arms,' he reasoned.

'You want her for a hostage?'

'No. No. But she might be good insurance.' He looked back at Lydia, who was staring at him, not knowing what to think. She didn't want to go with this man, but she was afraid of what would happen if she refused.

'Come on,' he told her. 'You'll be in London by morning if you come with me. And I swear I won't harm you. I'll take you to within half a mile of wherever you want to go and I'll leave you without a blemish or a stain.'

He held out his hand. Lydia glanced at the carter for guidance, but he only shrugged.

'Go if you want to,' he said. 'He'll certainly get you to London far quicker than I can.'

'Come on,' said the man irritably as he reached down and grasped hold of Lydia's arm. 'Don't make a scene,' he warned her as he propelled her through the crowd that was gathering around the bar.

Once out of the door, he called for his horse and when he let go of Lydia's arm to put on his hat and gloves, she wondered whether to run. But as she looked around, seeking a place of sanctuary, she realised she wouldn't get far before her ankle gave way again.

'Don't look so worried,' the man said. 'I won't harm you. Whereabouts in London are you heading?'

'Deptford,' she whispered.

'The naval dockyard?'

Lydia nodded.

'That's where the convict ships sail from. Why do you want to go there?'

'I've free passage on a ship if I get there before the seventh. I'm going to my father in New South Wales.'

'Alone?'

She shook her head. 'My mother went ahead with my brother and sister. I was delayed.'

'Are you in trouble?' he asked as the ostler led out his horse, a bay that was tossing its head and dancing sideways – an animal most unlike the thickset horses that had pulled the wagon.

'No,' replied Lydia.

'I don't believe you, but I'll not ask again,' he said as he grasped the reins and put his foot to the stirrup. 'You can ride with me or stay here and take your chances.'

Lydia knew that she needed to decide quickly. Now that the man was up on his horse she thought he might just ride off without her and part of her wouldn't be sorry, but his words had stuck in her mind: 'You'll be in London by morning.' Was it worth the risk?

'We'll outgallop any constables on this horse,' he told her. 'Even if they send a carriage after us they'll not catch us. Trust me.'

Lydia looked up at him. Could she trust him? She didn't know. But if it was the difference between reaching

Deptford in time and being left behind when the rest of her family sailed, surely it was worth the risk? She nodded and he reached out a hand to her.

'Put your foot in the stirrup,' he told her as he kicked his own free. 'I'll pull you up. You can ride behind me.'

Lydia pulled her cloak more closely around herself and lifted her foot to the stirrup. The man grasped her arm and she felt herself lifted upwards.

'Get astride!' he told her and somehow she managed to wriggle a leg over the horse's warm flank and pull herself upright. 'Put your arms around my waist and hold tight!'

Lydia did as she was told and was almost thrown backwards as the horse suddenly plunged forward. The hood of her cloak fell down and she could feel the muscles of the animal under her legs as the man urged it to a gallop. The night rushed past in a blur as she clung to the man's coat for dear life as she was bounced up and down on the animal's back. She heard the man laugh at her cry of terror. She heard the hoofbeats on the road and then, suddenly, she felt a rush of euphoria like she'd never felt in her life before.

Chapter Twenty-Three

On the Monday morning, more convict women arrived in chains and were brought below. Most of them looked weary and resigned and several had young children with them who looked bewildered and afraid as they stared at their new and unfamiliar surroundings.

As well as the women, the packages that Mrs Fry had promised them arrived. A few of the women, who were eager to take advantage of the opportunity to make quilts that they would be able to sell when they arrived in New South Wales, were keen to see what had been provided and began to unwrap the bundles and spread them out on one of the tables. Not wanting to seem unfriendly, Betty took Rose to sit with them and examine the fabric. She saw that there was a good amount of small pieces of bright, printed cottons along with needles, threads and scissors and some skeins of wool for knitting.

Betty knew that these women would be her companions for the next six months and that she would be very lonely if she shunned them. Besides, rather than judging them, as she'd been inclined to when she first came on board, Betty now realised from what she'd heard them say that many of the women around her were victims of circumstance, just as she was herself. They were the ones who had asked for work to be provided for them and who didn't want to spend the long voyage with idle hands. A few others were hardened criminals who boasted to each other about the crimes they'd committed, laughing and trying to outdo one another with tales of how they'd outwitted their employers or some shopkeeper who'd insulted them. They seemed to think they were entitled to help themselves to whatever they wanted when they saw that others had more and didn't deserve their good fortune. This group was the one who'd expressed their disdain for Mrs Fry and her attempts to help them better themselves. They'd been sullen during the hymn singing and silent through the prayers. And now that the materials had arrived, they remarked that they didn't see why they should work and had taken themselves to sit apart to play cards for the few pennies that they'd managed to conceal from every search they'd been subjected to.

But the rest were keen to show that they wanted to redeem themselves. One was a young lass of about Lydia's age. Betty felt drawn to the girl, wondering how she'd ended up on board the *Maria*.

'What's thy name?' she asked her after they'd threaded their needles and begun to stitch the squares of cotton.

'Charlotte,' she replied.

'Where do you come from?'

'Preston, in Lancashire,' she told her.

'I know it.' Betty nodded. 'What did tha do to end up here?' she asked.

'Stole some food,' replied Charlotte.

'Is that all?' exclaimed Betty, shocked.

Charlotte shrugged her skinny shoulders. 'I were hungry,' she explained. 'And I wanted to get something for my little brothers and sisters. They were hungry too.'

'What happened?' asked Betty, putting down her work and looking more closely at the whey-faced girl, who continued to run neat stitches through the fabric with nimble fingers that belied her bitten-down nails and jutting wrists in sleeves that were much too short for her.

'The baker turned around and saw me take a couple of loaves. I tried to run but they grasped hold of me and I was taken off to the lock-up.'

'What about thy brothers and sisters?' asked Betty. 'Do they have someone to care for them?'

Charlotte shook her head. 'I don't know what's happened to them,' she said. 'My mother died of sickness and my father went away to look for work and never came back.'

Betty reached out a hand and rested it on the girl's thin shoulder. Charlotte didn't respond. She seemed too sad to care any more as she went on with her stitching. She didn't even cry.

'I'm sorry,' said Betty. 'Happen a neighbour or friend will help them.'

The girl nodded and Betty could see that it was no comfort to her. She dreaded to contemplate what had happened to the children after their sister had been taken from them. The best they could hope for was the work-house. It was cruel, she thought. Most of these convict women didn't deserve to be on this ship and all she could do was hope that when they reached New South Wales, they would find opportunities to better themselves, as her husband Jimmy had.

'I have a daughter about thy age,' Betty told Charlotte.

'Where is she?' asked the girl, suddenly curious. 'Is she wed?'

'No. She's coming,' said Betty, hoping that it was true and that Lydia would find them in time. 'She'll be here any day.'

That night, as Betty lay in her bunk, she worried that their departure was imminent. Mrs Fry's visit had been a farewell, and now that all the bunks were filled she could see no reason for them to remain in Deptford any longer. And it wasn't just Lydia not coming that made her feel distraught. Betty was terrified that even if she did come, Mr Prosser or the captain might not allow her on board. Even worse than her not arriving in time would be to see her and be forced to leave her standing on the quayside. She could never do that, thought Betty. She couldn't leave her daughter behind like that. She would have to insist that they were let off the ship and they wouldn't go to New South Wales after all. Jimmy would be disappointed and so would she. But how could she go without Lydia?

Early the next morning she woke from a vivid dream, with her heart racing. Even when she realised that what had passed was not real, she still couldn't shake off the anxiety it had induced in her. She'd dreamt that Lydia was on the bank of a raging river, trapped behind iron bars, waving as their ship sailed past.

When Betty took Rose to see Mr Prosser for another dose of his medicine, she saw that he was in conversation with the captain, who had come down to the bay where the sickest women had been separated from the others.

There was an elderly woman, probably approaching sixty years of age who was so stricken with rheumatism and arthritis that she could barely walk. Goodness knows how she'd ever managed to clamber on board the ship at all, thought Betty as she watched the captain order her to move this way and that to assess her.

'I agree,' the captain said, turning back to Mr Prosser. 'There's no point taking her on the voyage. I think you're right that she should be put on the hospital ship before we leave. And which is the other one?' he asked, glancing at the papers that Mr Prosser held in his hand.

'Margaret Hoskins,' he replied. 'She has a badly ulcerated leg, syphilitic in nature, and she also has the habit of voiding her urine in bed whilst asleep. The woman is a perfect nuisance.'

'Then send her as well,' confirmed the captain. 'And all the rest are fit to undertake the voyage.'

'Aye, sir. They are.'

'Well, get these women off. Send a signal for the wherry. I'm not certain when we'll sail, but I expect orders at any moment. Are you ready?' the captain asked Mr Prosser.

'I am, sir.'

'I hope you'll find it a more pleasant voyage than being at war with the French,' the captain said. 'But don't underestimate any of these women. Govern them with a firm hand. They're a wily bunch.'

He frowned as he turned to leave and saw Betty just outside the doorway.

'What are you doing there?' he barked.

'Waiting to see the surgeon, sir. My daughter is unwell.'

'Mrs Knowles is one of our free passengers. She's going to join her husband,' explained Mr Prosser and Betty was glad of his intervention as she saw the captain's face soften.

'Well, good day to you,' he said as he passed to return to his duties.

'How soon will we leave?' Betty asked the surgeon. She was worried by the conversation that she'd overheard. 'My daughter hasn't come yet. My older daughter, Lydia. But there'll be room for her now, won't there? If these two women are not to come with us?'

'That would be up to the captain,' Mr Prosser told her as he put the papers down on his desk. 'Will you excuse me for a moment? I must make sure a boat is coming for these two.'

He waved a hand towards the sick women and hurried out of the door. Lydia heard him shouting orders to one of the sailors and felt the panic rising in her again.

'Can we be put in the boat with them if they're going ashore?' Betty asked the surgeon as soon as he returned.

'Why do you ask that?'

'I can't go without Lydia. I can't leave her here alone. What will happen to her if she's left behind in England to fend for herself?'

Betty didn't need to wait for an answer to know what happened to such girls. There were many amongst the convicts who sat around sullenly in the dark belly of the ship who she thought might not have fallen into lives of crime if they had been better provided for. She couldn't bear the thought of Lydia falling into a life of crime or worse.

'I don't think you realise how fortunate you and your children are to be given passage on this ship,' the surgeon told her. 'I would have expected you to be more grateful. You agreed to take the places and now you want to change your mind? I wouldn't mention such a thing to the captain. I doubt it would please him. And it's much too late to offer the berths to another family.'

'But Lydia—'

The surgeon held up a hand to silence her. 'I'll hear no more about this other daughter,' he told her. 'Allow me to treat the daughter you have with you, then please go back to your bunk. I am very busy!'

266

After Rose had swallowed her medicine, Betty took her and Simon up onto the deck of the ship. She gazed across the water towards the quayside and prayed that Lydia would somehow be there and that the captain would agree to her coming on board.

As she watched, she saw a boat being rowed towards the *Maria*. For a moment she allowed herself to believe that it was bringing Lydia to join them, but minutes later a man in naval uniform came aboard with a letter in his hand.

She watched in dismay as the captain came out of his cabin to greet him.

'Your orders, sir!' the man announced as he handed over the letter. 'You're to sail on the afternoon tide.'

Betty gasped as she heard the words. She couldn't believe that they were to leave so soon.

'Please, sir!' cried out Betty, approaching the captain. 'We have to get off! We have to go ashore! We can't go yet!' she told him.

The captain stared at her as if she was mad. 'You're the free woman,' he observed. 'Going to join your husband?'

'I was,' she agreed. 'But I can't go this afternoon. I'm waiting for my daughter and she hasn't come yet.'

The captain frowned. 'Everyone is aboard who should be aboard,' he told her firmly then turned to a sailor who was winding up a length of rope. 'Go and fetch Mr Prosser,' he instructed him. 'I want this woman taken below and kept there.'

Chapter Twenty-Four

Lydia clung to the man as they galloped. After a while her excitement ebbed and she became afraid that she might fall, but he soon reined in the horse and slowed it to a walk.

'We can't go at that speed all night,' he told her over his shoulder, 'but I thought you'd enjoy the thrill of it.' He laughed. 'You did well,' he added. 'The last maid I took up behind me screamed continuously in my ear until I was almost deafened, so I left her on the roadside.' He laughed again and Lydia wasn't sure whether or not to believe him. 'I know a place further on where we can rest awhile,' he told her. 'It's not as snug as a seat by the fire at the inn, but it'll be safer if they have sent anyone after us.

'What's your name?' he asked her.

'Lydia,' she told him, truthfully. 'What's yours?' she ventured, feeling brave.

He laughed. 'They call me Swift Stanley. But that's not my real name. You can call me Nicholas.'

Lydia didn't ask if that was his real name. She doubted it was.

They rode on at a slower pace until he pulled the horse up near what appeared to be a small abandoned shed a few hundred yards off the main road.

'It don't look much,' he admitted as he lifted her down, 'but it's one of my "homes", so to speak.'

Lydia watched as he jostled a key in the lock until it eventually turned with a click and he lifted the latch and pushed the door open.

'In you go,' he said. 'You'll find a candle and flint on a box. I'll just tie up the horse.'

Lydia felt her way across the stone floor until she came to the box. She found the candle already set in a holder so she struck the flint and lit the wick. In the light she could see that the small ramshackle building had probably been abandoned for a long time. Water was dripping down the far wall and the boards that covered the windows were rotten. She held the candle up and looked around the rest of it. There was a straw mattress and a couple of blankets arranged on the floor beside a makeshift hearth that was no more than a square pile of bricks with some dry twigs and sticks arranged inside it.

She heard Nicholas come in behind her and close the door.

'No one can see us from the road,' he told her. 'I'll light the fire.'

Smoke soon filled the space as the twigs took hold of the flame he'd kindled with some dry hay. It made Lydia cough.

'There's a hole in the roof that'll draw it up,' he said. 'But we'll have to quench it before daylight.'

'Are we going to stay here all night?' asked Lydia. She wanted to remind him that he'd promised he would get her to London by morning, but she didn't. She was wary of him.

'We'll leave as soon as it's light enough to see,' he told her. 'We'll snatch a few hours' sleep first.'

He moved some old rusted tools from the top of another box and drew it forward.

'Sit down,' he invited after giving it a wipe with a dirty cloth.

Lydia lowered herself onto it carefully. It looked flimsy, but it held her weight and he crouched down beside the fire, cupping his hands and blowing to encourage the blaze. She yawned, overcome with tiredness now that the thrill of the ride had left her.

'You look worn out,' he observed. 'Why not sleep for a few hours?'

'Where?'

'On the mattress. You'll be completely safe,' he told her. 'I'll prop myself against the door and doze.'

Lydia was unsure, but she felt exhausted and there was no way she could escape from this man so she decided that she would have to take the risk. She shook the mattress in case any rats or mice had got in and then lay down, pulling one of the blankets over her and leaving the other one for him.

The warmth from the fire bathed her face and she closed her eyes, but sleep evaded her at first as the wood crackled and burned and the man watched her. She wondered who he was and whether he really had robbed the women who'd come to the tollhouse. He certainly had the money for fine clothes, but this shed was no salubrious place to live, and it seemed he did live here for some of the time at least.

Eventually she must have slept because the next time she opened her eyes, she saw that the fire was out and the door stood part open. Outside she could just about make out the shapes of the trees, and the woodland was filled with the sound of birdsong. She sat up, still yawning, and raised her hands to tidy her hair. Nicholas came in a moment later and grinned at her.

'I thought I was going to have to rouse you,' he said. 'It's time to leave.'

Lydia got to her feet and told him that she must relieve herself first.

'Go into the woods. But not too far,' he told her.

Lydia hurried into the undergrowth, trying to avoid anything that might sting or bite her and looked about for a convenient place. Once she was sure she was out of the man's sight she crouched and emptied her bladder. As she did she wondered whether she should go back to him, or run and hide. She was afraid of him and was wary of crossing him, but she decided that she had to trust his word if she was to have any chance of reaching Deptford in time.

He was mounted on his horse, waiting for her, when she got back.

'Come on!' he said, reaching down for her. 'Up you get.'

Moments later she was astride the horse again with her arms around his waist and her face pressed against the warmth of his back as they cantered away. She knew little of men. She remembered her father holding her, but since he went away the only men she'd known were figures in authority over her like the men of the relief committee who had sent her away to Caton and the overlooker in the mill. She'd never been so physically close to a man since she was a child and as the hours passed she began to find pleasure in the feel of his body pressing against hers.

'Are you hungry?' he asked after a while in which they'd mostly kept off the road and followed tracks through woodlands and beside streams that he seemed to know well.

'I am.'

'There's a place up ahead where we can get some food,' he told her. 'It's not far.'

They rode on at a trot that bounced Lydia on the horse's back and jolted her against Nicholas.

'Whoa!' he called to the horse as they came to a small farm where a whitewashed cottage stood by the side of the road. A woman came to the door when she heard them, although it was still early and Lydia heard her cry of delight as she recognised the man.

'Nick!' she cried and before he'd dropped to the ground she was beside him and he gathered her in his arms and kissed her fiercely. 'Who's this?' she asked when he relinquished his grasp of her, looking up at Lydia, who was still astride the horse. The jealousy in her tone was unmistakable.

'Her name's Lydia. I'm taking her to London.' He laughed. 'No need to look so put out,' he told the woman. 'She's just an insurance policy.'

'Are you on the run?'

'Am I ever.' He sighed. 'And I swear that this time I've done nothing wrong. I've turned over a new leaf. I told you before.'

'You'd better come in,' said the woman, glancing up and down the road as if she expected trouble at any moment. Nick turned and held out to his arms to Lydia. She slid down into them and he whispered in her ear.

'Don't be jealous,' he said. 'But I need to keep Old Nell sweet.' Before he moved away he brushed his lips across Lydia's cheek and she felt a thrill run through her. 'Come on,' he said. 'She'll feed us.'

He tied up the horse and went into the kitchen of the house ahead of Lydia.

'Have you bacon?' he called, throwing his hat onto the table and going to sit beside the fire.

'For you, I have,' said the woman, casting a black look towards Lydia, whom she didn't invite to be seated.

'Then get it on to fry, woman!'

Lydia inched towards the scrubbed table and sat on the edge of a chair. Nick had called the woman Old Nell, but she wasn't old. She was older than Lydia but not as old as her mother and certainly not much older than Nick. Lydia watched as she put rashers of bacon into a pan and set it over the fire then came back to the table to cut thick slices of bread. As she watched, she heard a door open behind her and when she turned she saw a child – a little girl with bright blue eyes. She ignored Lydia but ran straight to Nick, who lifted her onto his knee and made much of her, producing a shiny coin that he pretended to pull from her ear before putting it in her hand and closing her fingers over it.

'What about me?' asked Nell.

'I've something for you, don't worry,' he said, pulling more coins from a purse and stacking them on the hearth.

'Where did they come from?' asked Nell doubtfully.

'Honest means!' he protested. 'Do you not want them?' he asked, reaching forwards as if to retrieve them.

'Leave 'em be!' she told him as she heaped bacon onto the bread and gave him the plate.

'Feed the girl as well.'

Nell frowned but prepared a smaller portion for Lydia, which she accepted with as much grace as she could muster then ate hungrily because it was the best thing she'd tasted in a long time.

'Don't mind Nell,' said Nick as they were riding away from the farmhouse. 'She doesn't like any competition.'

Lydia felt pleased that she might be viewed as *competition*. It was the first time that she'd been aware that another woman might see her as such. She'd always thought of herself as a child up until now and the unexpected comparison delighted her, offsetting the envy she'd felt as she'd watched Nick say a prolonged farewell to his friend.

It must have been around mid-morning when they were forced back onto the main road by the clusters of soot-grimed houses that now lined the route.

'We're approaching London,' Nick told her and pointed towards where a cloud of black smoke hung in the sky, belching from myriad chimneys.

The smell of burning coal filled the air. The roads converged and there seemed to be carts everywhere, clattering over the flagstones as street sweepers cleared horse dung into piles at the edges of the streets. As they rode on, past squares of newly built houses that looked like lines of palaces to Lydia, they came to streets filled with shops and passed crowds of people walking – some dressed in finery, others like herself clad in red cloaks and bonnets, and some who looked poorer than even the worst-off waifs back at home in Bolton. Carriages raced past them, making the horse uneasy and Lydia held on tightly to Nick as it skittishly danced beneath them.

As they turned down a narrow lane towards the river, Lydia saw baskets and crates piled up on the quayside and heard the raucous screams of seagulls as they circled around looking for an opportunity to steal food. She wondered if the *Maria* was close by and thought how glad she would be to see her mother.

'Are we nearly there?' she called out to Nick.

'I can leave you here if you want,' he called back, but Lydia was suddenly afraid of being set down amongst this seething mass of people without knowing if she was in the right place.

'I was told Deptford,' she replied.

'That's a bit further,' he said. 'I'll take you nearer.'

They rode on until the worst of the city life was left behind to be replaced by the sounds of sawing and hammering as they approached the dockyard.

'Here you are,' Nick said. 'Which one is yours?'

'It's named the *Maria*,' she replied. 'Can you see it?'

'It'll be one of those at anchor in the basin,' he replied and Lydia looked to where he pointed to the tiers of wooden ships, their masts moving on the rising tide as they swayed on the water. 'It could be that one,' he said. 'They're raising the sail.'

'But how will I reach it?' she asked, suddenly alarmed that she might be left on the shore as the vessel bore her mother and brother and sister away from her.

'By boat,' he said. 'Show your ticket at the office and they'll arrange a wherry to take you out.' He swung a leg over the horse's withers and slid to the ground before reaching up to lift her down. 'Best hurry. It's over there,' he said, pointing to a brick building with a sharply pointed roof some distance away.

'Thank you,' she said once he'd placed her on her feet. The horse turned its nose to her and she stroked its face, then straightened her cloak. She looked up at Nick, half hoping he might kiss her goodbye as she'd watched him kiss Nan, but he seemed agitated. His gaze was flickering this way and that as if he were on the lookout for trouble. Reluctantly, she began to walk away from him. Although she was eager to reach her family, part of her was sorry to leave this man. But when she glanced back, he'd remounted and was urging the horse on, disappearing into the warren of streets that made up the city. It was clear that she meant nothing to him. She'd served her purpose and she would never see him again. The disappointment almost overwhelmed her.

Lydia hurried past two huge ships with their hulls raised above the water to be repaired. Taking care to step around the barrels of provisions, sacks, and thick ropes coiled into high piles that seemed to fill the cobbled quayside, she gazed across the basin at the ships that were ranged three deep and the many smaller wherries that were taking goods out to be loaded onto them. She could see the names painted on the wooden hulls of the nearest ones, but none of them was the *Maria*. But she saw that the one Nick had pointed out to her was indeed raising its sails and she realised that she must hurry if she was to get aboard before it left.

She went on past the huge stone warehouse with its clock tower and towards the smaller brick building that had been pointed out to her. She was panting by the time she reached the door and she paused for a moment to catch her breath and arrange her cloak so that she looked respectable. As she did so, the door opened and a man in naval uniform came out, holding his hat under his arm. He glanced at her with a smile.

'Can I help you, ma'am?' he asked.

'I'm here to board a ship called the *Maria*,' he told him. 'Do you know which one it is?'

'The *Maria*? Yes, she's the far one.' He pointed. 'She's almost ready to depart.' He looked puzzled. 'I thought all the passengers had boarded,' he said.

'I was delayed. My family are already on board.'

'Then you'd better hurry.' He turned to hold the door open for her. 'Speak to the man at the desk and he will make the arrangements for you to be rowed out.'

'Thank you,' replied Lydia, slipping past him into the gloomy interior where she approached a clerk who was seated at an untidy desk, brimming with piles of paper-work that threatening to slide to the floor at any moment.

'Excuse me, sir,' she said after a moment when he didn't acknowledge her.

'What is it?' he snapped without looking up.

'I'm here to board the *Maria*.'

He stopped what he was doing and looked up at her, appraising her.

'The *Maria*?' he repeated after a moment.

'Yes, sir.'

'Do you have a ticket?' he asked as he studied her doubtfully.

Lydia shook her head. 'No, sir. My mother has it, I think. She's already on board. I was delayed,' she explained for the second time that morning.

'Name?' he asked as he began to shuffle around the piles of paper on his desk, making Lydia wonder how on earth he would ever find what he was looking for.

'Lydia Knowles. I'm to travel with my mother, Betty Knowles, and my brother and sister.'

She waited for what seemed an age as he looked through list after list, sighing as he did.

'I can find no record of any tickets,' he said eventually. 'Are you sure you have the right ship?'

'Yes. I think so,' she added. She'd been certain until a moment ago that Ann Booth had told her that the instruction her mother had been given was to board the *Maria*, but now she found that she was doubting herself.

'The *Maria* is set to sail on the afternoon tide,' he told her.

'What time is that?' asked Lydia. She'd heard the clock strike noon as she'd walked down the quayside.

'Fifteen minutes past four,' he replied and Lydia realised she had only a few hours to find a way of getting out to the ship before it was too late.

'How am I to get on board?' she asked.

'You can't,' he said, turning his attention back to his work. 'Not if you don't have a ticket.'

'But if I can reach the ship, my mother will show you the ticket.'

He shrugged briefly. 'Not my concern,' he told her. 'Come back to me with a ticket and I'll arrange a wherry.'

Lydia stared at the top of his head as he continued to make marks with his pen on the papers in front of him. She was unsure if he was stupid or being deliberately obtuse. The only way she could show him her ticket was by getting it from the ship, but the only way she could be rowed out to the ship was by showing him the ticket. It made no sense.

Frustrated, she turned away and back onto the quayside where she looked about at all the boats. Surely someone would take her out to the *Maria*?

As she stood, gazing out at the ships, she became aware that she was the only woman on the quayside. Every other person was a man, from the workers who were carrying sacks on their shoulders or rolling the huge barrels across the uneven stones to the waiting boats, to the naval officers who strode up and down with determined purpose. Suddenly Lydia felt afraid as she noticed that both the labourers and the officers were looking at her with undisguised curiosity. She wished that Nick had stayed with her until he'd seen her safely aboard the ship, but she realised that he wouldn't have wanted to take the risk and that it was not his concern anyway.

As she watched, she saw a wherry approaching the stone steps near to where she was standing. She saw that there were two women in the boat and as they came nearer, Lydia was shocked to see that their wrists and ankles were chained together. The sailors in the boat made a rope fast to an iron ring and the first of the women stood up in the boat and grasped for the handrail that was secured to the side of the steps. She hauled herself up with difficulty until her head was level with Lydia's.

'What are you starin' at?' she asked as Lydia stepped back to give her room.

'Are these for the hospital ship?' asked an officer who approached from behind.

'Aye, sir. But I don't know how this one'll get up,' called one of the sailors.

'Give her a push,' encouraged the officer as he watched the elderly woman struggle to her feet and try to get onto the steps.

'Get a move on, woman!' he shouted down at her as the sailor levered her up from below.

Lydia was shocked. She could see that the woman was struggling and that the officer was not prepared to help her. She went to the top of the steps and, reaching down, she offered the woman her hand and helped her climb up.

'Thank ye,' she said to Lydia when she manged to reach the quay. 'Tha's a good lass to an old woman. Bless ye.'

Lydia watched as the women were taken away, struggling to keep up with the officer, who walked far too fast for their infirmities and their chains.

'Don't look so worried,' said one of the sailors as he bounded up the steps to stand beside Lydia. 'They've got off lightly. They should have been on their way to New South Wales shortly.'

'On the *Maria*?' she asked.

'Aye. Been sent ashore. Too sick to travel.'

'Where will they go now?' she asked.

'Hospital ship. Cosy billet if you ask me.' He grinned as he looked Lydia up and down. 'And where are you bound?' he asked her.

'I need to get on board the *Maria*. Will you take me?'

'What have you got to pay me with?' he asked, winking his eye in a suggestive manner. Lydia felt herself blush and cursed herself for it. The sailor laughed.

'I'm not supposed to go out without orders,' he told her. 'Why do you want to go, anyway?' he asked. 'Keen to say goodbye to a sweetheart? It'll have to be a brisk farewell,' he warned her. 'The tide's almost up and she sails this afternoon.'

'I'm going to join my mother,' she told him, hoping that he would take pity on her. 'She's waiting for me. I'm going to New South Wales. My father has sent for us.'

The sailor hesitated as his companion came up the steps and passed them with a grin.

'I didn't know you had a sweetheart,' he said as he thumped the sailor Lydia was speaking to between the shoulder blades and laughed before he strode away.

'Like I said,' the sailor told Lydia, 'I shouldn't really and it'll be hard to row all on my own. But if you could offer some payment? A little kiss?'

'No.' She shook her head, repulsed by him. He looked disappointed and then began to walk away.

'Wait!' she called after him. 'All right then,' she agreed. 'But only after we're in the boat.'

He grinned again and skipped down the steps before offering her his hand. Lydia turned and went down backwards, holding on to the rail and only accepting his help when she had to step into the boat. Still unbalanced as she stood in the wherry, she felt him clasp her firmly and plant a kiss on her lips. His face felt rough and his breath was bad and she felt repulsed and relieved when he let her go and allowed her to sit down.

Seating himself opposite to her after untying the rope and tossing it into the boat, he grasped the oars and manoeuvred them away from the harbour wall. As they rowed out onto the river, Lydia worried that he might take her anywhere. The ships loomed around them and she still wasn't certain which one was the *Maria*. But his attention was taken up with steering the wherry in and out of the other boats that were busy toing and froing between the ships and the quayside. She was thankful for it and wiped her mouth on her cloak when he turned to look over his shoulder, wishing she could take away the taste of his tongue from hers.

'Here we are,' he announced after a few minutes as a wooden hull loomed above them. 'The *Maria*.'

'How will I get on board?' asked Lydia, seeing no way up.

'Climb the ladder,' he told her, pulling the boat in alongside the ship where a rope ladder hung down the side. Lydia stared up. The ladder seemed endless and she hoped that the sailor wasn't playing another trick on her. 'Grab hold and get your feet on the rungs,' he told her. 'If them old women can manage it there's nothing for you to fear.'

Not knowing what else to do, Lydia stood up, fearing for her balance in the bobbing boat, and reached out to the ladder. She managed to catch hold of it and pull herself closer. Then she put one foot on the edge of the wherry and felt for the ladder with her other one. The sailor laughed as he watched her and once she had both feet on the ladder he called out a farewell and began to row away. Lydia was left dangling, praying that he hadn't left her there deliberately and that it really was a way up onto the deck. Trembling with fear, she began to climb, rising higher with each step until, after what seemed an age, and with her legs trembling, she saw the top of the hull and gradually raised herself far enough to see over the edge. Some women were sitting around in a group and they watched as she grasped hold of the rail and managed to climb over before landing on the deck with a thud.

'Where have you come from?' demanded a man's voice and Lydia felt her arm grasped tightly as she was pulled to her feet. 'Were you trying to escape?' he demanded.

'No!' protested Lydia. 'I'm coming on board.'

'The hell you are!' replied the man. 'Fetch the captain!' he called to someone. 'I think I've caught a stowaway!'

Chapter Twenty-Five

Betty sat at a table below deck with Rose and Simon. She was still smarting from Mr Prosser's anger as he ordered her below and told her she was more of a nuisance to him than any of the convict women. Above, she could hear the preparations being made for them to sail. The rising tide was slapping against the hull and she was trying not to cry as she thought of Lydia. She mustn't upset her other two children, but the wretched feeling that she was abandoning her elder daughter to an unknown fate threatened to overwhelm her. She should never have allowed her to go to that mill at Caton. If only she'd kept her at home, they could have all left together and Lydia would have been with them now.

'Lydia isn't going to get here in time, is she?' asked Simon as he traced the pattern of a whorl in the wood with his finger. Betty searched for words to reassure him.

'Ann said she would care for her. Maybe she stayed with them.'

'Would she not have sent a letter?' he asked.

'Maybe it hasn't arrived yet. I'm not sure how reliable the post is to Deptford.'

'Are we just going to go without her?' he asked.

'I don't know,' replied Betty. All the hopes that she'd been desperately holding on to were unravelling by the minute. She didn't know how much longer was left before they set off, but when she heard footsteps on the wooden ladder and saw the convict women coming down, she knew that they must be almost ready to sail.

Betty desperately wanted to get off the ship. She didn't want to go without Lydia but she was slowly beginning to realise that there was nothing she could do to prevent it. By coming on board the *Maria*, she had committed herself and Simon and Rose to their fate – Lydia too, except that it was her fate to remain in England without any of her family to protect her.

She wondered if she should defy her orders and go back up the ladder now that the last of the convict women had come down and were sitting around in silent groups. Even the women who were usually brash and confident were subdued now that the moment of departure was imminent.

When she heard the rattling of the chain as the anchor was lifted, Betty knew that it was her last chance and that if she did nothing she would never forgive herself.

'Get our things together,' she told Simon and Rose. 'Pack the box. We're going ashore.'

Leaving the children to gather their possessions, Betty climbed the wooden ladder, determined to find a way to get off the ship. As her head crested the open hatch onto the deck, she saw a young girl in a red cloak being held fast by one of the sailors. Mr Prosser and the captain were firing questions at her and Betty heard them accusing her of being a stowaway and saying that they would send for a boat to put her ashore despite her protests that she had a ticket. A rush of hope filled Betty. If there was to be a boat to the shore then she was going to insist that she and her children were put on it as well.

She climbed the few remaining steps onto the deck and began to walk slowly towards where the men were standing. She saw Mr Prosser notice her and she shuddered, knowing that she would receive another tongue-lashing from him for disobeying his orders, but she braced herself for the onslaught, determined to insist that her decision was upheld. She was not one of the prisoners. She was free to leave if she chose to.

'Here is Mrs Knowles now,' Mr Prosser said.

The captain turned his attention to her. 'Do you know this girl?' he asked her as he gestured to the sailor to swing the captive around to face Betty.

'Mam!' Lydia cried as her face crumpled into tears of relief and she struggled to free herself from the sailor's grasp so that she could run to her mother.

'Lydia!' Betty exclaimed, barely able to believe what she was seeing. She hurried forward to wrap her arms around her daughter, eager to reassure herself that this time she was real and it wasn't one more bad dream where she would dissipate on touch. But she found herself restrained by Mr Prosser, who kept her at arm's length.

'It's my daughter, Lydia,' she protested, struggling to speak as tears of relief and joy threatened to overwhelm her.

The sight of Lydia was such a shock. She'd been praying for her to come, but she'd never imagined it would be like this with her daughter suddenly standing on the deck in front of her, as if summoned by magic.

'How did tha get on board?' she asked, her voice breaking with emotion as she spoke.

'A sailor rowed me out. But now they're saying I can't stay,' Lydia sobbed, her face forlorn with anguish. 'They want to send me back. Please don't go without me!'

Betty's heart broke at the desperation in Lydia's voice. She could see that her daughter's bottom lip was trembling and all she wanted to do was hug her close and never let her go ever again.

'If they put thee ashore, then we'll all go ashore!' Betty reassured her, wiping her own face and longing to dry her daughter's tears as well. She certainly wasn't going to sail without Lydia now that her daughter had arrived.

Mr Prosser glared at her and the captain looked from one to the other, seemingly unsure what to do.

'My daughter was listed on our ticket,' Betty told him, surprising herself by her boldness, but determined that she wouldn't be parted from her daughter again by men who had authority over her. 'She has the right to sail with us.'

'Is this true?' the captain asked Mr Prosser.

'I would need to check,' he said, although Betty was sure that he remembered perfectly well.

'Then check!' said the captain. 'And be quick about it. We have orders to sail on this tide and time is of an essence!' He watched as the surgeon hurried off to his cabin and then turned to the sailor who was holding Lydia. 'Let her go,' he ordered and as soon as she was released, Lydia ran into her mother's arms and Betty held her tightly and kissed her face again and again, trying to heal the hurt of their long separation.

Above them, the unfurled sails were flapping in the wind and the ship heaved as if eager to be off. Betty clung to her daughter, waiting to hear what their fate would be and praying that they would all be allowed to leave together to join Jimmy in New South Wales.

Moments later, Mr Prosser returned with the paper Betty had given him when she'd first arrived.

'It does list Lydia Knowles as a passenger,' he admitted, 'but because she wasn't present when the family came on board I allocated her place to an extra convict.' The captain frowned. 'We only have supplies for a set number,' Mr Prosser told him.

'I know that!' retorted the captain, clearly irritated. He seemed undecided about what to do.

'But two of the convict women were taken off,' said Betty as she clutched Lydia's hand.

'That's true,' agreed the captain. He paused thoughtfully and glanced towards the horizon. 'If we wait for a wherry to come out then we'll miss the tide,' he observed. 'I can't see any good reason to wait. We'll take the girl.'

Betty felt the relief flood through her as fresh tears welled in her eyes. She tried to thank the captain but words were beyond her.

'You'd better get below then,' Mr Prosser told her. 'The girl will have to share a bunk with you, unless you want her to sleep amongst the convicts.'

Betty could see that he wasn't pleased, but she didn't care. Lydia was here and that was all that mattered. It would be a cramped voyage, but Lydia could share a bunk with Rose and it was no worse than the straw mattresses on the floor that they'd become used to in their cottage back in Bolton.

–

Lydia followed her mother down a steep, narrow ladder that led to a hold below the deck. She was still trembling from the prospect of being sent back when she'd thought that getting onto the ship and finding her mother would solve everything. She rubbed her arm where the sailor had held her too tightly as she saw for the first time the place that was to be her home for the next six months. The ship was not what she'd expected. It was crowded and it smelled and when the hatch closed above them, the only light was from a couple of oil lanterns that were swinging from the wooden struts.

In the gloom she could make out dozens of women. Some sitting around tables, some sitting on the floor. The silence struck her more than anything. She'd never seen such a crowd of people with nothing to say, except for the rare occasions when she'd been to church. But even there the silence hadn't been as profound as this. She could feel the fear and as her eyes became accustomed to the dark she saw the terror on the women's faces.

Then she saw Simon and Rose with a box on the floor between them.

'Lydia!' Simon came to touch her, as if he couldn't quite believe she was real. She pulled him closer and hugged him. She'd never have believed that she'd be so glad to see her annoying little brother.

'How did tha get here?' he asked.

'I followed ye,' she told him, knowing that the longer explanations would have to wait.

Then she turned to her little sister. Rose looked frail, as if she'd been unwell, and Lydia embraced her too.

'I'm glad tha's come,' whispered Rose, clinging to her.

'So am I,' replied Lydia. 'So am I.'

She didn't say that she'd feared she would never see them again, although the thought had never been far from her mind during her difficult journey. But she'd made it, she reminded herself. Despite all the adversity and the setbacks, she'd arrived, just in time. And now no one could come after her and take her away from her family again.

'Did tha get the money I left for thee with Ann and Peter?' her mother asked her later, as the ship began to rise and fall on the water as they sailed down the Thames towards the open sea.

'I saw them. I went home looking for thee, but tha'd gone. I only just missed thee,' Lydia told her mother, thinking of the London coach that had passed Mr Haslam's cart.

'Was it enough for the ticket?' asked her mother.

'I got a coach part of the way,' Lydia told her. 'Then I got a lift.' She knew that there was a lot to tell her mother, but she wasn't sure yet how much of it she would reveal. There were some parts of her journey that she thought it better her mother knew nothing of.

'Well, thank goodness tha got here,' said her mother, stroking her hair.

'Would tha have left me behind?' asked Lydia. 'If I hadn't come?'

'Never!' her mother told her emphatically. 'I'd already asked to be put ashore so we could search for thee.'

'What about my father?' asked Lydia. 'He would have been disappointed.'

'We would have gone on another ship,' replied her mother. 'The only thing that matters is all of us being together.'

Epilogue

Betty listened as she heard the anchor being dropped: the clank of the chains and the thud as it hit the seabed. They were in shallow waters here and the ship was still, unlike the pitching and rolling that they'd become accustomed to for all those long months at sea.

She stared at the patchwork quilt that she'd only recently finished. Lydia and Rose had helped with it and when she looked at it closely she could pick out their stitches. Rose's were always neat and even. Lydia had less dexterity, but Betty thought no one else would notice a difference. Besides, she had no intention of selling this quilt. She intended it for the bed that she would share with her husband after all the lonely years apart.

Lovingly, she folded it and put it in the box with their other possessions, few though they were. Some of the convict women had brought more than she had. Betty closed the lid and looked around at the place that had been her home and the women who had become her friends on the long voyage. Some she would be happy never to see again, but others she would miss, like young Charlotte, who had become close to Lydia. She wished she could do more to keep the girl safe and hoped that she would find someone to take care of her. No one was sure what awaited the convicts once they left the boat.

'Mrs Knowles!' Betty looked up as she heard her name called. 'You and your family can come up on deck now,' Mr Prosser told her.

They climbed the ladder into bright sunshine. Simon and Lydia hauled up the box between them until it thumped onto the deck that was bone dry now that they were no longer at sea. The air was warm and there was a gentle wind that lifted strands of Betty's hair. She raised her hand to shield her eyes against the glare and saw that they were anchored in a cove. The boats that were coming and going between the bigger ships, ferrying goods and passengers to and from the shore, reminded her of Deptford, but that was where the similarities ended. This seemed a desolate place. There were some scattered buildings along the shoreline and larger houses higher on the hill, but beyond that there was thick forest as far as the eye could see.

Betty wondered where Jimmy was and if he was waiting for them. As if reading her thoughts, Mr Prosser answered them.

'Your husband has sent a boat for you,' he told her. 'He's waiting on the quayside.'

Betty's stomach fluttered as she thought of seeing him again. It was a dream she'd had for so many years, but now that it was only moments away, she was afraid. She watched as the box was lowered and her children climbed down into the boat. Jimmy would not recognise them, she thought. She hoped that he would recognise her.

As they were rowed ashore, her eyes scanned all the figures on the quay, but she couldn't be sure which one was Jimmy. She hoped he hadn't changed so much that she wouldn't know him. The tide was low and as they approached the jetty, Betty saw the water was lapping at a set of stone steps that led upwards. The wherry was tied to a ring set into the wall and Betty sent the children up first, taking a moment to compose herself, not knowing what to expect. Then she climbed, taking care not to slip or wet the hem of her petticoat. At the top, she stopped and raised her hand again against the sun. A man was coming towards her. He wasn't rushing. He seemed hesitant and unsure. She began to walk towards him. He looked different. He wore a wide-brimmed hat and he'd grown a moustache and his body had filled out with muscle and adequate food. His skin had darkened but his eyes twinkled with the same mischievous gleam that she'd always loved.

'Jimmy?'

He swept off his hat and she was relieved to see his hair was as thick as ever even though a few silver threads glinted in the sunlight.

'Jimmy.' She increased her pace and he held out his arms.

'Betty,' he said as he embraced her. 'Tha came!'

Author's Note

The Runaway Daughter is the final book in the Lancashire Girls series, which tells the stories of some of the convict families from Bolton who were mentioned in the letters of Thomas Holden.

Although plenty is known about Thomas Holden from his letters, the lives of the other men and their families are only sketchily recorded.

James Knowles was tried alongside Thomas Holden and thirteen other men at the special assize in Lancaster in May 1812. He was found guilty of swearing an illegal oath at a secret meeting. In fact, the senior judge at the trial, Baron Thompson said as he was sentencing him: 'You, James Knowles, too well observed the nature and purport of the oath, for you were one of those present when Holland Bowden was compelled to take it, and you were indicted for assisting in that act'. He was sentenced to seven years' transportation to New South Wales at the age of twenty-four.

The wives of the men from Bolton applied for permission to accompany their husbands when they were first convicted, but they were refused a free passage at that time. Later, the government realised that these families were a drain on the financial resources of local parishes and the convict reunion scheme was introduced in 1818 to allow wives and children to join their husbands. It was thought that the scheme would also help redress the gender imbalance in the new colony and that men would be more inclined to good behaviour if their families were with them.

Men who had received a ticket of leave or a pardon, which allowed them to work for themselves, were entitled to apply for their families to join them. Under the scheme, women and children were sent out free of charge on female convict ships. However, places depended on the number of available berths and not all those who wished to go were selected. The ones who were offered a place had to get themselves to the ship at their own expense, but records show that many parishes willingly paid for their travel to be rid of the longer term expense of paying out an allowance or keeping them in the workhouse.

In this final story, I wanted to portray a family who were offered this opportunity, as in the previous two books the convicted men came home. According to online records James Knowles was granted an absolute pardon on 22nd July 1817. Although there is no record of him sending for his wife to join him I hope he and his family found the happy ending I have portrayed in the book.

Acknowledgements

Thanks to my editor, Emily Bedford, Alicia Pountney, the copy editor, proofreader, cover designer and all the team at Canelo for their enthusiastic input whilst bringing this final book in the Lancashire Girls series to publication.